THE GOLDEN WOLF - BOOK 1

NEW YORK TIMES BESTSELLING AUTHOR

SHANNON MAYER

NEW YORK TIMES BESTSELLING AUTHOR

SHANNON MAYER

To all the women who think they can make a bad man into a good mate/partner/husband. You can't. But you can read a book about it. You're welcome for the biggest fantasy of all, men who can change!

Wait...what do you mean that's too mean? Oh, you mean honest. Fine, I'll lie.

To all the women who've loved the bad boy, seen him through his mental health issues, married him and helped him see the light via their unending love and sassy banter. I hope you enjoy this book, which really...isn't like either of these dedications! Psych!

CONTENTS

FUCK ME SIDEWAYS WITH A FORK

The dreams were always the same, though calling them dreams was maybe a bit of a stretch. That place between sleep and waking, where memories you'd rather not remember lived, that was where I was, stuck, unable to move forward or back.

Just like every other night.

Even though I could feel the soft flannel sheets around me, the steady rumble of my cat purring as he lay across my chest, there were also other sensations that hailed from the past—the ones that held me tighter even than the present.

The staccato pop, pop, pop of Richard's gun, the rush of air as I tried to throw myself to one side. Bullets laced with silver slamming into me. Right hip. Center of my belly. Left shoulder. My body spinning with the concus-

sive force. I landed face down in the mud of the river-bank, pain numbing my mind. I should have fought them harder. Should have figured out what they were up to. I turned down one of my older brother's advances, I should have known he would get rid of me. Fear and shame raged a war inside of me.

My fingers clutched at the sheets, and I scrunched my eyes harder, as if that would push the memories back and allow me to go to sleep.

But how could I have known that my own brothers would try to kill me? Even in our family, that was an extreme response. Or at least that's what I'd thought. The warmth of the blood, the sting of the bullets. I held my breath. There were times to fight, and times to hide. This was the latter, and both me and my wolf knew it.

"That should do it. Shove her in the river," Kieran said. "Bitch should have known her place."

A booted foot slammed into my side, flipping me over a full three hundred and sixty degrees so I was facedown again, only this time in the edge of the water.

My hip, belly, and shoulder were on fire, as if a flame had been set to a pool of gasoline. The silver was flooding my system, slowing my heart, and casting a fog over my mind. Kieran didn't have to waste any more of the bullets that were so hard to come by. Silver poisoning would do me in with a single bullet given enough time.

Another kick, the crack of my shoulder blade as I was booted fully into the river. I rolled with the current as my *lungs burned. Face up, I dared to open my eyes. The images were unclear through the water, but I knew the faces. I'd known them my whole life, but perhaps...I'd never truly known them at all.*

This was the hardest part of the dream, worse than the bullets or the fear of dying. No, reliving that moment when all my worst fears were confirmed about myself was the one that bit deep. I wasn't truly part of the family. I never had been part of the pack despite my parents being the alphas. I was the mistake, the oops, the turn your head and look away after Mother had an indiscretion that led to my birth. I'd never felt that truth so keenly as in that moment.

Richard, my oldest brother. Kieran, my second oldest brother. It was the third face that hurt the worst. Shipley was just a little older than me, the one person in my family I'd thought I could rely on and trust. The one brother I'd thought was my friend.

"Get rid of her," Shipley said, his voice wobbling through the water. "Or Mom will have our hides. You should never have tried to fuck her."

"You heard Mom; either she submitted to me, or she was out," Kieran snarled. "She had one chance to stay in the pack, that was it."

I jerked out of that in-between limbo as the remembered sensation of cold water rushed over me, the bouncing of my body against the rocks along the bottom of the river. My hands went to the scars on my left breast, just above my heart, tracing the ripples in my skin. Not much could leave a scar on a werewolf, silver shrapnel did the trick pretty nicely though.

My sheets were soaked with sweat and my pillow with the tears I'd shed while sleeping. Fucking-A. I could tell myself the sweat soaked sheets were from the muggy summer air, but the tears on my pillow were harder to explain away.

I leaned over to the fat gray cat lying stretched out on his half of the bed, obviously he'd gotten tired of my thrashing. "Will it ever stop, Martin? Don't answer that, I know, I know." I ran a hand over his sleek fur, and he opened one eye and gave me a rather disgusted look before going back to sleep with a yawn and a twitch of his tail. If he could have talked, I could only imagine what he'd say.

Probably something along the lines of 'take a Prozac and stop bothering me'.

Martin was used to my thrashing at night. A cat who didn't mind werewolves was a rare thing. Then again, we'd both nearly died in the river together that night. That was the kind of thing that bonded two beings together.

Running my hands over his fur, I let myself go back through the rest of my near death experience, try to pick out the bits and pieces that were good. To find the bright spots.

Sitting on the edge of my bed, I gathered Martin into my arms. "Remember how we met, Martin? I was washed up on the edge of the river, must have been at least ten miles away from where they dumped me. And that miserable old biddy, she had you in a sack, and was swinging you around in it?"

Martin yowled and tipped his head back, teeth chattering. I laughed. "I know. What a bitch, right? And she had the nerve to throw you into the river, with a brick tied to your sack!"

He growled and tried to burrow his head in the blankets. Meowing away, as if in answer to me.

She'd seen me and gotten scared and ran away, dropping the sack with Martin at my head. Mind you, I was probably pale as a fresh sheet of snow. I could still smell the burlap, feel it under my fingers if I thought about it. Martin had come out hissing and spitting mad. Seen me and had gone still. He'd licked my face and bounded away.

"But there are still good people in the world," I said softly. "Good people found us, Martin. That has to mean something, right?"

Two hunters out early had found me and Martin. Or more accurately, Martin had impossibly brought them back to me. They'd gathered me up and taken me to the nearest hospital.

Yeah, I know werewolves and hospitals don't normally mix, but there are always exceptions. The hospital near the pack had a couple of doctors who were in the know, and still kept the confidences of their less than human patients. Human themselves, but they'd had training in dealing with supernaturals. Martin began to purr again, making biscuits in the thick feather stuffed duvet.

I scratched him down his spine, then checked the clock on the bedside table.

Early, it was stupid early. Ass crack of dawn, nobody was going to be up for hours, that kind of early. Didn't matter, I knew I wouldn't be going back to sleep, even after my mini therapy session with Martin. I padded through to the bathroom and flicked the shower on full cold. That was the best thing at this point.

Stepping into the freezing spray, I gasped but held still as the water pounded over me, prickling my skin and sweeping away the fear- and pain-laced sweat. Not body pain, I'd healed from that years ago, but *heart* pain. It was a real bitch, and it seemed that the more I tried to put it behind me, the more it bubbled up. But let me tell you, trying to find a therapist for a middle-aged werewolf dealing with a murderous family wasn't as easy as it sounded.

Drying off, I dressed in jeans, over-the-knee boots with a lovely thick poof of black fur at the top of them, a long-sleeved flowy top that I tucked in just at the button of my jeans. The cream color was not something I'd wear to any other job, but this one allowed me to be a bit more... feminine.

I passed my roommates' room. They were shifters too, fox and bobcat, respectively, and did their own thing, in their own little bubble. Taini and Copper were cool, and we ate together maybe once a month. Roommates, not friends. I didn't let too many people get that close anymore. Survival and all that. Still, I paused at their doors and listened. The steady in and out of breath, the distinct rumble of Copper's light snore she swore didn't exist, and I nodded to myself.

I couldn't help the instincts that were in me. Protect. Protect. Protect.

I made my way downstairs and began flicking on lights.

This was the beauty of the apartment being attached to the bookstore I worked at. There was always a place to go when the dreams got too much, when the memories were too heavy. Books were a sanctuary, a place to hide even from the worst of my past.

Of not only what I'd survived, but of what I'd been made to do.

Row upon row of books were quickly illuminated, floor to ten-foot ceiling. The entire bottom half of the massive old house was store front and storeroom. As I walked, boots tapping on the tile, I trailed my fingers across the spines, letting the calm of this place soothe away the last of the memories.

"More dark stuff, huh?"

I didn't so much as flinch as the ghoul flowed out between the stacks of books, her body more corporeal than solid today. She'd been avoiding food again —I mean, I couldn't blame her. Ghouls were scavengers—the longer the thing had been dead and rotting, the better they liked it. Denna, though, had better taste, and it was making her fade.

"Good morning, Denna. And yes, more dreams, though... not. The usual, you know."

Denna was the previous manager of the bookstore... back when she was human. She'd been relegated to night-shift duties after changing into a ghoul. It turned out customers were sensitive to her existence, something Grant (the owner, also a somewhat questionable character), should have probably realized. Most humans couldn't see her, but she gave them the 'hibbity jiberty-fits', according to Bob, one of the regulars. So now she worked only at night, facing books and putting out new stock. I was pretty sure I was one of the few who could see her, and still talked to her.

I made my way over to the large wooden slab table that was set with all the makings for what a reader needed. Coffee, tea of every variety, packages of cookies that weren't greasy—couldn't have the pages smeared, sugar, honey, and real cream in the small fridge. A steamer, cappuccino machine, coffee grinder, and a small toaster. But that wasn't my favorite thing. Nope, the individual coffee cup warmers were. They looked like little coasters, and you just sat them down next to you.

Heaven, this place was heaven.

"Hardly morning." She pushed her big glasses up her face, though they didn't hide the brilliant yellow eyes that looked like small moons behind them. Solid yellow, no iris. "Why don't you just go back and take your mother's spot as the pack leader?"

I grimaced as I opened the coffee tin and began scooping in the required number for the largest pot. Seven if you must know, and I counted slowly in order to take my time and calm my irritation at the often-asked question. "It doesn't work that way. I can't just go in and take the pack. We've talked about this before."

"Right, but explain it to me again. You yourself said you were second in strength only to your mother, and she's the one causing all this shit. Yeah, you had a different father than the other kids, but that shouldn't matter."

I sighed and hit the start button on the coffee,

then went to the tea pot and started to boil water. I was not about to tell her that my one brother wanted to start a new dynasty with me as his bitch in the most literal of senses.

"It's really simple, Denna. I don't want to. The entire pack is broken, and I don't want to go back. They think I'm dead, and it's best to keep it that way. I don't want, nor do I need to run things."

"Not everyone is bad, I'm sure." She fiddled with the chain hanging from her glasses, the only noise she really made, or that I'd heard her make.

I looked at her kind of hovering behind the counter, gripping the edge with her toes. She was so damn quiet, she almost floated along.

Martin leapt up onto the counter, his baleful eyes locking on mine. "I can't read your mind, my man, what do you want?" I didn't look away. I was not submitting to a cat even though it wasn't really the same as doing so in a pack. He squinted his eyes—the closest he would get to giving in—and let out a loud yowl. One paw snaked out and patted a tin of tuna that was there just for him. He refused to eat real cat food.

"You got it." I cracked it open, and he stuck his face right in.

Denna's fingers clutched at the edge of the table, and she hoisted herself up, perching there like a gargoyle. "I still think you should go back. You said your sister was sweet."

My jaw ticked. My younger sister had been my mother, Juniper's, pride and joy before she'd even been born. I wasn't jealous of Meghan, not one bit, but she didn't need me. I was the one who was the black sheep, not her. Juniper would protect her 'real' daughter, I had no doubt about that.

The thing is, a black sheep in a werewolf pack doesn't last long. Making it all the way to adulthood had been a feat for me and in no small part to the man I called my father. No, not by blood but that didn't matter. He'd protected me all the same.

"Besides..." Denna peered closely at the coffee machine, a look of longing on her face. "I heard from Mary, who heard from Jakob, who heard from ..." The list of names went on and on. Ghouls seemed to communicate in an endless version of telephone. I'd learned not to put a lot of stock in her gossip since I never knew how much the stories had been twisted. "...Rachel, who said to Kevin, and he told me that your little sister is not happy. That she cries all the time."

"Not happy is not the same as in danger," I said even as my stomach rolled. "Besides, like I said. She is well loved. She'll be fine. Probably just had her heart broken by a first love. That happens." She would be what, eighteen now? I'd been 'killed' on the night of her eighth birthday. I'd held her tight and gifted her with a book of simple spells. Most wolves couldn't do magic, but some had the knack. I'd hoped for her sake she'd become the next healer of the pack. It would give her standing outside of the normal hierarchy of things. And if she chose, she could leave to another pack. Being a healer would give her the freedom to choose her life.

I couldn't spin a spell for the life of me, though my father had tried to teach me.

My heart did a strange thump, but I ignored it, chalking it up to floating bits of silver that could still be in my chest cavity. Ignoring the fact that I'd have been long dead if that were actually the case.

Denna gave a harrumph and slipped away. And me? I spent the morning going through inventory and getting some good research in so I could stop thinking about my past and the family who didn't want me and focus instead on my future.

And by inventory and research I meant I grabbed my current favorite book on mythologies around the world, snuggled up in the coziest chair in the place and chilled, letting the quiet of what was left of the night calm me. Werewolves, or wolf shifters if you prefer, are not meant to be loners. We do best when we have our family or pack around us. Which was only one more reason I didn't fit and never would.

Me? I found solace in the hours in which no one needed me.

Really, it was no wonder that I'd been 'killed' and tossed into the river. In our culture, it was anathema to a) contradict your alpha and their orders b) deny your pack access to you at any time and c) not fuck who you're told to fuck. I'll let you guess which of those I was guilty of.

Yup, all three.

When the light finally started to turn, and sun was coming through the front windows, I put down my book—I'd been fully immersed in reading about the Peruvian take on shifters—and made myself get up and prep the shop. I flicked on the open sign, and it wasn't long before the first few regulars trickled in.

George and Bob, a super cute couple who'd moved to Skagway only a few months after me, lived down the street and came in every morning for coffee. George ran the hardware store, and Bob was the only medium in town.

Not a real one, mind you, but both Denna and I humored him because he liked being a part of the supes community here. He had a run in with a witch when he was young, and it had opened his eyes to seeing more than the average human.

"We brought fresh cookies!" Bob clapped his hands together and plunked down the baked goods on the large table, as George headed over for the newspapers. Yesterday's, of course, but I knew from past experience he'd only grunt if I asked him if he'd prefer something newer. The man was quiet as a church mouse. Then again, Bob did enough talking for the two of them. "Lordy, lordy, I need to find a new office! The heat doesn't even work properly and you can imagine how that's going to go come winter. I'd have to take on another lease, though, and it just isn't worth it."

A longstanding complaint of Bob's. He'd never actually rented any space that I knew of. George gave a non-committal grunt that obviously meant something to Bob.

"Oh, George, you are so right! I'll ask her! Cin-cin, did you see the new guy in town? Hot, hot, hot!" Bob was pouring coffee for himself and George. "Oh my, he could put his shoes under my bed any day, all day, and at least half a night!"

George didn't even look up, just turned the page, the newspaper crinkling softly. I smiled at Bob from my spot behind the counter, my fingers smoothing out the bills from the float. The old cash register was clunky, but I liked it. Liked how the bell rang when the drawer popped open. Even if you didn't mean it to. I counted the float, making sure it was all there. "You trying to set me up again? My luck doesn't exactly runneth over in that department my very optimistic friend."

"Girl. *Girl.* I've known you for almost ten years, and I haven't seen you so much as blink at anyone. Man. Woman. Critter." He grinned and winked. "You'd better damn well blink at this one. Blink a few times if you catch my drift. Bat those beautiful eyes at him like you're trying to blow out a candle."

He came up to the counter, cookie crumbs falling everywhere. He motioned at me with the half-eaten confectionary.

"Unlikely." I swept off the crumbs, my eyes catching movement out front of the store.

"Ooh, the lady of the fates, I see your future with this one," Bob said through his cookie. "And I am never wrong."

The bell over the door tinkled softly, announcing a new arrival.

It felt like the half-dream from earlier had resumed, like I'd been sucked into the past without so much as a breath of a warning.

Shipley stepped through the door.

The youngest of my older brothers. The one I'd thought was my friend. I was sure my heart stopped as he turned and looked at me.

"Speak of the devil who wears Prada, there stands the object of desire right now. And is it just me, or do I sense chemistry?" Bob stage whispered.

Shipley's nostrils flared. His dark ginger hair was brushing his shoulders, longer than he'd ever worn it before. He'd been working out, and his muscles were almost to the point of being ridiculous, straining against the cloth of his shirt, pushing on the seams. That or he'd just bought clothes a size too small. That was possible too. He'd always loved the attention of the ladies. Loved being seen as the big man.

I didn't move, every part of me ready to fight or flee. I wasn't sure which.

Instinctually I knew that if I killed him, the others would come looking. If I ran, he would chase. The only other possibility was that he'd run from the pack...hope was a terrifying thing. Did I dare give myself that possibility, that my brother had run and...we could be friends again? The fantasy was bittersweet. How did you forgive someone for trying to kill you?

I supposed I was about to find out in three...two...one.

His eyes swept over me as if he didn't see me and then back so fast that he actually did a literal doubletake and stepped back. Nostrils flared, eyes wide. The pulse in his neck picked up, the staccato of his heart audible, at least to me.

Martin leapt up on the counter and let out a low rumbling growl, his body fluffing up to full height, which was saying something on a fat cat like him.

"Cin?" Shipley whispered my name. Fear? Shock? Maybe both.

I was moving forward, my wolf coming to the surface of my skin, begging to be unleashed on the traitor. So much for forgiveness. "Outside. Now," I growled.

Shipley stepped out quickly, moving backward, not turning away from me. Smart man. I had every reason to cut him down right there. Every reason to kill him.

"What in the fuck are you doing here?" I snapped.

"How... are you alive? Am I seeing things?" His eyes were wide, and his nostrils kept fluttering as he tried to scent me. As if he wasn't sure.

I snapped a fist out and punched him in the nose. "Does it feel like I'm dead, asshole?"

He grabbed at his face, blinking fast as the blood dripped onto his white shirt. "Jesus. Fuck. No."

"What. Are. You. Doing. Here?" I growled each word. He held up a hand, as if that would stop me. He was likely stronger than me in some ways, but his wolf would always be a submissive doormat when an alpha showed up. He wouldn't fight unless he was sure he had the upper hand and would win.

"I'm recruiting," he bit out. "Word came that there were some lone wolves up this way. Juniper wants to strengthen the pack before some big showdown."

I glared at him even as fear laced through my blood. Just like the silver poison. "This is *my* town. Get the fuck out before I break the rest of your face. Before I decide to make sure no one ever finds you."

He glared at me; gray eyes narrowed. As if there was a snowball's chance in hell that I'd back down from his bullshit. I might have been his younger sister, but we were not cut from the same cloth... I stepped close to him, so that we were nose to nose. "I'm dead, Shipley. Remember that when you get back to Grayling. I'm dead."

His lips curled into a snarl even as he dropped his eyes. "You think she won't smell a lie on me? You think she won't drag it out?"

"You say nothing about me. Tell them the lone wolf up here, because there is just one and it's me, is not fucking interested."

I let my wolf come up a little higher, until I knew my eyes would be wolfing out going from the hazel brown to a deep golden. His eyelashes fluttered, and he looked down again. It was so fast that anyone else might have missed it. But it was a submission.

He took a step back. "I won't throw..."

"Don't. Don't tell me you won't throw me under the bus," I growled. I'd heard those words before. When he said he'd always have my back, no matter what. That's what hurt, more than Kieran or Richard turning on me. My lip trembled, but I kept my voice hard. "Just go. Get the fuck out of here, and stay gone."

He slowly lifted both hands in mockingly real submission but said nothing else. Because, let's be honest, what was there to say? He'd fucked me over, thrown me out with the trash. He surely didn't expect me to play nice, did he?

I watched him walk down the street, his shoulders hunched. He didn't look back, but the tension in his body as he walked away said he fully expected me to attack him. I backed up and let myself into the bookstore.

"Well, how did it go?" Bob asked, hurrying up to me and staring out the glass of the door. "So cute. Totally bangable, we could double date—"

I put a gentle hand on my friend's shoulder. "He's a dangerous and completely disloyal werewolf, Bob. Steer clear of him. Okay? Promise me."

Bob's pale blue eyes popped wide and he looked from the door to me and back again. "What? You know him?"

I turned and stared at my brother's wide shoulders until he disappeared down a side street. I shook my head. "I thought I did, but I was wrong."

Bob pestered me with questions—how did I know him? Was he an old flame? Was he an alpha?

Bob, like so many humans, wanted to know more about the supernatural world. But I could only tell him so much without putting a mark on him. That was the deal.

They—the humans connected to the supernatural world—knew just enough to help keep them safe. Nothing more. Nothing less.

"Are you sure? Because I mean, fixing a broken man is an art form, I could teach you! He can't be that bad. Or maybe he is the bad boy, oh, I love me a good bad boy! Golden heart underneath maybe?"

"Bob, enough. He's my brother." I finally broke. Normally I'd have humored him, but I just couldn't. "Promise me you'll steer clear of him? He...hurt me badly, Bob."

George looked up over his paper. "Let her be, and listen to her, Bobby."

Bob stumbled over next to George then slumped into a chair. "Your brother? Well shit. Okay, I'll stay clear of him, I promise."

The rest of the day was a blur. Every time the door jangled, I had to fight not to spin and growl. Bob and George stayed for the entire day, not their usual time, but I appreciated that they were looking out for me.

Every part of me was wired, ready for action. I'd never stopped training, never stopped believing that at some point I would have to fight for my life again.

But I'll be honest, it had been long enough that I'd started to believe I was safe. That my pack would never find me. That I was finally free of them and all the fear they brought to this world.

I hated being wrong.

2

NO TIME FOR MENTAL
BREAKDOWNS

After twelve hours of the store being open, and me freaking out more than one customer with my partially bared teeth and my rapid-fire movements, I could finally flip the closed sign on.

Bob hugged me as he and George left. "You call us, day or night, right? You need us, we're here girly."

I hugged him tight, and was surprised when George pulled me into a bear hug, squeezing me hard enough that I was sure a rib popped out. He whispered in my ear. "I got a gun, and a few silver bullets left if you need them."

I couldn't have been more surprised. "George, those are hard to come by...how..."

He patted my cheek. "We all got a past, kid."

And then they were gone, and I was staring out

at them wondering about George in a way I'd never before.

Denna slid out from the back room. "Girlfriend, that was brutal."

I'd told her what had happened while on my one break to the back. Of all the people here, she was the one who knew my story inside and out. Everyone else had only heard the watered-down version. Family break up, starting over. My boss, George and Bob knew I was a werewolf. I tried to keep that knowledge on the down low for fear it would get back to the Grayling pack—exactly as it had.

A tap on the front door spun me around. In the semi-darkness stood Grant, the owner of the store. I sighed, more relieved than irritated. "Crap, I do not need this right now."

I went over to the door and unlocked it. "Grant. Checking up on me?"

He grinned, showing off his huge fangs. Which I have to say looked ridiculous in the body of a scrawny, forever nineteen-year-old who had a receding hairline and giant ears. Becoming a vampire had not made him any prettier.

"Cin, heard there was some trouble today?" His voice was a bit on the squeaky side, breaking with the changes that came during puberty. He just seemed to have hit all the shitty parts of that late teenage period. Between his voice and his appearance, people underestimated him, which he used to his advantage. He was a wickedly smart and savvy businessman.

I stepped back to give him room to come in. "Yeah. An old pack member showed up. I sent him on his way. With a solid threat."

Grant frowned and pursed his lips. "An old lover?"

"No." I turned my back on him and headed toward the stairs. "If I don't eat, my wolf is going to be a bitch."

Grant followed. I didn't mind. I wasn't afraid of him, and he'd been in my apartment before. There were some very big, very bad vampires out there. Grant was not one of them. He was in Alaska for the same reason as me. Hiding out. Flying under the radar.

Besides, the apartment felt empty without my roommates. Taini and Copper loved the music scene, and they'd left sometime earlier today for a festival in Vancouver. Did they say goodbye? Nope, they did not. That wasn't how our roommate situation worked.

I grabbed some leftover elk roast and didn't even bother to heat it up before I sat down at the small table in the kitchen and started shoveling the food in. I had been so wound up all day I'd not stopped to eat. Not smart when the full moon was coming on, tugging on my natural instincts to be wolfy.

Grant watched me. "Is there anything I can do to help?"

I shook my head as I tore into the meat, swallowing a hunk before I answered. "No. I'll just have to do some extra patrols, check in with the other shifters around here."

Denna crept up the stairs. "I can check in with the ghouls."

I nodded. "Please, thank you, Denna."

Grant took a seat and crossed his legs, linking his fingers over his knee. "Is he truly that dangerous?"

I struggled to swallow the mouthful, anxiety and fear making my mouth dry. Denna leapt over to the fridge and grabbed a bottle of water, which she tossed to me. I drank it down in three big gulps. "Yes and no. He... was one of the ones that drove me out. They thought I was dead. If he reports back that he found me here, alive, then I will have trouble. They don't like losing. If I'm alive, they will see that as me winning."

Grant frowned. "You think he will come back then?"

I shrugged and leaned on the table. "If he does, it won't be on his own. I told him off, told him none of the shifters wanted him here. But... he's on orders, he's looking for recruits."

Denna tapped the plate with a long fingernail, and I sliced her off a hunk. She grabbed it and stuffed it into her mouth, grimacing. Too fresh, no doubt for her ghoulish taste buds. She spoke around the meat. "The question is, why would they send him all the way up here to recruit? That seems like a long way."

I blew out a slow breath, because she'd just asked the question that had been rumbling around in my head for the entire day while I'd tried not to jump every time the door opened. "Something must have changed within the packs. He said something about a big showdown. So it could be that a big fight is coming; they would want to shore up their weak spots."

Grant stood and tucked his hands into his pockets. "You'd be safer at my place. They don't know where I live. It would give you a few days to plan."

Denna snickered. "And you'd just let her sleep in the bed with you? Naked, of course."

Grant smiled, totally unflustered as he winked at me. The man had balls. "Not a bad idea."

I shook my head before he even finished speaking. "No. They'd scent me all the way to your lair, and then we'd both be marked. I'll be okay here."

Grant frowned—apparently he hadn't thought it was as bad as I was making it out to be, or he'd never have offered his place to me. He began a slow pace across the kitchen as his tune changed rapidly. "I don't want my store burning down, Cin. And if they are as good as you think they are, that will happen."

I washed my hands, then dried them on the tea towel. "You telling me not so subtly you want me to go? No offers of a bed now?" I smiled to soften the words. Because I did understand.

His pacing stopped. "I think you should leave. Not for me, but because if you don't, and you're right about them, then you will end up dead for real. And this world... would be a duller place without your soul brightening it."

Denna sighed. "Oh, I wish someone would talk to me that way."

I just stared at Grant, because he didn't know me. He didn't know what I'd had to do to survive those first forty years of my life. I might not have looked my age, but that was a werewolf for you. He looked at me like I was an innocent, because my age didn't show in my face, or body. If he did know what I was capable of, maybe he wouldn't be so quick to worry about my soul.

He nodded as he leaned on the counter. "I'm not a strong vampire, I never will be. But I'm not stupid. I wouldn't have lasted this long if I were not able to outsmart the stronger ones. You have to be smart when you are outnumbered, Cin."

I'd never once thought he was stupid. A sigh slid

out of me. "Fuck, I know you're right. I just hate that they're driving me out, this...this is my home."

Grant reached over and put his hand on mine, his skin cool, dry. "This will always be your home, Cinniúint, daughter of destiny, bearer of fate."

Well shit, he even said it right. Sin-ew-ee-ent. Not that many people called me by my full name, it was a fucking mouthful. "How long have you known my name?" I asked.

He grinned. "Day you arrived."

"And you waited this long to spill the beans?" Denna said.

He shrugged. "I told you, I'm long lived for a reason."

I gave him a nod. He'd researched me, and found me right away—probably then he knew some of what I was capable of. Apparently, I wasn't as well hidden as I'd always thought. More than that though, he'd held my secret for ten years.

Trust is a thing hard earned, especially when it came to men, and Grant had proven his trust more than ever in that moment.

I went to my room and stuffed a couple of bags full of clothes, a couple of books, and a bag of cat food aka canned tuna. Martin leapt up on the bed and glared at me, smacking my hands while I packed. "Yes, you're coming with me, Martin. I can't leave you."

"Where will you go?" Denna crept into my room, her yellow eyes glowing in the semi-darkness. Good question. Where could I go and keep my ass hidden?

"I'll head to Vancouver. Taini and Copper are still there for that concert. They can help set me up again. I'll head to Europe. France, maybe, always wanted to see the Eiffel tower. I probably should have moved off the continent a long time ago." I scrounged under the bed and grabbed the cat carrier. Martin clawed at it until I let him in, and then he curled up and glared at me. I stuffed one of my sweaters in with him to help keep him warm on the ride.

"I don't know why you're glaring at me, my man. You're coming!" I patted the top of the carrier for good measure.

Out of my room and back into the living area, I stared at the place that I'd called home, and felt mostly safe, for the last ten years. Sure, I had nightmares, but I suspected I'd have them no matter where I went. Fucking hell, I hated that Juniper and the pack were still ruining my life. I pulled my phone out of my back pocket and stared at it. Pulling up the number of the pack house in Grayling, I punched it in, saved it, and gave it its own ring tone. Just in case.

"Where will you go?" Grant held out a hand, and

I took it as I tucked my phone away. His skin was cool, and his grip firm.

"Maybe Europe?" I forced a smile. "I've been reading a lot about the old mythologies there. I could go see where they were born. England. France. Italy. Norway. Greece."

He tugged me into a hug, surprising me. "I wish I were strong enough to protect you, Cin. You deserve a man like that."

I hugged him back. "You've been a good friend, Grant. Don't be a hero. If they show up, just tell them I left. Let them search the rooms. There's nothing here that will trace me."

He let me go, and I took a step back.

"Um." Denna cleared her throat. "Can I come with you? I've always wanted to go to Europe, and you know I can help keep you up on supernatural gossip through the ghoul lines."

Grant was shaking his head. "And who can I get to run the store? I obviously can't." He waved a hand at his scrawny, trapped-at-nineteen body as if that were the issue and not his fangs or the fact that he couldn't come out in daylight.

"Bob," I said immediately. "He loves this place. And he can do his mediumship out of upstairs. Tell him it's haunted, and he'll be all over it." Also, there was George who apparently would blow a hole in a werewolf given the opportunity.

"Haunted?" Grant's eyebrows shot up. "Seriously?"

"Yeah, he'll love that, tell him that I sensed the ghost as I left." I smiled as I gave him Bob and George's number, and then I was hurrying out of the place I'd called home long enough to feel like I was a part of something again.

Grant and Denna followed me downstairs, then out of the back of the building to where my motorcycle sat under a small overhang. "Are you sure you don't want to just stay with me?" Grant asked softly as I slung a leg over. Denna crawled up behind me, her overlong, thin limbs gripping the edges of the seat.

I put Martin's cat carrier onto the passenger seat and strapped it down. He squinted up at me and beaked off. Denna nodded along as though she understood him.

"Of course she's sure," Denna said. "I mean, I'm sure. I've already put the notice out that we're looking for a place to crash. We'll find something."

Grant was shaking his head. "And you have money?"

"It's all under a fake name," I said. "They won't be able to trace it, not right away."

I could see the hesitation in him. I knew that if I said the word, he'd do his best to hide me, to use his resources and connections, but... the cost was too high. He was a friend, and I didn't want to put someone else in danger.

Not again, anyway. I pushed those darker memories away before they could surface. Starting up the bike, I walked it out from under the overhang, then slipped on my helmet, handing one to Denna.

"I don't need this. I'm already dead, remember?"

"And I don't need one either, but the last thing we need is a cop pulling us over and putting us into the system. Put it on."

"Bossy bitch," she muttered, but put the helmet on.

Grant opened his mouth, and I revved the engine, blocking out whatever it was he was about to say. Goodbyes were the worst, and I did my best to avoid them. Which is why I let myself idle by Bob and George's house.

A figure came to the window and lifted the curtain. George. He lifted his hand and gave me a single nod. He'd look after Bob.

Without another look back, I took off, heading to the highway.

We drove south until the morning, getting us a solid nine hours away from where my brother had seen me, and stopped in a Podunk town just off the highway. A crappy little motel was all I could find. I tucked the bike in the parking at the back, hiding it as best I could. I lifted Martin's carrier off and opened the door.

"I didn't bring litter, so you'd better go do your business," I instructed him.

If cats could roll their eyes, that was his move. He strutted away, tail in the air.

"He'll come back," Denna said. "He knows who holds the tuna tin."

I laughed at her. "You are not wrong."

A few minutes later Martin was back and leapt up into my arms.

"You really think that he'll track you that fast, your brother, I mean?" Denna pulled her helmet off and crawled from the bike. She sniffed the air, and I followed her, doing the same. The faint smell of rotting meat hung in the air.

"Shit," she whispered. "Sorry, gotta go."

Before I could answer her, she was gone, the smell of rotting meat too much for her to resist.

I blew out a breath and buried my nose in Martin's fur. "Worse, Dee, he'll try to finish what they started all those years ago."

3

REPEAT AFTER ME. JUST 'CAUSE HE'S HOT DOESN'T MEAN HE'S WORTH BANGING

T hree weeks later, I was set up in a small house on the outskirts of Edmonton. A city big enough to get lost in, and currently there were no werewolf packs in the area, the closest one was in Lethbridge near the US border masquerading as holier than thou churchies, so I wasn't about to get scented.

Taini and Copper made a very good point as they helped me find the place.

"They'll expect you to run hard, to get on a plane and jet," Copper said, her creamy complexion dusted with sparkles. Her deep brown eyes reflected those of her animal that resided under her skin. "Lay low, pick a few other cities. Stay a few weeks in each."

Taini slid her slender fingers through her hair,

standing the red ends straight up. "I agree. Then we can meet you in Paris. We'll go to London first, then we'll use the train. We can tour Europe together."

I'd stared at them, back and forth. "You...are willing to uproot your lives to come with me?"

Copper grinned. "Hard to find good roommates. You know we can hear you stop by our door, every morning, every night, checking on us? You know we don't pack up like wolves but...we're outcasts too. So why the fuck not?"

Why the fuck not?

The words had echoed in me, the plan solid. I would work in Edmonton for a few weeks, then I'd fly across Canada to Quebec. Shift, cross the border and slide down into Maine. From there I'd pick up the new ID that Copper would have in place for me, Denna and Martin would have all their paperwork by then and we'd fly out in a little over two months.

By the way plans went, I couldn't see many cracks in it.

And I still felt the warmth of my roomies wanting to be part of...my pack. Yup, life was shifting right for once.

As long as I could keep my nose clean between now and then, I'd be good.

I paused in my morning jog, a smell rather closer than I'd like it to be, one that tugged on my feet.

The faintest hint of wolf.

My nostrils flared as I took the smell in, deep, identifying it.

Male, not related to me, and all alone. A lone wolf was less of an issue. The scent wasn't fresh—weeks old, I was betting. I drew in another breath because something about it was... tantalizing. I was probably safe to go check it out, as long as I was careful not to touch anything.

Denna poked out from behind a garbage can on the park loop. "I smell it too, and you're stupid if you go looking for trouble. We just got settled here, and you have a great job! You need to keep it long enough for our next flight."

I grimaced. "I wouldn't call it a great job." Working nightshift as a part-time bartender was... it was a job, and one that didn't require credentials other than the ability to sling a drink and not piss off the patrons.

Musk curled up my nose, tugging me forward. Curiosity got the better of me—my father had always said I was part cat—and I found myself following the smell of the male wolf.

"I won't touch anything, so there will be nothing for him to pick up on," I said as I got closer to the source of his smell. No, that was not entirely honest. My scent would be there, lingering in the air, off the bottom of my shoes even.

The sound of voices caught my ears long before I

saw the two who were talking. A gruff man and a woman whose sobs and hitching breath told me she was scared. I picked up my pace. Much as I didn't want to draw attention to myself, I wouldn't leave another woman in trouble if I could help her.

"You have to hide." His voice was deep and had a thick accent that I couldn't quite place. European, maybe? "I can't keep you safe if you don't hide. I'm doing all I can to stop him from finding you, and you have to do your part. You have to keep hiding, keep moving."

She sobbed softly, her hair platinum blonde to the point of being silvery, trailing all the way down to her butt. "I can't keep running, I'm so tired. I just... I just want it to be over. Terrance keeps getting hurt, trying to protect me."

I slowed my feet and found a tree to lean against. From there, I peeked up from under my lashes. The man was dressed all in black, angular and slim, hunched over. He moved as if he were old and in pain.

She, on the other hand, was younger than me—probably in her early thirties. Her frame was slight, with generous curves and skin that reflected the sunlight to the point of nearly glowing. Whatever products she used, I would have bet they cost her a bundle.

"She's stunning," Denna whispered.

The man jerked around and stared across the thirty or so paces between us. "What the fuck are you looking at?"

Well, shit. My wolf immediately rose to the surface of my body, ready to fight, ready to protect someone else. I blew out a slow breath, calming myself and my inner bitch. "Just making sure you aren't hurting her."

The woman in question shook her head, silvery hair floating. "I have to go, I'm sorry I'm not good at this."

She took off at a hurried walk, pulling her jacket tight around her tiny waist. The man stood there watching her go, then turned to me.

A snarl slid out of him, and his face twisted into a grimace that didn't look quite human. The eyes and lips were wrong, the skin shadowed under his hooded eyes seemed off too, though I couldn't quite pinpoint the reason.

"He ain't human," Denna muttered under her breath. "I'd bet my glasses on it. Think he's going to follow her?"

My jaw tightened, and I locked eyes with him. Both me and my wolf were spoiling for a good fight, and this one... he was begging for an ass kicking.

But he didn't step toward me.

"Stay out of business that isn't yours, bitch." He growled, then turned and was gone with a swirl of his cloak, limping away. I waited a beat and then approached where they'd been standing. Right on top of the male wolf's scent.

Was that just coincidence?

The male wolf had been here probably ten days or so before, touching the bench, the garbage can, the trees, all of it. Why? Marking his territory? Covering another scent?

The mystery was a wonderful distraction from the feeling that my brother was closing in on me. No, I hadn't seen or heard from him, but I *knew* Shipley. He liked the hunt more than the kill, and Juniper would have set him on me with full measures to bring me in.

Despite my warning, he would have told her everything. Which was the entire reason I'd left.

"Satisfied? Can we go?" Denna said. "It's getting cold."

I gave her a quick nod, and we turned to leave. As we walked back along the path, headed home, the hair on the back of my neck rose and I stole a glance over my shoulder.

In the shadow of the tree where I'd stood was a wolf, fur black as night, eyes blazing with hate. His lips curled back, flashing perfect white teeth.

Denna squeaked and grabbed my arm, dragging me away even as I snarled back at him.

"What are you doing? He could be working for

your brother!" Denna's words got through to me, digging in past my instincts. She was right. This was a terrible idea and I needed to move.

Whoever the wolf was, I needed to get the hell out of there and away from him.

I picked up a jog, and Denna loped along beside me, her strange limbs folding and unfolding, kind of looking like a small camel keeping pace.

At the edge of the park, just before I stepped onto pavement, the howl of the wolf behind me ripped through the air. Marking his territory.

My thoughts scattered, dust on the wind.

That howl cut through my body, dropping me to my knees. The sound reverberated against my bones and rippled my skin in a most delicious fashion... everywhere. My clit throbbed, shocking me with the ache that grew along with the howl. What the shit fuck damn *was* this magic? I could barely think. I sucked wind and struggled to breathe, and the bastard seemed to know what he was doing, because the howl stretched and grew until I was panting.

I dug my fingers into the soil, barely holding myself together on my hands and knees. The urge to rock with the way the howl touched me, the need to move against it, to push harder was brutal.

By sheer force of will, I clung to my control, even though a whimper slid out of my lips as the howl eased off.

Shuddering, I got to my feet and forced myself to move, stumbling the first few steps as my body protested. Blue balls had nothing on me.

"We need to leave," I bit out. "Tomorrow."

"Um yeah, how about tonight?" Denna said. "You just about orgasmed on the sidewalk, my friend, from a howl. Like sound alone? That's some powerful juju."

Even though I knew she was not wrong, my sense of responsibility was strong. I was a pack creature after all. "I have a shift at the bar. I get home at one, and I'll sleep a few hours, and then we'll leave, forget the flight, we'll drive across to Quebec."

She side-eyed me, but I chose to ignore her.

My shift at the bar was blessedly quiet which gave me time to try and figure out what had happened earlier.

What did the woman and the angry man have to do with the blue-eyed wolf? Anything? I realized then that I'd not picked up a scent on the angry man. The woman smelled of summertime, and flowers, even though she also smelled of tears. She was less the concern than the grump. There wasn't a person in the world, human or supernatural, that could hide their scent unless they had a spell.

Which meant he was what, a mage or shaman of some sort.

Fucking magic wielders were always causing shit.

"You're all done?" My manager, Josh, tapped the bar as I was cleaning up. He was tattooed on every piece of skin I could see, with a big beard and an even bigger belly. But he was easy going.

"Yeah," I said. "Won't be back tomorrow. Family shit I gotta deal with."

He grunted. "Well, you come back this way, you got a job. You're good with people."

I shook his hand, and he handed me my tips. "Luck to you, Sasha."

Sasha, false name number twelve.

I left, the city quiet as it would ever be just before one in the morning, the cool air rushing around me, bringing me all sorts of scents as I drove.

Including the male wolf again. Only this time, it was fresher. Sharper. Right there, not far off the road. My body tensed, remembering his howl and how it had affected me. How his scent had drawn me close even though he was an obvious danger to me. I swallowed hard at the thought of what he could do to my body, naked and begging for his touch, if his howl could send me to my knees and push me toward an orgasm. Anything. I'd probably let him do anything to me, given the chance.

Sue me, it had been a long, long dry spell.

I didn't slow my bike down, just kept on going,

letting my little fantasy play out in my head. I was old enough to know better. Honest.

There may have been a glimmer of movement, but I kept on staring straight ahead. Got to my rental, parked my bike in the garage and took myself inside, locking the door behind me. The urge to turn around and go check him out on foot was strong, and my wolf agreed that it wouldn't be a terrible thing.

Only I'd be leaving behind a perfect marker for my brothers to track, which was completely unacceptable.

I forced myself upstairs, showered—keeping it cold helped—and threw myself into bed. Martin hopped up beside me, teeth chattering as he chided me for being late. I smiled and grabbed him around the middle. "Come here, fluff butt."

He wriggled a little, then gave up and let me hold him. His motor started and the rumble of it soothed some of the ragged edges of the day, and it wasn't long before I was asleep. Dreaming of a black werewolf with eyes made of chips of blue ice and hatred.

4

WELL, THAT WAS FUN WHILE IT LASTED

In the End by Linkin Park jerked me out of a deep sleep.

The ringtone that was tied to only one place.

The pack phone in Grayling. My distant past and the family I never wanted to return to—yet here I was, answering the phone before I could think better of it, barely with it. I got the phone to my ear before words started pouring out of my sister's mouth.

"Cin, you have to come home. Mom's going to kill me. I'm going to die if you don't come home." Meghan's voice cracked, and not because of the distance. Her sobs shattered me like nothing else could have done.

Grown up, she sounded so grown up from the eight-year-old little sister I'd left behind.

Wait, how the fuck did she find my number? I'd changed it a half a dozen times in the last ten years. It had to be Shipley. Once they knew I was alive, they would have hunted for any way to track me.

Including my phone.

I sat up in bed, scrambling for clothes even as I kept the phone pressed to my ear, because I knew she wasn't exaggerating or speaking in metaphors. This wasn't, *OMG, Mom's totally going to kill us for going out after curfew* or *holy crap, I'm pregnant, Mom's going to kill me*. Our mother wasn't the type to soften or bend or compromise.

If my little sister said our mother was going to kill her, that was *exactly* what she meant.

"Fuck, I'm awake, I'm awake. Tell me what's happening." I glanced at the clock beside my bed. Three in the morning. I'd been asleep less than two hours. Everyone in the Grayling pack would be asleep. That explained the timing of the call at least, but not the *why* of it. Why would Meghan be on the chopping block? Weren't they all out hunting for me?

Meghan was the spitting image of Mom, and in the past she'd never stepped out of line, which had unintentionally made her a favorite of the head bitch. It was the one solace I'd had after my brothers tried to kill me. I'd believed Juniper—our mother—wouldn't ever lay a hand on her mini-me.

I'd have put all my hard earned fifty grand in the bank on it.

"What happened? Are you hurt? Was it Dick or Kieran?" I looked at the phone call. Under a minute. If they were tracking me, I had time.

Her voice lowered to a level that no human ears could have detected. "No, it's not the boys. Mom slept with the wrong guy, and his wife is a witch," Meghan hiccupped back a sob. Witch, she said witch, not bitch. "She doesn't know that... that I overheard what... what is going to happen. His wife is really a witch, Cin, with some serious standing. She's demanding compensation. A death for the trespass of sleeping with her husband. I didn't know who else to call. The witch said it had to be Juniper or me. Shipley said he found you and I found your number... and... ."

"Fuck," I whispered, both because of the situation, and the confirmation that Shipley was indeed fucking me over. Again. "It was always the wrong guy with her." I'll admit, part of me hoped this would be the end of Juniper. This could be the answer to my constant vigilance, to running from my own family. My brothers might hate me, but they were too fucking lazy to keep hunting for me if Juniper wasn't pushing them. "I'm coming."

"Hurry. Please."

"I'll get there as fast as I can, but listen to me,

you need to hide. Go to the western side of the forest, to the base of the Rockies. I need you to stay hidden, like when you were little, okay? Near the river, the sound will help hide you. Get in the water if you think they're close, tuck under the reeds at the edge. Remember how we used to do that? How we used to practice breathing through the reeds?"

Her crying cut through me, especially since she was making a solid effort to stay quiet, sniffling and fighting the sobs. "Okay, how will I know you're there?"

"Magpie call," I said. "Take supplies with you."

She sucked in a shuddering breath. "How long?"

I knew the distance from Skagway like the back of my hand. It would be thirty-three hours to Grayling, Montana, if I were driving like a normal person. But from Edmonton? I wasn't as sure. Half that if I were lucky.

But as a werewolf with no need to worry about a crash? I could cut hours off no problem, maybe more than a few. "I'll try for nine hours, but that will be hard, probably closer to ten."

There was no other option; I didn't tell her what to do if I didn't make it, because if that was the case, we'd both be dead.

The phone clicked off before she could say anything else, and the line went silent.

I didn't try calling her back. I knew why she'd hung up.

Someone had been getting close, and she'd cut and run. She'd have to hurry now to get to the river without being caught. I tried not to think about how tough it would be for her to stay hidden for that long. I peeled open the back of my phone and pulled the SIM card, then tossed both onto the bed.

My mind raced as I yanked clothes on—jeans, a long-sleeved shirt, and leather boots—barely paying attention to what I was doing. If I could get Meghan out, then Juniper would be forced to take her own punishment, and the world would be a better place without her special brand of crazy sauce. Even though I knew Meg was the favorite, there was no way Juniper would die for anyone, certainly not one of her children.

"What's going on?" Denna grumbled. "I thought we were leaving in the morning."

"Rescue mission. I need to save my sister. You stay here with Martin, okay? I might be a couple days." I gave her a thumbs up. "Use my extra bank card if you need to get anything."

I ran through the kitchen, grabbed my keys, and was out the door in seconds into the already crisp-fall-is-coming-soon air.

"You know it could be a trap!" Denna yelled out

after me. Martin bolted down the stairs and jumped up to sit in front of me.

I paused, sitting astride the bike. "Yes, I know. But it's my *sister*, Denna. The only person there who's worth anything, as far as I'm concerned. Even if there's a 5% chance it's not a trap, I'm going. And the chances that it's a trap are low. Meg isn't like the others. She's going to be killed if I don't get her out of there." I picked Martin up and set him on the ground. "Stay with Denna."

He stood on his back legs, clawing at my pants, yowling his face off. I ran a hand over his head. "Martin, be a good cat, okay?"

Denna gripped the doorframe, her claw fingers digging in hard. "If you aren't back in two days, I'm going to come looking for you."

Martin sneezed, as if in agreement.

I grinned at her. "You're a good friend, Denna. But I'll be back. Take care of Martin, please."

I had to believe that what I was telling her was the truth. I was about to march my ass right into the lion's den, not that they would see me coming. Shipley was out in Alaska snooping around for me. Hopefully all three boys would be out looking for me. That was why, more than any other reason, I was willing to go. I could kill Juniper if I needed to. Fuck, she'd trained me to be that bitch.

"Hang on, Meggie." I turned the key, and my bike

rumbled to life under me. Movement out of the top corner of my eye drew my attention to the other side of the street.

Gods-damned. The big black wolf sat quietly, watching me. I swallowed hard and fought to keep eye contact, finally breaking our stare down and looking at my bike. How long had it been since I'd been unable to keep a stare up? It rankled me and I raised my eyes, locking our stares again.

At least he was seeing me go. "Peace out, mother fucker!" I flashed him a rocker sign.

He let out a low growl and took a step toward me. Nope, not tonight.

I lifted my kickstand and rolled my wrist, taking off with a deep roar of my bike that still made my blood sing after years of owning it.

Hurry, hurry, hurry. I hadn't seen Meghan in over ten years, but I would not deny my little sister. She was an adult now, and if she wanted to leave the Grayling Pack, the decision should be hers. Well, maybe I wasn't framing the situation quite right. It didn't sound like she was being given a decision at all, other than stay and die or leave and maybe live.

The hours blurred together as I drove at the top speed my bike would go, taking curves and driving around other vehicles as if they weren't there. I was not one to let fear drive me, but Meghan was my little sister and the one person I wished I'd been able to keep from our family.

Born late to our mother, I'd been an adult for a long time when Juniper had announced she was pregnant for the fifth time.

Memories roared through me, taking me back to the time when the pack in Grayling had been my world.

One of the strongest packs on the continent, Juniper and Mars had been the alphas that everyone looked too.

No one ever told me who my father actually was, but it didn't matter. Mars looked out for me as if I were his little girl, teaching me to fight, teaching me how to track and hunt, and the rules of the pack. He protected me when no one else would have. To the end.

My eyes watered as I thought about losing Mars. It had been my fault that he'd left, and we all knew it.

Eighteen-year-old me stood in front of the mirror. My birthday and my induction into the pack as an adult. I was wearing a sleek black dress, and my hair was twisted into an updo, leaving my neck and collarbone clear, where the mark of the pack would be set on my left side.

"Well, well, little one." Mars let himself into my room, smiling at me. His hair was an unusual color, deep gray

throughout, just like the coat of his wolf. "You ready for this?"

I grinned at him, butterflies going wild in my belly. "Yes. Of course!"

He pulled me into a hug and whispered into my ear. "No matter what, hold your ground. You know who you are, Cinniúint, you were named for a reason." *He stepped back and held me at arm's length.* "I cannot believe you are the same girl that I took hunting, that I rocked to sleep after nightmares. I just can't." *He smiled, pulled me close, and kissed me on the forehead.*

"I knew it." *The words cut through the moment, and we turned to see Juniper glaring at us.*

"June," *Mars said.*

Her hand snaked out, and she grabbed the edge of my dress, tearing it from my body. "Don't you dare try to pretend you haven't been fucking her!" *Her scream echoed through the room.*

I scrambled to cover myself up, Mars stepped in front of me. "Juniper. Have you lost your mind? She's my daughter!"

"She is not your daughter and now you're just going to replace me!"

The screaming went on and on as I managed to grab a t-shirt and yank it over my head before I was dragged out in front of the entire pack. Shamed. Beaten. Forced into a confession that wasn't real.

Mars tried to stop it, but he was held tight, chained with silver.

I never saw him after that night. He left, and I couldn't blame him. Not one bit.

I stopped on the road only to eat and fuel up the bike, to try and ignore the memories that were demanding my attention.

My first kill at Juniper's command. Then the second and third. Trying to find a way to escape. Thinking Shipley would help, might even come with me.

Pain radiated from each memory, and I pushed it all down and away. I had to focus on what was ahead of me now—Meghan and getting her the fuck out of Grayling.

Nine and a half hours later, I was rolling into the outskirts of a place I never thought I'd come back to. Before I reached the first outpost where Juniper would have the Delta guards watching, I pulled my bike to the side of the dirt road. Flicking off the engine, I pushed the bike just deep into the bush that ran next to the road that I could cover it with a few well-placed branches. Using a bottle of rubbing alcohol, I doused the seat and handlebars and rubbed the back down, cleaning it of my scent more than anything else. I rubbed my hands with the alcohol, then quickly ran them over my neck, behind my ears, and over my pits. I even ran my hands between my legs. The alcohol would kill my scent for a short time and soften its impact. That would help me sneak in, I hoped. And it would help hide my bike too. Any shifter would sniff out the gasoline and steel in a flash, but if they weren't looking, they wouldn't notice it without the scent of wolf attached to it.

It was no spell of hiding, but it was better than nothing.

I shouldered my backpack and headed into the trees on foot, avoiding downed branches, sticks, and dry leaves, and crept silently toward the meeting place—the bend in the river near the northern edge of the pack lands. I'd taken Meghan there a hundred times as a child, teaching her to swim, teaching her about the plants and animals as Mars had taught me before he'd left. Teaching her, more than anything, how to hide and stay silent and safe—something that had become more important than ever for pack wolves by the time she was born. Although I never wanted to say it out loud back then, I'd known that I was always in danger from my family—all because of Juniper. I'd seen it in my brother's eyes when they looked at me, and even back then, I'd known that I would have to leave at some point.

Mind you, leaving on my own would've been a hell of a lot nicer than being nearly murdered. But there you go, that was my family for you.

Breathing deep, scenting the air, I adjusted my direction. The wind was at my back, pushing my scent out to anyone who might be ahead of me, and I couldn't have that. I swept wide to the left, doused myself with some more rubbing alcohol, and prayed the wind would change in my favor.

The urge to shift to my four-legged form was strong this deep in the woods, but that would mean stripping, leaving my clothes, and praying I didn't have to do any fast shifting back to two legs. Basically, a total nope for a rescue mission.

The late morning air was still cool, and I drew the familiar smells into my lungs, constantly checking for anyone else who might be wandering about. Which is the only reason why I had the small warning I did—miniscule at best.

A faint whiff of ogre beer tickled the back of my throat, the wind playing on my cheek. Richard, my eldest brother. It didn't really surprise me that the drunk got left behind off a hunt.

I dropped flat to my belly, holding my breath, and went completely silent. Likely he was out here looking for Meghan. The question was, would he be alone? Probably, no one really liked him.

There was an exhale of air to my right. I rolled my eyes in that direction, straining to catch movement, praying my scent didn't break through the rubbing alcohol. If Dick had been drinking, then I had a chance. He was the sloppiest of my three brothers when it came to getting shit done. More so when he'd been into the ogre beer, which was a daily event.

Another exhale of breath that was farther away, the distant crack of a branch.

I waited for a solid three minutes—a long time when you are trying to alternately hold and control your breath without gasping for air—before I pushed back into a crouch.

Moving as fast as I could, cognizant that my luck wouldn't hold out forever, I worked my way toward the bend in the river, where Meghan would be waiting for me. Hiding from our family.

My plan was simple. Once I had her with me, we'd make a full tilt run for it. Smaller than the boys, we were faster too. Or at least I was, and I was banking on Meg being the same as me with youth and vigor to back her up.

Richard, Kieran, and Shipley, they were all bulky, thick-muscled and just enough slower that —

Movement in front of me at the river, a flash of long red hair, a flower tied into the ends. Still the same Meg, still tying flowers to her hair.

Denna's fears that I was being set up came back to me, and I slowed my run, crouching within a section of thick wild roses, their scent helping cover my own. I hadn't wanted to think that Meghan would help set me up. Then again, I'd been away a long time.

Still, my mind rejected the idea, hard. My little sister had always looked up to me, wanted to be like me, and she'd been afraid of the boys and fearful of Juniper, even though Juniper hadn't treated her poorly.

Meg would know I didn't leave the pack on my own. That I'd been rejected for standing up to Juniper. Just like Mars had been rejected for standing up for me.

Movement again drew my eyes. Meg crouched by the river as Richard stepped out from the right side. His dark reddish-brown hair was swept back and held at the nape of his neck in a ponytail. The slight hitch to his stride spoke volumes about how much ogre beer he'd taken in. And before lunch too.

"Meg, hiding are we, little bitch?" He swung a hand toward her.

"Go away, Richard!" Meg stumbled back to the water's edge and then stepped farther, out into the river itself. The tremble in her body and the fear in her eyes said it all. This was no ruse. She was in danger.

There was no turning back now. I sprinted out of the bushes and leapt onto Richard's back.

"Hello, you ugly Dick," I growled as I locked my

forearm around his neck, bearing down on all the blood flowing to his fat, beer-filled head.

He clawed at my arms, but my jacket kept his nails from scoring flesh. I wrapped my legs around his thick waist and squeezed with all I had, my thigh muscles tightening as he thrashed and grappled with me.

"Bitch," he wheezed out.

"Always the original one," I growled in his ear as he began to slump, his body going limp until he finally passed out. We'd have twenty seconds at best before he came around. I jumped off his back and turned to Meghan. She was beautiful all grown up, her blue-green eyes wide, her hair caught in a shaft of morning light, but it was her hands that I couldn't look away from.

Her hands, and the gun in them.

"Meg, he's out cold. We can go. Come on." I took a step toward her, and she squeezed the trigger.

5

GOLDEN HOUR MY ASS

S low motion is a funny thing in real life. I swear I could see the bullet as it raced toward me, and I twisted to the side so that it ended up hitting me in the left side of my belly instead of dead center. Probably not that much better since the silver shards still ripped a line through me. The burn and bite of them was exactly as I remembered. But the pain in my heart was totally new.

Not Meg too. Of all my family members, I thought she was the best of them.

I hit the ground, spun on my knees as she cocked the gun again, her face streaming with tears.

I'd been gods-damned duped. Just like Denna had warned.

I was a fucking idiot for believing in anyone.

The gun went off again as I lurched away, and a

series of howls went up all around us as the pack began to close in.

I did the only thing I could.

I shifted.

It took me about ten seconds, faster than anyone else in the pack, but those ten seconds cost me precious escape time.

As soon as I was on four feet, I scrambled out of my clothes and took off as fast as my injured guts could go. Nose out, ears swivelling as I strained to listen to my pursuers, I turned on the speed, my limbs stretching as far as they could as I ran for my life.

There wasn't a lot of time for me to process the shock that my little sister had shot me. Not really. I'd felt the pull to her, felt her fear as I'd gotten closer, and I'd believed it. I'd thought... well, I'd thought my little sister needed me.

I thought I needed to protect her.

"You can't escape this time!"

A shudder slid through me with the deep timbre of Kieran's voice. He'd been my best friend at one time, my protector and then... something had changed. When Mars had left. He'd turned on me, lashing out. He'd beaten me within an inch of my life weeks before my brothers' joint attack, setting me on a path that would have driven me from my family even if it hadn't driven me from the pack.

Panting, I struggled to breathe as I streaked back toward my bike, the wound in my side throbbing with each beat of my heart. I slipped under a series of low-hanging branches—

A noose slid around my neck and tightened before I could take a last breath, and I went down in a heap, tongue out, eyes searching, because I knew she wouldn't let me go down without watching. Without letting me know that it had been her choice to end my life.

"Good job, boys." Juniper stepped into my line of sight as darkness crept in at the edges. "It's about time she made a sacrifice for the family."

WELL, fuck. I was on my knees in the mud in Grayling, Montana, my shitty family surrounding me, and a woman who was obviously the wrong witch to cross in front of me, her straying husband next to her. They wore cloaks that should have been cliché and looked... cliché.

He was tall and slim, his face covered by the edges of his hood. She was of average shape though she looked like she'd had a boob job at some point, and then strapped them in a push up corset. The tops of them fairly jiggled with every breath she took. Her hair was pulled back in a severe bun, blonde, streaked with gray.

"Matriarch of the Grayling Clan," the witch said, "you have made a wise decision. Which of your daughters shall carry the curse and die to save the rest of your pack in compensation for your... indiscretion?"

My hands were tied firmly with ropes woven with silver threads, and a ball gag shoved deep in my mouth, I knew there wasn't a single thing I could do about what was happening. The burn of the silver bullet fragments made the world fuzzy, and my joints throbbed as if I were three hundred, not in my early fifties.

My side ached, blood still flowing freely.

At least I could see and hear, though to be totally and completely honest, I kinda wish I didn't know what was going down. I pushed on the ball gag with my tongue, but it just rolled away, smearing spit over the edges of my lips. My mother's hand dug into my hair and dragged me to my feet. My neck burned where the silver-laced noose hung loose, and my entire body was pebbled with goose flesh.

"This is my child. She will be the one to pay the penance. To compensate you."

Penance. Compensation. Moon goddess above, they could have my bank balance if it got me out of this mess. Though I doubted that even fifty grand would have been enough.

I would have kicked Juniper in the cooter if my feet weren't also tied together. Or my left leg wasn't snapped through the shin. I wasn't sure when it had happened, but judging by the bruising all over my body, my brothers had taken out some rage on my unconscious form.

I closed my eyes and let myself sense my way through my body. Nope, nobody had violated me. That was a bonus.

I ground my teeth over the ball gag, a growl all I could manage, the sound rumbling out and reverberating in my chest.

"Pet, are you sure you wish to do this?" the warlock asked softly, his voice barely above a whisper. "It was a mistake. On my part too."

His wife snapped a fist back, driving it into his sternum, forcing a blast of air from him. "Shut your mouth."

If I could have grimaced, I would have. I could see why he'd taken to my mother—he obviously had a type. Nasty women. Some people just fell toward their abusers with open arms, unable to see the monsters that waited for them.

His eyes swept to mine. Pale green and full of sadness. He even mouthed the words, *I'm sorry*.

Movement pulled my eyes away from the pitiful

warlock. Juniper's long bright red hair curled wildly, reaching out around her as if alive in the wind that blew down from the mountain passes. Her vibrant green eyes and flawless pale skin had ensnared many a man since Mars had disappeared. He'd been the only person who could keep her in check. After he left, her crazy had been completely unleashed.

And a few women had fallen under her spell too, truth be told. My mother was not picky about her bed partners' gender. They needed only one thing to hold her attention—power.

Look where that had gotten her. No, let's be real, where it had gotten *me*.

Was I freaking out, panicking? Not yet. Sure, I was buck naked in front of two magic users, one of whom was apparently ready to kill me for the sins of my mother; I had a broken leg, gunshot wound, and silver lacing my blood. But I wasn't dead yet.

Survival was in my blood along with the silver.

I made myself look at the warlock standing in front of me. He had a slim build, and his dark hair appeared to sweep his shoulders, though I couldn't fully be sure seeing as he had pulled the hood of his cloak up. A small part of my brain wondered just what my mother had thought she was going to get by fucking a married warlock. Had she *actually* believed she wouldn't be caught?

He wasn't the problem though and my eyes slid to the left.

His wife, a powerful witch in her own right, was, and she was pissed with a capital P.

She stood to the left of me, between my mother and her one-night stand who had turned out to be my freaking doom.

The witch was all but vibrating with energy, her eyes narrowing on me. "She does not look like you."

I grinned around the ball gag. And there it was. Juniper having to prove I was one of hers when I didn't have a single feature that tied us together.

The three boys and Meg all looked like her side, but I'd taken after my father. Dark brown hair, light hazel eyes, a slim and tall build unlike my mother's voluptuous curvy one.

Juniper grabbed the back of my head and yanked me around. "You want blood, Petunia, you have her. Take her or take *nothing*."

Petunia's eyes did this strange twitch around the edges. "You would dare to dictate the terms of your punishment? You would dare to cross me?" She paused. "Again? After all I've done for you, you stupid bitch?"

The warlock stepped forward, his voice even and smooth. Was there a charmer under there, after all? "We will curse the daughter you are presenting. The very curse made for you. Your family is marked,

Juniper. Cross myself or my wife a third time and, as the Americans say…"

"Three strikes, you're out!" Richard slurred from somewhere behind me. Then the sound of a punch landing.

Was it Kieran or Shipley who'd shut Richard up this time? It couldn't be Shipley. Had to be Kieran. Shipley was still out hunting for me.

The witch snapped her hand out toward me, the very tips of her fingers lighting up as if she had little green lightbulbs under her nails. I couldn't look away as she started to speak.

"Let the shame lie heavy on you all, for she shall die a whining bitch. As you should have, Juniper. As you likely still will, one day, given that I have my way."

The ball gag snapped free. My mouth was moving, but it was too late to deny my parentage or try to talk my way out of this. The spell on her fingers drove into me in a streak of deep green light, straight into my mouth and down into my belly. It knocked the wind right out of me as I fell back, the restraints blasting off my limbs. I didn't understand why they'd bothered to take the ropes off, but it didn't matter. I couldn't move anyway.

"She shouldn't have to die," the warlock said softly, and then it felt like he spoke only to me. "I will do what I can to save you, wolf. You have a life ahead of you still, I think. A destiny that even I can see."

Save me?

His pale green eyes were all I could see as the witch screamed with rage.

Talk about a domestic situation I did not want to be caught in the middle of, and yet here I was. Clowns on the left of me, jokers on the right.

The wound in my side no longer had my attention. It was nothing to the tearing and lurching from that green light. It felt like my body was being twisted and turned inside out as the green light pulsed behind my eyes.

Meghan was crying, her sobs cutting through me. Richard was laughing.

The last thing I saw was my mother's horrified face as she stared down at me. I closed my eyes, and the green of the witch's magic faded, my world slipping into gold.

Or rather should I say, golden.

6

NO PADDLES UP THIS SHIT CREEK

I woke up on hard concrete, to the smell of shit and piss and vomit and... dog food? My nose twitched, and I groaned as I pushed shakily onto four feet, trying to place myself. Okay, so I was in my wolf form, that was good at least. On four feet, I could tackle everything except maybe doorknobs. And my bite force could snap bones.

I didn't pick up any scents from my family, that was a major bonus.

I'd heal faster in this form too, which I needed after the gunshot wound and the silver... only there was no silver in my system. Eyes still closed; I took stock of my body. From the way my belly muscles flexed, I judged the wound in my side was mostly healed. Painful, but no longer torn. And the silver wasn't burning through my blood stream. Good deal all around.

Go me.

I wrinkled my nose and took another deep sniff before I opened my eyes.

Lots of dogs had been here, and... cats too? There was also the distinct scent of a rooster, though it was older, and rats. Fuck, I hated rats. Blinking, I tried to put the pieces together. My vision was blurry, like that time Richard had hit me in the back of the head with a bat, claiming there had been a bee in my hair. The world had been loopy for days after that.

Slowly, painfully, my eyes came into focus.

Concrete walls, bars, other dogs across from me, also in cages, signs on the bars. Names. Breeds. Ages.

I blinked and shook my head as if I could clear away the image in front of me. Then I dropped my head to catch my breath and found myself looking down at my front legs.

Holy toasted fucks.

I suddenly couldn't breathe, and it had nothing to do with the wound in my side that still throbbed lightly, or the tension around my neck from the silver-laced noose that I'd been mostly strangled with. Nope, those things were... minimal compared with what I was staring at, unable to fully comprehend what I was seeing.

Long, fluffy golden hair coated my legs down to paws much smaller than I was used to. No big were-wolf's claws at the end of the pads, but instead nicely shorn dog nails. I whipped my head around and looked down the length of my torso.

Golden. A sea of soft, feathery fur, waves and waves of it rippling in the breeze off the ventilation system.

"Not happening, this is not happening," I whispered.

Shorter, darker golden fur floated over my body. Everywhere I looked, no matter how many times I closed and then opened my eyes, it was the same. I was the same.

Golden fur, everywhere, fading in places to a near platinum blonde, wispy like fairy wings. A whine slipped past my lips because I couldn't even find the words to express the horror. Just an animal-istic fear that was tying me up into knots.

Distantly, my brain was trying to remind me that I could have been dead. That the alternative was far worse than this monstrosity I'd become. Yet the wolf in me was freaking the fuck out. Because she was buried under all this too, same as me.

And I could barely connect with her. Strike that, there was *no* connection to my wolf. I could feel her very distantly, could sense her fear, but other than that, there was nothing.

What I felt now? The urge to make someone happy. The undiluted desire to have my ears scratched.

My panting ratcheted up to the point that my vision fogged. I scrunched my eyes shut, and then looked again.

"Please be a dream," I whispered.

Nope.

It was still there. All that golden fur, down to the tip of my long-haired, slightly wagging tail.

Golden retriever. I was a dog. Panic panting ensued until I was drooling on the floor.

My tail had a life of its own and continued its slow wag. Was that all a golden retriever thought about? Happy things?

No, no. I was a werewolf! I tipped my head back, opened my mouth and... yipped? No deep-throated, awe-inspiring howl. A toasted fuck of a yip.

I closed my eyes, bowed my head, and gagged, my whole-body convulsing until I was lurching forward, all my weight on my front legs.

This *was* worse than death. I was in some sort of kennel where no doubt I'd be euthanized, dying in the body of a dog. How would I get to the halls of my family? This was no warrior's death.

"You see the cost now?"

I stumbled sideways into the bars of my cage. Petunia stood outside the door, her eyes tracking me, narrow and calculating. Where had she come from? "Shameful, isn't it? A once proud, fierce wolf, turned into a fluffy little dog. What is worse, do you think? To die as a whining dog, or to be forced to live as one for the rest of your life? If not for my husband's soft heart, you'd already be dead."

Fuck me right up my golden ass. She couldn't mean what I thought she meant, did she?

Except... *of course* they meant for me to spend my life like this. Until I was euthanized. Or died of shame. It was hard to say which would happen first in my current state.

She smiled, and for a minute I saw a woman who'd be beautiful, maybe even stunning, if she wasn't so busy being a miserable cunt, but it was gone in a flash, her anger stealing beauty from her. "I think that your suffering will be greater alive, but I suppose it will depend solely on if anyone wants you. Perhaps you will die here, in time. Perhaps they will just euthanize you."

I barked at her. *Fucking barked*. Like the dog I was —that a goddamn witch named after a flower that I could crush with one finger had made me. "When I get out of here, I'm going to hunt you down and gut you!" I was screaming at her. But my screams to her came out as nothing but barks and yips.

She clapped her hands together. "Why? Your mother, I would have killed outright. But the pain of watching your child suffer is a greater consequence than anything I could ever do to her. Trust me, I know what it is to lose a child."

My jaw dropped. Did she really think Juniper gave a single loose-as-a-goose shit about me? "She hates me, you damn fool! You'd have saved the pack if you'd killed her! You fucking twat! Get rid of the man if he cheats on you like this, he isn't worth it!"

I tried several more times to explain, wishing she could understand me. But the witch didn't grasp the full impact of my swearing at her as I barked and barked and barked.

Petunia lowered herself so that she was face to face with me. "I want you to remember that your *mother* did this to you. Until the day you die, whenever that comes. Perhaps you should make friends with your new companions. For what life you have left, at least it won't be alone." Without another word, she turned and walked away, leaving me there in a cage. Unable to shift to two legs.

In a cage next to other dogs.

A pit-bull mix. German shepherd. Several mutts. The German shepherd snarled and lunged at me and I... I tucked my tail between my legs.

I couldn't even lift my lips at him.

Apparently, it was no longer in my DNA to fight back.

Talk about an existential crisis. Had the werewolf

in me made me strong then? Was I just a weak-willed soul under all this fluffy fucking fur? Another round of dry heaving left me flat on the concrete, panting at high speed until the world blurred again.

As the panic rolled, I tried to put the pieces together, forming a plan that would help me out of this enormous mess. After a few minutes, my panting slowed, and I could think a little clearer. Focus on the first step first.

My best bet would be to get someone to choose me. To get me out of here. Then I could make a run for it and... and what? I wasn't sure that there was an answer. My thoughts were interrupted by a new voice.

"Hey, what you in for?"

Shivering, my whole body shaking, I looked up to see a cat strolling down the catwalk above us, a structure which could not be more aptly named in that moment. She was a gray-ish tabby, with cream down her chest and around her nose, and she was exceptionally petite. She looked like a kitten more than a full-grown cat.

I swallowed hard. "You can... talk. And I can understand you. Can you understand me?"

Her one ear flicked. "Well, it's not like the humans talk, but yeah, dummy. We can talk. Think of it like Disney on crack, full of fuck this and fuck that." She started grooming her front legs as the German shepherd leapt up from under her, teeth snapping. I was impressed that she didn't so much as blink. "Of course, not everyone can talk, just us poor schmucks who were cursed. You know, souls trapped in animals."

Others like us... like me? Jesus Christ on a motorbike. I *wasn't* alone. That's what Petunia meant?

The German Shepherd leapt again, slamming himself against the bars. The cat barely flicked her tail in his direction.

"Pansy dogs," she muttered. "What are you in for? The last talker in here had made a literal deal with the devil." A shudder rippled down to the tip of her tail. "I don't suggest that, I think his soul was eaten. Totally gross."

Hesitating, I stared up at her. Did it matter now who knew what had happened? The likelihood of me dying in the shelter was high. "Witch turned me into a dog," I finally said. "For something I didn't do. My mother fucked the witch's husband."

Her eyes widened, and she leaned toward me. "Fuck me up the tail, Petunia got you too?"

I was on my feet in a flash, tail irritatingly wagging away. "What do you mean, *you too*? You... what were you... before you were, are, a cat?"

Was this another werewolf gone wrong? Maybe,

just maybe, we could work together to get out of here.

"A woman with a taste for flashy men." She sighed and her eyes fluttered half closed. "He was a right sexy piece of ass, kinda worth it, I think. I still think back to those nights, and the screaming, panty tearing orgasms that left me weak and useless for days, and while I wish I wasn't here, I'm not totally sure I'd change anything. I've never come so hard I blacked out before."

A shiver rolled through me, thinking about how that howl had roiled through me back in Edmonton and what would have happened if he'd been closer, or I'd not been able to block that sound? No, that wasn't going to help me now. "How long have you been in here?"

"Little over six months. I made nice with the workers, so they haven't fried my ass yet. I can slip in and out of the different rooms through that little tunnel there." She sat, balancing precariously above the other dogs and flicked her tail at the ceiling where an opening had been made.

Speaking of making nice... a worker came in, interrupting us. He stared up at her and motioned at her to get down.

"Skittles, you're going to get eaten one of these days!" he shouted up at the cat.

She gave him a long, pain-filled meow. "Only if I'm very, very lucky."

I wrinkled my nose and let out a sneeze.

The worker continued toward me. He wore a pair of green army pants and a lighter green shirt that had his name—Tad—etched into it above the main logo.

Street Angel Saviors.

"Good day, beautiful girl, we need a name for you." His Aussie accent was so horrible, it was obviously fake. Who was he trying to be, Steve Irwin? Nobody replaced Steve. "Yup, a pretty little Sheila you are, aren't you?"

This time I did manage to curl my lips—okay, I managed to keep my mouth from its stupid wide grin—and backed away from the main door until my butt was up against the far wall. Where it nicely hid my equally stupid tail that refused to stop its constant wag of happiness even when I sat on it.

"Don't be like that, no need to be scared." He smiled, and I managed the smallest of snarls. I'm not sure that he even realized I was unhappy with his presence. I knew I needed to make nice, but I was feeling more than a little traumatized.

Fuckwit just kept on coming in.

Did he think that it would help him pick up girls, saying he worked with animals and faking a Steve

Irwin impression? Yeah, probably. I'd heard of worse pick-up lines.

Yes, I was also thinking about him and his dating record rather than my situation, because what in the actual hell was I supposed to do? Petunia obviously had a thing for turning the women her man banged, or their nearest and supposedly dearest, into shelter animals. But maybe that would help me? Maybe I could get Skittles—star gods help me not end up with a name like that—to help me navigate this clusterfuck.

That witch had turned me into a golden-fucking-retriever. Man's best friend. Well behaved. Loves everyone. No bite force. But as Tad reached for me, there was a moment when I pulled my shit together. I did not want him touching me.

Skittles let out a small hiss. "No, be nice to him! He's—"

Too late. Tad put his hand forward as he came in the door, and I lunged at him, hackles up as much as possible with four-inch-long, loose hair. He took a step back, his hands well out of my reach. "Easy, little spicy. Just going to get you some food."

He slid a silver bowl across the floor to where it ended up between us.

Dog food. Cheap ass dry kibble that smelled like wax and dirt and some fake processed-to-hell meat.

My nose twitched and my stomach rumbled, but I wasn't desperate enough for that, not yet.

Tad muttered away at me, and then he finally left me alone, clanging the kennel door behind him. Though alone wasn't quite right. There were other dogs in the *Street Angel Saviors* kennel club.

And of course, there was Skittles. Who really had no fear.

She dropped down into my kennel and strolled up to me, her nose butting right into mine in greeting.

"Aren't you afraid I'll snap you in half?" I asked as she circled around me.

"Did you fuck him? I know you said your mother did, but ..."

I gagged. I couldn't help it. "No. My mother did, this isn't a new thing for her, banging men she shouldn't."

"Oh, super Shakespearean of you to take the punishment." She bobbed her head, reached out and patted me on the nose with a paw.

I snorted on her, splattering her with saliva, much to my satisfaction and her obvious irritation. "I did not. The curse was forced on me. After my sister shot me and I was choked out, gagged, and handed to the witch."

Let her chew on that.

"Damn, and I thought my family was terrible!

You win that award my new friend." She smiled at me. "You aren't alone, kid. Just be glad you didn't get shoved into the body that Hammy did."

I didn't want to know. Skittles told me anyway.

"Guinea pigs don't get much freedom. At least you and I can wander about. And being a goldy, you will get chosen for sure. And then out you go into the world."

I finally found my teeth and snapped at her. "You think I can wander about? I'm in a cage! And the chances of us getting picked are pretty fucking slim." This part I'd already been thinking about. I'd never seen the name of this rescue. "Petunia didn't put us in this particular kennel by accident. What do you want to bet that they have a high euthanasia rate and a non-existent adoption rate?"

Her yellow-green eyes widened. "Oh my god. That makes sense. So, I've just been super lucky? Mind you, I know when they are coming for me, so I always make like a tree and leaf."

I snorted. "Yeah. Something like that. How do you know when they are coming for you?"

"They aren't quiet about it," she said. "Fucking Skittles! That's what they start yelling."

All that yelling and barking at her had set off the other dogs, who were barking in a cacophony that rebounded off the cement walls. She glared at the other dogs. "That one, the German shepherd, he'd like to eat you. Just running it through his head, over and over. The pit-bull wants to be friends. But she's sweet. Only wants love."

Said pit-bull had stuffed her face through the bars, which pushed her lips back in a ridiculous grin.

Shivering, I lay down, head on my paws. Skittles sighed and tucked herself in between my front legs and under my chin. "You are so warm. This is better than that cat room. Mildly stinking of dog, but I can deal." She was quiet a moment. "If you're right about the whole euthanasia thing, then we need to find you a way out fast."

"Why would you help me?" I mumbled.

"Why not?" she shot back. I guess she didn't want to tell me why. Fair enough.

I closed my eyes, the shivering intensifying until my teeth were rattling. I couldn't help it though. My wolf was panicking. Loss of freedom, entrapment, unable to shift. Those were the things my wolf feared most, much like the human side of me feared what had already happened. Meg, looking at me over the gun. My brothers, consigning me to that river. Losing Denna and Martin.

Skittles started to purr, her front paws kneading at my legs. The vibration of her rumble slowed my shivering. It made me miss Martin more.

With my eyes closed, all I could see was my

sister. She'd been crying while she shot me. How had they forced her to turn on me? And how the fuck was I going to get out of here?

Denna might come looking for me, but she wouldn't be looking for a golden retriever. Same issue for Grant if Denna managed to reach him. They'd be looking for a werewolf. Not a dog.

Taini and Copper would be in London by now. We'd agreed not to reach out to one another, just in case...something like this happened. Though I didn't think any of us actually thought *this* was a possibility.

My friends would have no chance at saving me, so I couldn't put any hope in them.

My thoughts were scrambled as I tried to put together what my family would do now. If they knew what had been done with me, would they let me go? No, I didn't think so. I had to assume they knew I was alive, and they would do their best to end that.

If I were a betting girl, I'd bet that at least one of my brothers would be sent looking for me to finish the job. And as a goldie? I was well and royally fucked. There would be no fighting my way out of that.

The hours ticked by. Night came and went, and by the next morning things did not look better.

I was still a fucking dog in a shelter of some sort, my only friend a scrawny cat with a spicy attitude.

But at least none of my family members had shown up. That had to count for something, right?

"We have to get out of here," I muttered as I stood and stretched. The night had given me the healing time I'd needed, but now there was just one goal.

To get the hell out of dodge.

The pit-bull gave a soft whine and pushed herself closer to the bars of the cage until her lips were all pushed back, making her look like a clown.

I turned away. The other animals were animals. I was not like them, and I couldn't save them.

Tad flung the door open a few minutes later. "Well, hello my beauties, we have someone coming to look for a new companion! First in a month, so let's see what we can do for him, yeah?"

Skittles stretched languidly. "Probably not here for a cat, but this is your chance."

"He's looking for a lovely doggo." Tad slid food into the cages. I once more ignored mine.

Skittles sniffed the food that I surely was not going to touch and gagged so hard her tongue stuck out. "That's worse than the cat food."

Tad scratched out a label and stuck it to the front of my cage.

"What does it say?" I pressed myself close, trying to read it.

Skittles slipped through the bars and stood up

on her back legs. Then she started to laugh. "Your name. He named you Princess."

I grimaced but didn't have time to do more. The door opened again, only this time it wasn't Tad. It was a prospective accomplice—a way out. I refused to think of the person as an owner.

My only way out of this place was to make someone like me, get them to 'adopt' me and then, at the earliest moment, break free of the human family. From there, my plan was a little foggy, but I figured I'd find a shaman within another wolf pack. How I was going to get him or her to understand me, I wasn't sure. But that was my starting point. A goal.

That was the plan, until I got a good look at *him*. The prospective owner, that is.

Well over six feet tall, he had shoulder-length sandy blond hair that had been mussed by the wind, bright blue eyes, and a chiseled jaw. He wore jeans that were just a touch too small so that I could see every line of muscle, and a button-down shirt that he'd rolled up at the sleeves and left the top couple of buttons open. I half expected flip flops, but he was wearing a nice pair of cowboy boots to finish off the look.

On two legs, I could have happily dry humped his leg all day long. On four, I just wanted him to get me the hell out of here. Okay, I'd still have humped his leg given the chance.

"Holy cat nip, he could be Cavill's blond brother!"

No shit.

Okay, time to lay on the damn charm.

I gave a soft woof, drawing his eyes to me, wagging my tail as I blinked up at him, all but fluttering my eyelashes. But other than a quick look, he didn't stop. He went past me, straight to the German shepherd. "What's this one like? Good dog? Strong dog?"

"Oh, that accent!" Skittles all but swooned at my feet. "I don't know what the fuck it is, but I want to rub my face on his crotch!"

"Skittles, we need him to get us out of here!" I muttered under my breath.

I ran to the side of the cage that was closest to the German shepherd. I gave a soft whine—damn it, I sounded pathetic, and I knew it. But who knew when we'd get another prospective adopter? If this guy was really the only person who'd shown up in a month, I needed him to choose me. Now. I ran so that I was right close to him, pressed against the bars. Another low whine.

He reached in through the bars and patted my head, and a rush of electricity buzzed through his fingers and straight into my skin. What the actual hell was that? It felt... familiar? How was that possible?

He paused and looked down at me, eyes searching mine even as he rubbed behind my ears.

"Sorry, Princess. Can't take you, too dangerous," he rumbled with the accent I could not quite place.

Tad stepped into the room. "That GSD is... well he'll be tough. What is it you're looking for? A guard dog?"

The pretty man stood up and ran a hand through his hair, messing it up further. "I would like to do some hunting. I need a dog that is exceptional at tracking other animals, at picking up scents."

Tad lit up, and I'd have hugged him if I'd been able to, because I knew what was coming. "Oh, shit, I have the perfect girl! She was just surrendered last night! And if it's a nose you need..."

I spun in a circle, already knowing that he was talking about me. Goldies had the best noses, and they were all about the sport of hunting. We—meaning Mars—had actually brought one into the pack once, to help us learn how to track scents better. Watching that golden retriever work had taught our pack a ton. Though I never would have thought then that I'd end up as one myself one day.

I gave a woof, and then the door was opening. I couldn't help myself, I leapt up and into the handsome man's arms, forcing him to grab hold of me. Might have licked his face too before he got me back onto the ground, a hand curled into the ruff of my neck.

That same pulse of electricity was there, and I couldn't keep my nose from twitching. I couldn't quite pick up his scent—he was heavily layered in soaps and a lovely musky cologne, but those things only made me more eager to tease it out. Or was it a spell? Fuck, that was it. He had something hiding his scent.

"You really think this one? Very sweet. Perhaps not very clever?" the handsome man said. "I need a smart dog. One that can learn quickly."

Shit. I had to convince him.

I sat down hard, doing my best to remain still. My fucking tail kept wagging though.

"Um, eager much?" Skittles stepped up between my front paws again.

"You telling me you wouldn't want to sleep in his bed? He's my way out," I muttered between gritted teeth.

She laughed, a funny mewling noise. "Girl, you're a dog. You're going to watch him bang however many pretty women he brings home!"

"Don't care, just want out of here." I lay down, then rolled onto my back, sat back up and tried to think of something else that a dog should do on command.

"Try shake a paw," Skittles suggested.

I held one paw out, then the other. His blue eyes went over me several times. "Good hunting dog, are you sure?"

"Best nose, better even than a wolf's!" Tad exclaimed like a fucking champ, and the pretty man smiled, his eyes locking on mine.

"I'll take her."

7

PRETTY, DANGEROUS, AND LICK-WORTHY

I couldn't stop myself from bouncing. Literally. I told my body not to jump around, but here I was leaping and dancing on my back legs like a damn fool. The wolf in me was cringing, maybe even dying a little inside at my antics

The golden? Freaking ecstatic.

"Here." Tad shoved something at the pretty man. The clink of something metallic.

And then a linked choke collar connected to a leash settled over my neck. There was a brief moment of silence, a pause where the world didn't move and my breath froze.

I sat so still I was sure my heart had stopped beating.

This wasn't real silver, but it didn't matter—once more I felt the silver rope tightening, yanking me off my feet, dropping me to the forest floor. Cutting off the air to my lungs as Juniper stood over me. Trapping me, dooming me.

If I'd been on two legs, I would have been screaming my face off, scratching at my own neck in a frantic attempt to free myself.

As it was, a pitiful excuse for a yelping scream was all I could manage as I thrashed at the end of the line like a hooked fish.

"Easy, easy." Hands pressed down on my body, gently pinning me to the ground. Whimpers slid out of me as my teeth clacked and chattered. I rolled my eyes up.

Handsome man knelt on one knee beside me, his hands buried deep in the fur around my neck, massaging gently. He did not take the leash off.

"She'll get used to it," Tad said. "Probably just needs a little help."

"Indeed," the blue-eyed man said. If I didn't know better, I'd swear he had magic in his hands, because the fear slid away and I was able to breathe again. "Better?"

As if I could answer.

I gave a soft woof, and he smiled as he stood. The loss of his touch was... painful. An ache deep in my bones that I didn't understand. Did I want to hump his leg? Sure. But this was a bottomless ache that I'd never felt before. Not even when I'd left my pack had I felt the loss this keenly.

Was this how dogs felt around their humans?

I couldn't help the gag that erupted out of me.

"I believe she will stay at my side without this," the handsome man said softly, his voice rolling through my body.

The collar slipped off and I lay flat on the floor, staring up at him. He didn't frown or even yell. His eyes were thoughtful. Intense.

"You will be a good girl for me, won't you? Come."

That one-word command, and I belly crawled to him, all but plastering myself to his leg. Again, my mind raced. This had to be how dogs felt then, because the need to be with him was... well, the only word I had was overwhelming. Like I couldn't breathe without touching him.

I expected my wolf to be royally pissed, but she was quiet, curled up deep in the corner of my mind.

Tad sputtered, "You can't take her without a leash. That's against the rules."

"Obviously I can and unless you want to return my... significant donation, I suggest you move out of my way." He snapped his fingers, and I stayed glued to his side. The energy that rolled off him was strong, confident, demanding. Edgy and dangerous.

Hot as fuck.

"Beautiful, stay with me." His voice was still raspy with irritation at Tad, and I had no problem obeying him.

Skittles watched us go. "Totally jealous. How come he didn't want me?"

I could have just left her behind. Could have just gone with him and gotten the hell out of there. But that wasn't really my thing. She'd kept me company when I was losing my marbles, something she hadn't needed to do. Besides, she was the only person who could understand me.

"He's not looking," I muttered. "Stay under me, no one will see through all this damn hair."

Skittles didn't need to be asked twice, and that's how I escaped the shelter and helped a fellow inmate escape with me. No one so much as blinked.

The minute we were outside on the street, Skittles was off like a shot. "I'm free, free!"

She slid to a stop twenty feet away and looked back at me. "Girlfriend, aren't you coming with? I mean, I know he's damn lickable, but let's go!"

Oh, I tried to leave him there. I really did. I went so far as to lean my head away from him, but my paws wouldn't move. My body wouldn't listen. The word *stay* echoed inside my head.

That one word had me unable to disobey.

"My feet won't move!" I yelped as I struggled against the insane urge to just... stay with him.

But just like my stupid tail that wouldn't stop wagging, my body didn't want to listen to me either. The golden in me was too fucking obedient.

The handsome man reached down and slid his hand over my head, tucking one finger behind my ear and scratching me gently. "Good girl." His deep voice rumbled through me, lighting up nerve endings that I'd thought were dead and gone after my last attempt at a relationship.

Fuck. Me. Two words out of his mouth, and I was toasted, buttered and ready to be eaten. A puddle just waiting to be told what to do. Again, I thought my wolf would be freaking the fuck out, chewing her own leg off to escape this man-made trap.

But then I got my first good sniff of him from the hand that was petting me, his wrist right by my nose, and his scent finally broke through everything he was using to hide it. Through the cologne, through the clothing and the smells of the other dogs, through the heavy scent of traffic and cars, I finally understood.

I drew in the smell that was uniquely him as he flagged down a cab, and I, of course, followed him right in and sat at his feet. To be fair, I was following my nose, unable to stop processing what I was picking up on. The impossibility of it. How could this be happening?

Skittles shot in and stuffed herself under my ridiculous tail, but I barely reacted to her.

Because it suddenly made sense why I couldn't leave his side.

The undertones of wolf were there at his wrist, so subtle he'd managed to cover it with all the other scents around us. I suspected that if I'd not been a golden, I would have missed it completely. The smell burrowed deep under my skin, and I closed my eyes. He didn't just smell like wolf, he smelled like... home.

Not home like the Grayling pack.

Home like my fated mate.

I sucked in a deeper breath, kind of a gasp.

I'd always thought the stories about fated mates were no better than fairy tales. Because mates were supposed to be forever, and Mars had left, which meant that the whole thing had to be a crock of shit. Sure, the story was that he'd disappeared, but we knew the truth: Juniper had been too much, even for that mate bond, and he'd left her after the show down with me. That was pretty telling. I'd seen the way he had looked at Juniper. He'd loved her, loved her beyond reason, and in the end that love hadn't been enough for him to deal with her flaws. So, he'd saved himself and left us behind.

You didn't leave your mate. You most certainly did not leave the children of that union. If you were an alpha, you most certainly didn't leave your pack. No matter what.

Not for anything. Which meant mate bonds were not real in my estimation, no matter what anyone else said.

If the stories had been true, my father would still be in Grayling, and we'd maybe have survived Juniper's reign of terror together. Because it was after he left that Juniper's chaos and violence had truly ramped up. Or maybe he'd seen it coming and had left while he could.

But this feeling... there was no denying its power. My heart felt as if this pretty man—*my mate*—had reached into my chest and taken hold of it instead of simply resting his hand on my head. Equal parts terror and joy slid through me.

A mate could be someone to depend on, to see you through life. To have children with if you were so inclined. But... I did not want to have my heart ripped out. Once upon a time I would have wanted the fairy tale, but I was too jaded now. Not after seeing Mars leave and Juniper turn into an even bigger bitch. I couldn't bear the thought of that happening to me. I did not want to be wanted for a period of time and then cast aside when life got hard.

Never mind the current state of my body, which

was most assuredly not that of a woman or a werewolf.

I dropped my chin on his knee and stared up at him, not caring if I looked sappy, or stupid, or like a dog. Just that simple touch was enough to lock me onto him.

He was my mate.

Holy fucking hell.

8

WEST COAST WEIRDNESS

Now that we were sitting still in the cab, I catalogued just what I was looking at. Just how gorgeous my mate was, at least to my eyes.

He'd shaved probably the day before, so light stubble was visible across his jaw and cheeks. Most of it was dark, but there was a lighter patch that went from the middle of his bottom lip, down over his chin. Like a white stripe. The lines of his face were indeed reminiscent of Henry Cavill, I could totally see Skittles' point. And now that I knew he was a wolf shifter under all that, I could see the signs of his animal too. The tension around his eyes, the way one side of his lip curled as scents he didn't like flowed past his nose. The way he tapped one hand on his opposite knee, unable to just sit still. The shaggier hair, even the cowboy boots. Easy to slide out of, faster than laced up shoes when you needed to shift.

"I cannot believe I snuck in with you!" Skittles whispered from somewhere under my tail.

I thumped her once with the giant fluffy thing to shut her up. But handsome man had not so much as glanced her way. I slid my head across to his other leg and under his tapping hand.

Begging for his touch.

Bob would have been ecstatic, egging me on to 'get some, girl'. I'd never begged for a man to look my way. I wasn't as much of a beauty as my mother, but I had the legs and ass of a runner, and my lightly curling long dark hair and light hazel eyes had always drawn men to me, not the other way around.

I didn't care though, not in that moment. His touch soothed the ragged edges of my soul, soothed my fear of being stuck like this, of my mother coming to hunt me down. For the first time in a very long time, I was where I belonged. Even if I was in the wrong body.

I had no doubt one of my brothers would be sent to finish Juniper's dirty work. If I'd been in that shelter, they could have 'adopted' me, and I'd have been dead by rights, theirs to do as they pleased. The horror of it choked me.

The cab lurched to a stop.

"696 Ocean Front, this you?" the cabbie rasped out.

"Ya, it is. Thank you." Handsome man handed over a couple of twenty-dollar bills that I hadn't even seen him pull out of his pocket because I was too busy drooling on his knee as I stared up at his face.

He opened the door, and I hopped out, did a circle and sat at his feet.

The sound of waves snapped my head around. Waves.

Water.

Ocean.

I let out a bark. Or at least that's what it sounded like to my mate. To Skittles, I was saying, "Where the fuck are we? I was in Montana just yesterday!"

She stuck close to my side where she couldn't be seen. "Venice Beach, you ding dong. Petunia sends all her creations to the west coast for some reason. Or at least she did to the other ones I met. I was from New York. Hammie was an Ohio boy. I mean, if what you're suggesting is true, then that shelter was set up just to be a euthanasia shelter."

I let out several barks, mostly because I couldn't help myself. What the fuck? What the actual fuck? Even if I did get free of the handsome man—which let's be honest, I wasn't sure I wanted to do now that I knew he was my mate—I wouldn't know where to go, who to ask for help. What packs were even out here? I knew of two on the west coast. One in Seattle, and the other way south, close to the Mexican border.

A hand settled on my head. "It's okay, Princess. Come, let us go and see your new home. Ya?"

I wouldn't have stopped myself from following him straight to the house that faced the ocean even if I'd been able to. The guy had money—he had to in order to have beachfront property.

Hot. Loaded. Fated to be my mate. What in the world could be wrong with any of this?

Right. Stuck as a dog. I forgot that bit for, like, half a second.

"Fuck me up, baby, this is amazing!" Skittles breathed out.

I looked at the house and wasn't sure we were looking at the same thing. Squarish. That was the only word I had. Maybe boxy. Someone else would probably call it modern. But I just saw a cardboard box on steroids. Maybe if... no, not if, *when* I found a way out of this fucking dog body, I could convince him to move to Alaska with me.

What wolf wouldn't love the icy, bracing cold, the forests, the wildlife to chase? We could get an amazing place up there, a big timber framed house with the money he'd get for this... box on the ocean.

The dreams were spinning through my mind, but they scattered as soon as he opened the door.

He pressed his thumb against the keypad, and a series of locks slid open. Not one, not two or three. Four.

Four big bolts slid open.

If I could have frowned... but again, golden retriever faces don't frown. The best I could do was close my damn mouth and stop smiling widely. That was a lot of locks, and high security for a werewolf.

I had three locks on my place in Alaska. Including solid steel bars that I could drop across the doors on the main floor.

And I had that because of my family and my fear of them showing up.

So, what was he afraid of?

I stepped inside the house with him, the air conditioning hitting me first, followed by the smell of something amazing cooking, which stole every thought from my head and replaced them with one.

I was starving.

"Hello, motherfucker."

I cringed at the deep sonorous voice and did my best to growl and bare my teeth. Came out like a cringing whine, but I *did* lift my top lip a little. Go me. Because I knew that voice. But from where?

"Sven, you're scaring my new dog," Handsome Man said softly. And then he bent down and *picked me up* in his arms, flipping me onto my back so I was staring up at him. Blue eyes locked with mine. The intensity was too much. I was a dog.

He was my mate.

But there was no way he'd know, and I... I had to find a way out of this body. Not that it hadn't been on my to-do list, but the need just amped up further.

I rolled my head to see Skittles ducking into the hallway closet before either of the men saw her.

"Loki's ass! What the hell did you do now?" the other man snapped, punctuating his words with the smack of something wooden on the counter. Yup, I knew that voice. But where from? How?

I blinked a few times as I was carried up the steps and then set down on the tile floor of the main part of the house. Kitchen, living area, and a series of windows staring out to the ocean. But I was more fascinated with the incredibly skinny man who seemed to be made of... tree bark? No, that wasn't quite right.

Sven slapped his hands—and they did slap kinda like skin despite looking barky—on the countertop. "You said no more dogs! NAH! Fooey! Terrible idea!"

"I said *one* more. And this one has the best nose in the business. This will work, Sven. We can't give up now. She is so close."

Sven glared across the counter at me. If I'd been in my wolf body, I'd have glared right the fuck back and maybe even put him in his place with a sold push of my energy.

Golden me? Not so much.

I pushed up against Pretty Boy, all but wrapping myself around his legs, and lowered my head, unable to look Sven in the eye.

"Just look at her! What will happen when your brother shows up swinging an axe straight for your fat head? Huh? She will cower and run!" Sven yelled, flinging his hands and a few bits of whatever he was cooking into the air. "This is worse even than your last idea, Han. Worse and worse."

One tidbit of meat came my way, and I leapt up, snapping it out of the air before it hit the ground. Yup, that was worth it. Even though I was immediately cringing again.

I understood clearly that I needed Sven to like me. He was the food guy.

"I need her nose. It does not matter to me that she has no heart for a fight, my old friend."

Sven rolled his eyes. "Loki's fucking ass cheeks! You need protection too, Han. You have no pack! And you pick a dog to be your helper? You have lost it completely!"

His name was Han, like as in Han Solo? I blinked up at him. Maybe I could be his Princess Leia.

I gave a soft woof, and Han snapped his fingers at

me as he left the room, telling me to follow without words. As if he needed to ask.

"I'm going to shower and get changed," he called out to his friend. "We will go tonight to search the beach where we last saw our quarry. I have her shirt, so Princess here can pick up the scent."

Shower. That meant he was about to get naked. The rest of his words meant nothing because of what I was anticipating.

Yes, I followed him through the house, barely noticing the minimalist design, barely noticing anything but my mate.

I shuddered, unable to help the fear. He might have been mine, but was this a good idea? Did I really want a mate? I mean, I wanted to fuck him, but I didn't want to have my heart stomped on, thank you very much, do not pass go, do not collect two hundred dollars.

I mean, even if I wanted more than a romp, he couldn't see me inside the golden retriever.

Burning shit could not have made my nose wrinkle more.

There would be a way out of this, I just had to figure it out. Certainly, Petunia and her husband weren't going to reverse the curse they'd placed on me. Not by a long shot. I had to find a shaman. That was my only hope.

Maybe the shaman's name could be Obi Wan and we'd complete the Star Wars world.

Han started stripping the second he walked over the threshold to his bedroom. And he talked to me while he did it. Which meant I was no longer thinking about anything but bare skin and muscles as they were revealed to me a section at a time.

Star gods were surely looking down kindly on me in that moment.

"Princess, I hope I am not wrong about you." His shirt fell to the floor, unveiling every perfect muscle across his back, and a scar running from left to right on a sharp diagonal that was too clean of a cut for a claw mark. A sword maybe? No, that was ridiculous, no one used swords anymore. Guns were far more efficient at killing even supernaturals, given the correct ammo.

"I need you to help me find someone. Someone very precious to me," Han said. "Someone I have been hunting for a long time. Manner of speaking."

The jeans slid off next, and the man did not wear anything beneath them, which meant I was staring at his perfectly shaped ass. I was panting away as if the air conditioning wasn't down to, like, sixty degrees. His skin hadn't even pebbled in the cold.

And he certainly hadn't lost any... size... where it counted. He stretched his arms over his head and flexed so that even his perfect (yes, I realize I'm using this word a lot, but damn it, perfect is perfect) ass flexed, glutes jumping.

When would I get this chance again? Maybe never.

I couldn't help myself. I leapt toward him and licked an ass cheek, mouth open, and considered a nip while I was at it.

He laughed and pushed me away. "Nah, none of that, Princess. No nipping."

I snorted and took another swipe anyway. Because damn it, there had to be perks to being stuck like this.

And being able to get away with licking his flexing butt cheeks? Yeah, that was one of them. However, the show I got next, *that* was even better.

Maybe being stuck as a golden wasn't so bad after all.

9

WET, WILD, AND FULL OF PUSSY

Han gently pushed my nose away as he laughed at me. "Princess, go lie down," and then stepped into the shower in the en suite bathroom without closing the door.

I did as I was told immediately and lay as close as I could to the shower while still getting a full view of him. This was voyeurism at its best. He didn't even know he was being ogled.

"Thank every god that ever was in existence that it's an open shower with no curtain," Skittles whispered from behind me.

I whipped around and saw her nose peeking out from under the bed, then whipped back to the scene in front of me.

"Don't distract me. There are not a lot of perks for me right now, stuck in this fucking body, but this scene right here is one of them." I lay on my belly and put my head on my front paws. Drew in a breath and let the smell of musk and smoke fill me up. His wolf scent was stronger now, issuing forth with the heat of the water.

Wolf. Smoke. Fire. Fir trees. I could have sniffed him all day.

"Oh, he's soaping up." Skittles almost moaned. I did not blame her.

He had big hands—gentle hands, from the way he'd patted me—and he slid them over his body in slow, sweeping movements that really just pushed the suds around and around. Not that I was complaining. Hopefully, he took multiple showers a day. Long showers.

Han slid his hands down between his legs and over his... I did a double blink. He was bigger now. Maybe the cold had been affecting him after all, which meant...

"He's hung like a god," I whispered.

"If we were on two legs, I think he could take us both," she whispered.

I snapped my teeth. "I don't share."

"I'd share. Just to get my pussy wrapped around that monstrous..." She sucked in a slow breath.

I held mine.

He was taking his time washing his monstrous... cock-a-doodle-doo. Damn, a small part of me said look away. The rest told that part to shut the fuck up and enjoy the show because the wolf moon only knew when I'd get laid again. Maybe never at this rate unless it was some over eager standard poodle loose from his owner hoping to make a doodle.

Han put one hand on the shower wall, the water spraying down his back as he slid his other hand up and down his shaft, slowly at first. I could have even said he was just washing, only I knew that wasn't the case, not with the way he lingered, his fingers splayed and then tightening.

I licked my lips. Oh, to not be stuck like this. To have it be my hands on him, sliding around in all that soapy temptation, feeling the silken skin against my palms, against my body.

His fist tightened over his shaft, and there was no mistaking that this was no longer just a wash and rinse job, but a very different kind of job. He flicked his thumb over the tip of his cock every time he reached it. Then slid his hand down to the base. He turned a little, and damned if the view didn't improve.

Shifting his feet, he spread his legs, bracing himself as his movements sped up, grip tight and fingers sliding over the tip and then back down to the base of the shaft, the soft shush of soap and water the only sounds.

"I need you," he whispered, his breath hitching

around the words. My body tightened, and I struggled not to let out a whimper.

I'd never been about watching anyone get it on before. I wasn't into porn, it did nothing for me. But this, *this* I could watch all day. The view in front of me had me strung tight, need battering at me. Need that there was no way to fulfill in my current situation.

A groan left his lips as he stroked harder yet, leaning into the wall with his forearm now, one leg back.

"Is it bigger? Fuck me, I think it's bigger," Skittle whispered.

"Shut the fuck up," I snapped at Skittles, but didn't dare look away. I should have been jealous or weirded out that she was watching him take matters into his own hands, but honestly, I was too mesmerized by the sight of him touching himself. By the rhythmic sound of his hand on his own flesh, paired with the noises escaping his mouth.

Sounds I wanted to draw from him with my own body given the chance.

I didn't think his movements could get any faster, but his hand was suddenly a blur, and his hips started to move in time with his strokes, thrusting hard.

Another groan, this one turning into a deep growl that I felt all the way to my lower belly, wrapped itself around me. If I'd had panties on, they'd have been soaked as he came hard and fast, cum mixing with the soap as he pounded into his hand, his body tight as he climaxed, only slowly relaxing after another thirty seconds of lazier stroking. I almost wondered if he was going to go another round.

I wasn't sure my body could take it if he did.

"Is he going to... again?" Skittles asked.

"I don't know," I breathed out.

Han didn't move from his position on the wall for what felt like a long time, the water spraying down his back and his muscles still tense, his hand lazily stroking up and down, his hips giving the occasional jerk forward as if he could come again if he wanted to.

"I need to get laid," he said softly.

To himself of course, but both Skittles and I heard him.

"I volunteer as tribute!" she screeched as she ran toward him. Perhaps forgetting that she was the wrong kind of pussy.

I lunged and grabbed her by the tail, flinging her back over my shoulder so that she sailed over the bed and landed on the other side, out of sight, with a light thump. No doubt landing on her feet.

"He's mine until I say otherwise!" I turned back in time to see Han wrapping a towel around his waist, much to my disappointment. He strode across to me, still dripping wet. His hand slid over my head and this time down my back to the base of my tail.

Which I was still wagging like a fool. Oh, to be on two legs so I could ride him all night long, so I could feel his hand at the nape of my neck, pinning me down.

"Up." He patted the bed next, and I was there like a shot. He stretched out and I crawled up so that I lay along the length of him.

Once more, that sense of home, of being with my mate, rolled over me—so strong I couldn't deny that what I was feeling was real. Han was who belonged to me, and I to him.

Insta love, here we come, am I right? Fear rose with the need to be close to him and I squirmed. His arm pinned me tight, and I wasn't sure if that made it better or worse.

Gods. It would be my luck to not even...with my mate right here...why?

His breathing deepened, and in moments he was fast asleep. Skittles crept up onto the bed, glaring at me.

"Bitch."

"Pussy," I growled back. "Let me be clear. He is *my* mate. You can look, but you can't touch until I figure out if I want to keep him."

She snickered. "You can't touch either, dumbass.

What are you going to do about that little problem you have there, being a dog? Even if you are his mate, which fine, whatever, you're screwed."

I closed my eyes and lowered my head so that it rested across his abs. He reached an arm around me in his sleep. Did he feel a strange pull to me too? I didn't doubt it, even if he couldn't possibly understand why. I mean, what wolf would want to be stuck with a golden retriever? None. Zero. Zilch.

Of course, it would also make him uncomfortable as fuck if he felt drawn to a dog.

Not that he'd done anything to me that any owner wouldn't. Pet my head. Have me sleep in bed with him. Call me princess. Fuck his hand so hard in front of me that I'd felt an orgasm growing in my own body. And it was still there, just humming under my skin.

I closed my eyes, exhausted by the day's events, and, let's be honest, the wound in my heart made by Meg. I grimaced, and Han's hand tightened on me as if he knew I was hurting.

Skittles snuck up close to me and lay down. "You know, if a witch could do this to us, maybe a witch could reverse it?"

"And if they make it worse, because that's what witches do?" I asked around a yawn. Of all the creatures in the supernatural world, witches were the worst to deal with because they always twisted things. You'd ask for a drink of water, and they'd throw you into the middle of a lake, knowing you couldn't swim.

Skittles sighed. "Okay, so what do we do? How do we get out of this shit?"

"If I could find another pack, they have shamans. They might be able to help," I muttered, sharing my half-baked plan. "Usually there's a way to break a curse, right? But we don't have any parameters. Did Petunia say anything to you? Like maybe gave you a time frame, or told you what to do, like 'you have to learn to truly love' or some shit?"

She snorted. "She told me that she hoped I died in a dark alley, eaten by a dog while I was still alive."

I grimaced. "Yeah, not helpful."

Back to the shaman plan. "A pack might have a shaman, like I said."

"A pack? A pack of what?" Skittles yawned and curled up tighter.

"Werewolves."

She snickered. "Where-whats? Are you kidding me?"

I looked at her. "You want to mock werewolves when a witch turned you into a literal pussy?"

Skittles crinkled up her nose. "Right, fair enough. Let's start over. My real name is Bebe. I am thirty-five years old, a part time model, part time barista at a popular coffee shop chain and have been stuck like this for around six months. I was running out of time at the shelter. Another few days, and I'd have been killed. And I didn't have much to do with the supernatural peoples. Basically, I just heard what was in the news. I didn't know Lukey, that's that guy I was banging, was a magic man. Other than what he could do with his mouth, of course."

I drew in a slow breath. Like so many humans, believing the things that were fake, and ignoring the ones that were real. "My real name is Cin. Spelled with a C, pronounced like Sin. I am fifty-one, but that's young in werewolf years. Basically, we don't age like normal people. I lived in Alaska and ran a small bookstore and coffee shop."

"Oh, look at us, twinning as baristas!" Skittles— strike that, Bebe—butted her head against mine. "I like the name, very... Sinful."

I rolled my eyes. "We need to find a way back to our bodies, Bebe."

"Agreed. But I gotta be honest. I was human before, and so this whole crazy world has been a trip. A nightmare. I don't really know how to get us help. Like, are psychics real? Maybe one could give us some direction."

I let out a sigh. "A pack is our best shot. Assuming I could find one... and that someone there could understand me. Psychics can be real, but like the rest of the supe community, they are rare. Hard to convince to help for anything other than a first-born child."

In order for me to find a pack, I'd need to get to some open space and do some tracking. And that was assuming there was a pack out here on the ocean—which I was pretty sure there wasn't. Most of us liked secluded, rural areas where we could shift into our wolf forms without being caught by humans.

Worst case... I could go with Bebe's idea and look for another witch. I fought a grimace. A witch would be a last resort. But most cities had at least one at hand. Out on the coast here, there was a good chance of a few.

An hour ticked by while Han dozed, and I did the same. My mind continued to flick through the possibilities. What could Han be looking for that he needed a golden retriever's nose? He was a wolf under all that muscle, so in theory he could just use his own nose. But if it wasn't good enough, then the scent had to be faint. A woman. He was looking for a woman that had been what, missing? Maybe she was a total twat like Juniper and it was a revenge thing? No, he'd been too soft when he'd spoken of her.

Maybe his sniffer was broken? Or maybe someone was trying to hide their scent from him? That would do the trick too. Not all wolves had the skill to be sniffers.

Was it possible that he didn't know he was a werewolf? It happened from time to time, where the wolf would be buried so deep it never came out until something traumatic happened.

That would explain the whole mate connection not freaking him out. Though again, he might not be feeling it as much as me, because of my current form. I dismissed the idea though, he'd been careful about his scent, I was sure of it.

The creak of the bedroom door had me lifting my head and turning to see Sven slipping into the room.

I tried to growl.

Ended up whining. But it had the desired effect. Han woke up.

"Sven, it is time already?"

"Sun's down, best time to find her is when she's sleeping. You know that, boy." He glared at me. "I give that one three days. Maybe two."

She, who was she? Was this who we were looking for?

I found myself spinning on the bed and, by sheer force of will, sat my ass down to listen to the men talk. And where did I know Sven from, anyway? His movement and the rumble of his voice tugged at my memories.

The swoosh of my tail across the bedsheets was the only sound I made.

"Soleil." Han said her name in a way that made my tail stop moving—he had a strong affection for her, maybe even love...maybe, worse than that...*need*. "I will find her. I know we are very close. Come on, Princess. Time to work."

He snapped his fingers, and I leapt off the bed, even as my heart was gripped with a funny pang. He needed this woman in a way that I wasn't sure I liked —even if I was still considering whether or not I even wanted a mate. Han dressed swiftly in black army pants, a thick leather belt, and a black tank top covered by a vest laced with several weapons. Like he was going to war. And we were going to walk down the street like this?

Bebe crouched down in the bed sheets, almost invisible against the gray satin. "Don't be a hero, Cin. I need you to help me get back to two legs. So I can pursue a man who isn't a magic man."

I could have given her a snappy response, but to be honest, I wasn't really sure what was going on other than we were looking for a woman named Soleil. "I doubt it will be dangerous for me. I'm just the dog. We're looking for a woman, not hunting down an army."

Though I had to admit Han looked ready to take on the world. I was worried about him, and we hadn't even left the house.

The urge to protect him was there, even as a

golden.

He snapped his fingers again, and I followed him out of the bedroom, down the hall and the stairs, and to the front door.

"Sven, lock it down, and keep an eye out for my brother," Han said as we stepped out into the dark of the early evening. Things kind of had a soft glow around us, probably from the distant glimmering of streetlights. There were none near us. Where we stood, darkness stood too.

It was hard to believe I was even here. That I wasn't having an incredibly wild dream that had taken me from Alberta, to Montana, to California in the space of a few short days.

No, no, I had to believe it. I was not in Alaska, and I was not in Montana or even Alberta. I was here, and I had to find a way back to two legs, just like Skittles—strike that, Bebe—had said. Because no matter who this Soleil person was to Han, *I* was his mate. I was sure of it, even if I wasn't sure of what I wanted to do with that knowledge.

So, no matter how he felt about Soleil now, I was just going to take it one day at a time.

I was not going to get my heart broken by tying myself to a mate that I didn't even know. No matter how good his touch felt.

I followed Han, looking up at him every few seconds. I couldn't help it, even though I was trying not to be stupid, he made me want things I knew were dangerous. Things like love. A family. A pack.

He didn't hail a cab, but instead took me across the street to the beach.

The sand still held heat, and it warmed the pads of my paws as we strode across it, all the way down to the water's edge, the waves washing along, a steady shush back and forth. From there, he turned to the right and kept moving, staying close to the water line.

"Princess, we have to find Soleil before my brother does. He...he can't be allowed to find her first. What he'd do to her, it is not something I can even..."

He didn't exactly choke up, but he shook his head. "He's a very bad man, Princess. I know you are not a fighter; you don't have the heart for it. But should you ever meet him, you must fight for your life. For *my* life. Can you do that?"

The words sunk into me. Apparently, I was not the only one with an asshole family.

I gave a soft woof of agreement.

"Good girl." He patted me on the head, and I let out a long sigh. "I hate to ask it of you, but I know that you will fight him with all you have."

No. Nope. Don't be throwing yourself in front of a speeding bullet for a man you just met!

I woofed again.

"Listen, I know you can't understand, but I'll do my best. You might be my mate, but...mates aren't always all they're cracked up to be."

The independent me was slowly losing what was left of her marbles. That part of me could not believe I'd fallen down the rabbit hole of fated mates and instant love. This wasn't me. Not at all.

And yet... my reaction to him made it plausible, even likely. Why else would I be happily traipsing along Venice Beach next to this man, pretending quite happily that this was some sort of weird first date.

Crazy, I know. Maybe it was a stress-induced reaction. That was possible. Or was I just leaning into the magic of a mate bond?

We walked for about an hour before he slowed to a stop. Across the road from us was another *beauty* of a house and I grimaced, wrinkling my nose at the boxy structure. Completely white from top to bottom, the windows were dark, and there was no movement around it that I could see. Han started toward it.

My hackles lifted as we got close.

There was a smell that I didn't like being this close to, stuck as a golden retriever.

Distinct, clear, and without a doubt, we were walking onto someone else's territory.

A pack of wolves had been here.

10

HOUSTON, WE HAVE A PROBLEM

P art of me was excited. A pack of wolves meant the possibility of a shaman, yet I suspected this pack wouldn't want anything to do with me. Why?

Because Han did not seem happy about being there, and I watched him sniff the air. "Pack's been here. Not good."

So, he wasn't friends with the local pack and now I smelled like him. Just fucking peachy.

"Come," Han said softly to me as he stood in the threshold of the back door. The big house reeked of werewolves, of a pack that I did not know.

I crunched my jaw together and forced my feet to follow him into the house. Laundry room was first, and it was torn to shreds. Claw marks covered the walls, gouged through the steel of the washing machine, and even through the metal door, which was hanging by only one hinge.

"She tried to hide here. My brother beat me to this place, but I do not think he took her. Not yet anyway." His voice was low, barely a whisper.

My claws clicked on the tile floor, and my nose caught the first whiff of blood as we stepped into the kitchen, driving the questions out of my mind. A perfectly white kitchen if not for the blood that had splattered the surfaces. I stepped up and sniffed the bit closest to me.

Human. Male. Lower testosterone levels, so likely in his late forties.

The next bit was also human, though from a female. Younger, late twenties at best.

I let my nose lead me through the room. In the kitchen alone, I pulled up the scents of at least four humans, varying in ages and gender. The amount of blood of the one—the first man—told me he was probably dead.

The others I wasn't sure about. Injured, but not as badly as the first.

Han didn't say anything else. He just let me roam through the house as I followed my nose. Fuck yeah, it was more sensitive than my wolf's nose—I could even tell that the young woman had recently had sex, not that I wanted to know that, but there you go. I made my way through the living room, where there were only a few splotches of blood on the cushions, and then up the stairs to the bedrooms.

At the top of the stairs, I froze and tilted my head. I could have sworn I heard an intake of breath, the slightest shush of air.

Another intake. Male. And a big guy by the sounds of the tremor in his chest.

I looked over my shoulder and saw Han at the bottom of the stairs, watching me, giving me nothing.

Wolf me was like *get the fuck in there, and deal with this shit. Fuck up the bad guys.*

Golden me was almost peeing, the fear was so strong.

A wet, throaty cough cut through the silence.

Han bolted up past me, taking the decision out of my hands—paws, whatever.

He slammed his shoulder into the door on the right, bursting through. The pop of gunfire had me running back downstairs before I could stop myself.

The wolf in me howled to get back to my mate. To help protect him.

I slid to a stop, shaking. I had to learn to fight off this urge to be a coward. I was *not* a coward!

Cringing every step of the way, I slunk back up the stairs and peeked into the room on the right. Han was crouched next to the body of a man whom I identified with a single intake of air as the one from the kitchen, the one who should have been dead.

I mean, he *was* dead now, but I was shocked that he'd been alive enough to fight after losing so much blood.

I had to help Han clear the house, he didn't have to tell me that, I knew from years of...Juniper's training. He didn't look at me as I moved past him, forcing my feet down the hall, sniffing along the edges of the doors until I reached the one at the far left.

The master bedroom, if the sound of running water was any indication. There was a bathroom in there somewhere.

I poked my head through the open door and drew in a deep breath. The smell of a woman was the first thing that hit me, and I knew instinctively that she was the woman Han was looking for. She smelled like heaven. She smelled like stars and light, and beauty.

I didn't like that.

Nope, I did not like her at all... unless she was his sister.

I sniffed again. I knew her smell. Summertime. Sunshine.

The woman I'd seen crying all the way in Edmonton? What had she been doing there, and now here? How had our paths crossed?

All sorts of questions, no answers.

Swallowing hard, I crept through the room. There was not as much blood splatter here, and none of it belonged to this Soleil woman. The blood was from a man again. My nose tickled.

A cat? Where was that — "Where the fuck are we?" came a whisper that had my heart in my fucking throat, and I strangled back a yelp.

I leapt straight up in the air and spun, landing in a crouch to see Bebe behind me.

"What the fuck are you doing here?" I growled even as my legs shook and my knees tried to buckle.

"I followed you, and you were so caught up in your man, that you didn't even notice. Han is pick pocketing that dead guy back there, you know? Found something he liked too, because he took the guy's phone." Her chartreuse eyes did a slow blink. "Maybe he makes his money by stealing from the dead? Kinda weird if you ask me. I mean, don't get me wrong, I'd still bang his fucking eyeballs out of his head given the chance, but it's super creepy."

I shook my head and started again toward the bathroom. The water was running, and as I drew close, the carpet squished under my toe nails. Toe nails, not even really claws. Pitiful.

The creak of the bathroom door tipped my head sideways, and I went as still as if my body had been turned to stone.

A pair of boots could be seen just behind the door, the toes casting a shadow. Was there someone... *in* them? Or were they just boots that had been left behind? I sniffed the air. Ice. He smelled like snow and ice, and he was most certainly in those boots. An impossible but undeniable scent, flavored by the faintest whiff of a wolf. And there was more than a passing resemblance to Han, a hint of a connection.

The smell gave no doubt of just who this was behind the door.

Fuck.

Bebe let out a long, low hiss.

She had more guts than my stupid golden body.

The boots moved. The world around me seemed to slow as he stepped out from behind the door. He was enormous, and I took him in with a single look even as my hackles fought to stand up.

Black clothing, top to bottom, raven black hair, black eyes with the exception of a fleck of silver in the left. A scar ran across his left eye from his forehead to the middle of his cheek. And he held a giant fucking two-headed ax in his right hand.

Oh, and it was dripping with blood. He squinted down at me, his nostrils flaring, but said nothing.

I couldn't move.

Bebe hissed and spat at him, dancing her way in

front of me, drawing his attention and breaking the spell of silence.

He took a swing at her with a boot, and that unlocked me. I was still scared, but I wouldn't let Bebe be hurt. Apparently goldies were cowards, but my loyalty to Bebe overrode my fear.

Goldens protected their people too, it looked like.

I started barking like mad, leaping about, trying to draw his attention to me.

Which worked better than I could have hoped.

"Fucking mutt," he growled, his accent thicker than Han's. But I knew without a doubt this was his brother, the one he'd said I'd have to protect him from. The one who wanted to kill my mate.

He swung the axe toward me, and I flattened to the floor, feeling the deadly blade skim across my back. Where was Han? I yelped and barked louder, dancing around the room until I got to the door and scrambled out, Bebe right at my side.

"Who the fuck is that monster?" she screeched. "He's huge!"

"Han's brother! Bad guy! He's the bad guy!" I yelped out the words as I hit the stairs, going so fast I tripped over my own feet and tumbled all the way to the bottom, landing in a heap of legs and fur.

Han's brother leapt down the stairs and then slid between me and the exit. "Dog. Let me guess, my brother got you from the shelter? Saved you?" He let out a low chuckle. "Where is my little brother, anyway? Coward that he is."

That was an excellent question. I barked—couldn't seem to manage a growl—and scrambled to my feet. I had no choice but to make a dash for the living room. To get out, I'd have to go through the kitchen and out the back door.

Once more the ax swung toward me, this time skimming off a bunch of hair and the tip of my ear. I yelped and howled, throwing myself to the side even though I knew if I stopped running, he'd cut me in half with that thing. Warmth trickled down my ear, blood splattering from the nick.

Bebe leapt up onto the back of the couch, puffed up to maybe twice her size and let out a yowl that stopped the man in his tracks.

"Cat, you want to die too?" he growled. "Fine by me."

"Fuck you, you fucking fuckity fucker face!" She screeched the words as he swung toward her. I couldn't let her die. Not for me.

I shot forward and grabbed his leg, yanking him to the side and dropping him to one knee. Apparently, I still had something of my wolf left in me. I kept jerking on his leg until he was on his hands and knees. He swung his head around and snarled at me, his wolf coming through strong. Violent. Full of anger.

Our eyes locked, and terror ripped through me. Even *my* wolf cowered from this one.

Monster. This werewolf was a monster.

"Run!" I yelped at Bebe, and we bolted for the kitchen. We would have shot out the door, too, but it was shut. Han had left and shut the door behind him.

"Oh shit, oh shit, oh shit!" Bebe was screeching as she clawed at the door. We had seconds at best.

The top of the door was glass. The question was, how strong? Would I knock myself out? At least if I was out cold, I might not feel the death blow of the ax.

Only one way to find out. I backed up as the bellow from Han's brother ripped through the house. A bellow that turned into a howl that cut through me, shaking my body.

I didn't slow. Running full steam, I leapt up and hit the glass in the door. It shattered, and I fell through, my underbelly slashed on a large chunk of glass left in the frame.

Yelping, I hit the ground but didn't stop— survival was on the line. Bebe was out the door after me, and then we were running full speed away from the house.

"Is he behind us?" she screeched.

I looked over my shoulder. The dark-haired man —no, monster—was on the street, watching us go. Lifting a walkie-talkie to his mouth. I couldn't lead him back to Han.

When I picked up Han's scent a moment later, I realized he'd veered left, away from the house. I followed my nose and my mate, praying that he was okay. Was he injured? I didn't think so.

Han's scent wove through the streets around Venice Beach, and it took me over an hour to reach him. By then I was on my last bit of energy.

The good side? Han had finally come to a stop. The bad?

At a restaurant. What was he doing at a restaurant after killing that man and narrowly escaping his wicked brother? Was I missing something? Even while I was questioning what the hell he'd been thinking leaving me there at the murder house. Did he mean to? Had he chased after Soleil?

That seemed the most likely reason. He'd taken the dead man's phone. I'd be willing to bet he'd found a lead.

I didn't understand, and the blood loss was catching up to me, making me feel lethargic and sloppy. All I could do was sit at the door of the restaurant—a Chinese Buffet, no less—and bark.

And bark.

And bark.

Until someone finally came to the door.

"Someone leave their golden doodle thing out here?" The woman who answered the door yelled back into the restaurant.

Han was out in a flash. "Gods, Princess! What happened? I thought you'd run away!"

He scooped me up, and that was that, I was out cold.

Again.

11

WOUNDED, BODY AND SOUL

I woke up in a sterile white place that smelled like sanitizer, death, and dog shit. Not a great combo. For a moment I thought I was back in the shelter. Maybe Han had sent me back because that was easier. Not like I'd managed to find the woman, Soleil. All I'd done was get cut up. Bleed everywhere. Question my mate.

"Will she be okay?"

Han's voice near my right ear settled my worries. He'd thought I'd run away.

"She lost a lot of blood. I've stitched her up, and we gave her an infusion. No work for a few weeks." The second voice was low and melodic.

I managed to open my eyes.

The woman was as round as a beach ball with a kindly face and beautiful brown eyes. She adjusted her glasses and blushed up at Han. I didn't blame her. He was one handsome fucker.

I opened my mouth and gave a soft chuffing woof.

"Oh, she came out of that fast!" The woman, a veterinarian, maybe, came to my side and checked me over, her hands careful, gentle. "I had to trim much of her belly fur, but it will grow back. I can't understand how she lost some of her back fur, though? The cut is precise, like what you'd get from a razor blade. The same with the nick on her ear."

I'd forgotten about those parts. They didn't hurt like the belly gash, which seemed to have dug into the same spot as my gunshot wound.

"I'm sure she just tangled with the wrong dog," Han murmured. "May I take her home?"

Home. He wasn't getting rid of me.

Mind you, what came next made me wonder if I wanted to be there.

"Perhaps you'd like to come with us? Have a drink with me? The least I can do since you've opened your home and practice in the dead of night." He smiled at her, taking her hand in his and covering it with his other hand.

Was he...propositioning the vet?

Her stammering reply said it all. He *was*. And if she was any sort of a woman, she wouldn't turn him down.

Golden

Which is how I ended up locked in one of the spare bedrooms back at the house, listening to the vet make all sorts of noises as Han took his time with her.

Bebe was still right with me. At this point, I'd stopped wondering how she was going unnoticed by Sven and Han. Maybe they just didn't care. Maybe I was seeing things and she wasn't even real.

"Jesus, he's really giving it to her." Bebe lay curled up between my front legs. "Like the rhythm is really good. A solid pounding."

I groaned and wished the sedatives were better. I couldn't move, but I could still hear perfectly fine.

"Kill me now," I whispered. "He doesn't even know that I'm his mate. Not that I'm sure I want him."

"No way, we make a totally kick-ass team. You were awesome back there! Ducking and weaving. I think all that hair distracted the big fuck, made it harder for him to hit you."

I closed my eyes. The werewolf pack in town was tied to Han's brother, I was sure of it. I'd smelled the wolves; Han had been unhappy with the fact that there had been wolves there at all. I knew already that even if they had a shaman, there was no way they would help me. Help me and Bebe. Which meant we were going straight to the last resort.

"Let's find a witch," I whispered. "I can't...I can't

135

listen to him shagging women every night. We need to find a witch so I can explain to him...what I am." Then we could go from there, figure out if we were truly meant to be, or if I was going to call it before it even happened.

"Seriously?" She lifted her head. "I thought you said that was a no go? That witches were a bad idea."

It was a terrible idea, but my predicament was even worse. As long as I was stuck like this, there was no way that Han would even realize I existed. There was no way for me to have a life, let alone with him.

Worse, how did I tell him about his brother and the wicked ax? I was reasonably sure his brother had murdered that entire household. Maybe Han knew that, maybe not. Either way, I had no way of telling him.

The only way to get my mate safe was to make a deal with a devil.

"Find a witch, Bebe," I repeated. "Hurry. Please."

"Okay, okay...um...how?"

It was a good question. "Look for a place with symbols. Moons, stars, etched into the building. A painted door. Not red, something else. Green, that would be good." Green witches were the best of the bunch. Red was a terrible idea.

"Are all painted doors belonging to witches?" Bebe whispered.

I blinked once. "No. Combination of etches, no

pentagrams. Moons. Stars. Blue or green door. Herb garden out front." I sucked in a slow breath. "Ask the strays who scares them."

"Yeah, I can do that. And once I've found us a witch?"

"Then it's our turn to make a deal with the devil," I whispered.

That was the only encouragement it took for Bebe to all but fly from the room and down the hall. Maybe Sven let her out? I didn't know, didn't care. I just closed my eyes and prayed that she found a witch fast, so I would never have to listen to my mate fuck anyone but me again.

12

WHICH WAY, WITCH?

So, there was one good werewolf talent that I'd hung onto. I healed as fast as ever, my quasi-immortal werewolf blood closed the wounds in a single night.

"How is this possible?" Han rolled me onto my back and ran his hand over my belly—which was completely covered in fur again. "Unless..."

My tongue lolled out as he scratched up under my front legs, and then I was on my feet. I gave a woof. I was hungry.

Also, I wanted to see how Sven reacted to the vet, seeing as he didn't much like me, and I was just a dog in his territory. What did he think about a woman in Han's bed?

But the kindly, beautiful-eyed woman who'd stitched me up was not there. And Sven was as disgruntled as ever as he placed a plate of ground beef and chicken livers—cooked, thank you very much—on the floor and slid it across to me. "The night did not go well?"

"Her home was demolished, dead everywhere. I think Princess here took on Havoc."

Havoc. Was that his brother?

I felt Sven look at me, and I lifted my head and licked my chops. He squinted one eye. "But she's still alive. How is she not dead?"

"Exactly." Han sounded...happy? Proud? Either way, it made my tail wag. "I will take her out again tonight. See if she can pick up Soleil's scent now that she's been in the house."

"How will you make her understand?" Sven grumbled. "She's just a dog."

"I'm not so sure of that." Han took a sip of his coffee, the smell curling around me. What I wouldn't give for some of the good stuff right then.

Ah, fuck it.

I stood on my back legs and stuck my tongue deep into the cup, lapping it up.

Sven snorted. "I will get you a bowl, idiot dog."

I dropped back down and waited as he poured me a cereal bowl of coffee. Then I waited. He rolled his eyes. "Cream?"

Two woofs.

Two dollops of cream were dispensed by a rather disgruntled Sven.

I waited.

"Loki's ass! You want sugar too?" He roared.

I was proud that I managed to keep from cringing from him. The truth was, he seemed more amused than angry. Or maybe I was just hoping he was warming up to me.

I let out two barks in response to his question about sugar. I wouldn't drink straight-up black coffee unless desperate.

"Freya kill me now, I'm serving a dog her morning coffee. Me. ME, the last of my kind, the veritable king of the forest!" Sven grumbled as Han laughed.

Two spoonfuls of sugar later, I was lapping up my coffee while Han continued to chuckle behind me. "I like this one. She has...spice. Fire in there somewhere."

"You think she's not a dog though?"

Han grunted.

Sven squinted at me. "What dog asks for a double-double?"

My heart all but stopped in my chest, but my tongue kept on lapping up the coffee. Han was onto me.

"A special dog. Healed fast though. Maybe there is

a bit of something else in her? She could be part fae or even part shifter? Who knows? There is no magic in her that I can actually sense. But she survived her first encounter with Havoc. That alone is unheard of. I wish I had seen it." He stood and stretched. "Sven, make sure you clean up, will you? Give the place a good scrubbing. I'm going to take Princess for a walk."

For a walk? No, I didn't believe it was just a walk. He was a man with purpose.

He pulled his shirt up over his head and dropped it, baring his abs. "See if we can find someone to talk to near the house."

Damn, he was going to use his body to get contacts and information.

I could roll with that. Once we were outside, I paced along at his side, my newest scar itching like mad, but I ignored it for the fact that I needed to figure out a way to be more than just a dog.

Bebe had not come back yet. I was hoping that she would have an answer for me. A solution. But even I knew that pinpointing a witch could take some time.

Because I couldn't seem to leave Han's side, even if I wanted to.

Frustration rippled through me. This mate bond was *stupid*. I should have been furious with him for fucking the vet last night. Even if he didn't know what I was, or who I was, I still should have been jealous. But I didn't feel that way.

Which, I'll be honest, wasn't like me. I was a jealous bitch when it came to my man, like most werewolves. Territorial. Possessive. That was normal. I didn't share. And it had been so long since I'd even had a man that I should have been a slavering fool. Was this because I was a golden now? Had that made me less territorial about my mate?

Horror flickered through me. "I fucking well hope not," I grumbled under my breath.

We were out on the beach now, and Han picked up a jog that I easily matched. His muscles quickly grew damp with sweat, and he fairly glistened in the sunlight, his tanned and toned body drawing more than a few looks.

He didn't have any tattoos, and no real scars that I could see other than the one across his back.

I kept close to him, my eyes sweeping the area, watching as closely as I could for danger while drawing in deep breaths to scent the air. I did not want to be running into Havoc again without plenty of warning. But all I was getting was sun tan lotion, a range of human scents and the ocean.

Han slowed as we drew near the murder house. It was all taped off with yellow, and police cars, a black van, and a white tent had been set up outside the house.

Lots of people were gathered at the edge of the street, jostling to get a better view. Maybe see some blood or a body bag or other gruesome souvenir.

"Scavengers," someone muttered.

"Agreed," Han said, stepping close to the back of the human pack. "Does anyone know the people who lived there? I heard a woman made it out alive, are the rest okay?"

He knew they most certainly were not okay.

Soleil...he was hoping someone had a tip on her he could follow. Smart, I'd give him that.

A couple of women turned, saw Han, and immediately launched into fictional accounts of the former residents as they reached out, touching his arms.

I could smell the lies on them. Hopefully Han could to. I took a step away from Han, testing the proximity thing as a new scent caught my nose. Oh, now *this* was interesting. I was able to step away from him and into the crowd.

Why?

I didn't know, but I kept moving, following the smell. Because what were the chances?

The scent of grave dirt is not common. Very few supernaturals would use it in their magic—which made it more than likely that a witch was involved with this smell. I shouldn't have been surprised. A murder house would be a temptation to a witch, there would be plenty of raw ingredients left behind, and all doused with fear and pain.

I drew a breath, glanced over my shoulder at Han, and saw that he was completely distracted, busy with the women. Two had hands on him, he kept pointing left and right of the house. Looking for a direction on Soleil.

Good enough. I knew my way back to the house, I'd find my way back later. Nose to the ground—okay, not literally—I scented my way down the street. The smell of the grave was now mixed with a floral scent, one that was pungent, sweet, and deadly.

Belladonna.

Yeah, I don't know how I knew it was that kind of flower. The image popped up in my head, like my brain was full of scent categories. The deep purple petals swept out into a six-pointed star with a bright yellow center. "Fucking trippy," I muttered under my breath.

I'd told Bebe to smell for herbs, and this was an herb alright. A powerful, killing, kind of an herb.

I kept up my pace, trotting along, not really paying attention to where I was going as I followed the probable witch's smell. Which was growing in strength until my nose was full of nothing but her, and I was standing in front of a doorway.

Painted purple, the wooden door looked rickety, the paint chipped and faded. A moon and a series of stars had been etched into the top of the door frame, all the way around. A bunch of garbage cans banged down the alley from me, and I flinched, sliding down the few steps that led to the door, staring out into the space where the noise had originated.

Something large, dark, and incredibly wolfy stepped out of the shadows. Blue eyes stared down at me. The slight breeze was pushing my scent toward him, not the other way around.

Fuck. Fuck, fuckity, fuck.

That was the same wolf from up north, with the howl that tripped my clit out, and threatened my mere existence.

I spun and scratched frantically at the door, paint peeling off under my wimpy fucking toe nails.

The sound of his padded feet headed my way had me barking and all but throwing myself at the door.

I didn't look over my shoulder, but I knew he was closing in.

I closed my eyes as I imagined the sensation of teeth biting into my neck, bones snapping, life ending.

The door yanked open, and I fell in.

"Moon cursed, get thee gone from my doorway you brat! I've had enough of wolves and their terrible behavior!"

I scrambled inside as the large black wolf

reached the top step. He stared down at me, his lips curled back, blue eyes locked on me. I was on his turf, apparently. Again. Though I doubted he knew I was the woman who'd seen him in Edmonton. I doubted I smelled the same stuck in my golden body.

The door was slammed shut and the woman—witch—turned with her hands on her hips. Her hair was a classic red, curly, and loose as could be, falling well past her shoulders. She was a petite woman with big curves that she'd accentuated with a thick brown leather belt around her waist. A soft blue blouse on top, deep cut over her largest assets, had been paired with a billowing skirt speckled with star bursts against a blue night sky material that swirled around her legs. I would put her in her forties, but witches tended to age slowly, so appearances could be deceiving. Her green eyes flashed. "What in the name... what do I need a dog for? This is what I get for wandering down to the beach, isn't it?"

Swallowing hard, I sat up and woofed softly at her.

"I'm not a dog. I'm a woman. A werewolf trapped like this, and I need help. Please. *Please* help me."

Goddess of the moon and night, how did I get her to understand me? I'd kinda just assumed she'd know what I was, being a witch and all.

Her eyes narrowed as my tail thumped softly on

the ground. Crouching slowly, she put a hand on either side of my face and stared into my eyes, tipping my head this way and that. "Well, I'll be buggered with a splintered broomstick. Petunia has got another of you? She's a menace, that witch! A complete and total menace!"

She knew.

I lost it. I went mental, yipping and licking her face. Yeah, there was not a lot of control when I got excited. Someone knew and understood, someone who could maybe help me.

The witch pushed me off. "I can't turn you all the way back, wolf. I see you, but Petunia is stronger than me by a long shot. At best, I could soften this. I can't fix it."

All that excitement slid away, like water off an umbrella. A whine slid out of me, and I pushed my nose into her hands, begging.

"Please, anything is better than this. My mate is in trouble. This punishment wasn't mine to take. It was forced on me."

She sighed. "I know. I can see it all, my young friend, the whole story. But what would you have from me? I can give you, at best, maybe two hours a day on two legs. And then you'd be back to this. But if I do that, I'm not sure if the original curse can be broken. Not that Petunia gives that option usually." She patted my head. "Let me think on this. Come back tomorrow. I will have something ready for you."

Tomorrow. No, I would stay, and she would help me. Also if I left I was most certain that other wolf would still be there. Probably he was from the pack that Havoc was tied to, and that was enough to keep me from leaving.

I lay down on the floor, put my head on my legs and woofed.

She wrinkled her face at me. "Nowhere to go? Damn it. I suppose you aren't friends with big boy out there?"

I shook my head. I most certainly was not, even if his first howl at me had literally brought me to my knees.

"Well." Her hands were on her hips again. "Fine. You can stay. But you cannot see my secrets. Can't have more competition here than I already have, you know?"

I immediately closed my eyes.

Her laugh was soft. "Good enough. My name is Georgia. I came out west to get away from the politics of my sisters." Eyes still closed, I listened to the shush of her skirts, the clang of pots and wooden spoons, the spin of a container's lid as it was flicked off, and the soft ping of seeds dropping into a metal bowl. "You aren't the first to be attacked by Petunia. I'm betting it had something to do with that luscious man of hers? He is a fine one. I'll bet he looks good in and out of his clothes if you know what I mean."

My eyes opened, and I stared at her, horrified. "He's a wimp!" I barked. "No balls whatsoever if he can't even stand up for himself! If he had, I wouldn't be stuck like this!"

Her mouth dropped open, and her green eyes swung my way. "You think he was wimpy?"

I rolled my eyes, then realized that she'd really *heard* me. "I mean... he saved me from being killed, I guess. But honestly, he seems to go for powerful women who are absolute bitches. He fucked my mother, the queen bitch herself. He has a type and obviously needs therapy, hours and hours of therapy."

She huffed. "I suppose there is always room for improvement. You think he really has a type?"

I stared at her, realizing two things very quickly —she had a crush on Petunia's husband, and she was most certainly not his type. I stared up at her, cocking my head to the side. "Why else would he stay with Petunia? She's cruel and jealous. And why would he be with my mother? Sure, she's got looks and the moves apparently, but she's a raging psycho. Something must be missing in his life. Or his brain. Something is broken."

Georgia huffed as she dumped a bunch of something that smelled like sage into her metal bowl. "I suppose. But he's been with other women too, you know. Good women. Kind women."

I shrugged, thinking of Bebe. "But he stays with the horrible one. And what happened to those good women? Petunia got them too, didn't she?"

Her sigh filled the air. "If I could save him, I would. But he's not one who wants to be saved. He has a path that is not easily understood."

She opened the fridge and pulled out a wine bottle, though the shimmering deep blue liquid inside was most assuredly not wine. There were things sparkling and dancing in the liquid. Tiny creatures? I could swear that one waved at me. I couldn't look away.

"There will need to be a contract," Georgia said softly. "Much as I wish I could do things for free, because of the guild, I cannot. You know this?"

Here it was. The twisted part of every witch. They had to take something. Had to, and the more value the better.

"I'll pay whatever you want," I woofed. "I have money."

"Never in coin, you should know that. It's a bargain, a trade." She began stirring the concoction, her hand waving over the bowl as she worked. "A give and take, if you will."

"Well, I got nothing from Petunia," I snapped. "Except more hair than I ever wanted."

Georgia paused in her stirring, the smell rolling off the concoction heavily influenced by the sage.

"But it was a trade. She didn't kill your mother, and in trade, you got this." She smiled at me as if *this* was the deal of the century.

"Again, it was not a trade I had any part in. Isn't there something in the guild about that?" I asked.

Georgia gave a slow nod. "That's why he was able to help you. The trade wasn't a true trade. He could interfere."

She kept adding things, stirring, muttering under her breath. Sometimes her voice deepened and took on a tone that didn't fit her petite frame. I'd never seen a witch actually work, and I couldn't help but be intrigued by the process. She didn't remind me not to look, so I was taking in the sights. It was interesting.

She paused and looked down at me. "This is why I hoped you would go for the night, so that we could both think on what thing of value you could offer me. Something you can live without of course. Something... simple."

Simple.

I frowned up at her. "You want a post-dated check?"

Her laugh was soft and tinkling in the air. "I told you, not money. The thing you give must have value, value to *you*." Her eyes were distant. "Be quiet now, the rest is going to take all my concentration."

She kept muttering under her breath. I curled up and flipped my tail over my nose. Because it was obvious that she was done talking with me and needed me silent so she could concentrate.

There was nothing I could do now but wait, and hope that the price she extracted wasn't too high.

13

ALL WITCHES ARE BITCHES

I slept fitfully. The sound of Georgia in the kitchen, whipping up her spell for me, was apparently the white noise I needed to get some rest. My body was sore—despite what Han thought about me healing fast. There were layers and layers to healing. I would still need a few days at least for the muscles to fully come back together and feel myself again.

A dish of water and a plate of hot dogs were stuffed in front of me around dinner. I looked up at Georgia, her face bright with pleasure. "I figured more protein is better, right? You should keep that in mind, from here on out. Stick with protein."

I nodded my thanks and gulped the hot dogs down. Who would have thought cold hot dogs could taste so good? Of course, I was starving, and the healing took its own kind of toll, draining me of energy and even muscle tone if I didn't eat enough. Almost as much as shifting back and forth from two legs to four.

The night seemed to come swiftly after dinner, and Georgia didn't slow in her spell making.

Once more, I watched her closely. Sweat beaded across her forehead as she stirred and wiggled her fingers. She had no familiar that I could see. I was fully expecting a crow or a cat to show up at some point, but her house remained empty except for the two of us.

Around midnight, I fell into a deeper sleep. My dreams mashed up the past and the present, and instead of Richard and Kieran shooting me, Havoc and Han tossed my body in the river and high-fived as I floated away.

I woke with a start when the morning light splashed over my face. My heart ticked along at high speed as if I'd been running in my sleep.

"Bad dreams?" Georgia asked.

"Always," I mumbled as I sat up and stretched. "How's it going?"

"I have it all ready, and now we must discuss the terms of the agreement." Georgia smiled as she stirred a cup of tea on the table. "The bargain is simple. You get your legs back from sundown to sunup. You have to stay a golden during the day, I couldn't do better than that, though I tried."

My tongue lolled out as my jaw dropped. "That's a hell of a lot more than a couple of hours! That's amazing!"

She flushed pink. "I wish I could do more. When you are on two legs, you won't be able to shift to your dog form and vice versa. You will not have that ability."

I nodded.

Her smile faltered. "For that much time, I have to take something of great value from you, Cin. Great value."

Heart racing, I stared up at her, already knowing what she would want. "My soul?" What else did I have?

"Goddess, no! I don't want your soul! They are finicky, hard to keep happy and alive. No. You must give me your voice."

I blinked up at her. "My... voice?"

"No barking, yipping, singing, talking, nothing. Nada. Zip. Zilch." She tapped her spoon on the rim of her cup and set it aside. Her eyes were soft as she looked me over. "Very old school, don't you think?"

Very old school indeed, but it was the only chance I had. I mean, not very many people could hear me now as it was. And when I was on two legs, I could write down my words or type them into a device. Manageable.

"Will I ever be able to get my voice back?" I asked.

Georgia took a sip of her tea before she answered. "There are magics in this world that I cannot fathom or control. For instance, the magic of the moon gives power to the werewolves, and as such you praise your moon goddess. Perhaps a deity that has more power than a witch could change the curse, or give you back your voice. But again, what would the cost be? Worth it? That will be up to you when the time comes."

When, not if.

I squinted my eyes at her. "When?"

"A manner of speaking." She waved her hand, her fingers wiggling, but I was watching her eyes. She knew something that she was most definitely not telling me.

That was annoying, obviously, but it also told me this might not be the end of what my mother and Petunia had started. Hope flared in my chest. Despite everything, I'd landed on a path that had led me to my mate, and I might yet have a future with him.

Georgia had invoked the moon goddess, just by speaking of her. That was a good sign.

I dipped my head. "I accept."

She laid out a piece of parchment on the floor, and next to it she sat a pad of black ink. "Nose or pawprint, whichever you like."

I dabbed my nose into the ink pad, immediately regretting it since I could smell the ink so strongly it covered everything else. Without asking, Georgia swiped a cloth across my nose.

"Should have thought that through."

I wasn't sure if she meant me or her. Either way, I put my paw to the ink and then pressed it into the paper. The second my paw left the paper, the print flared gold, then the parchment curled up into Georgia's hand with a snap. She smiled down at me.

"Is there any way I can break Petunia's curse on my own?" I whispered as Georgia stood and scooped up my water bowl. She took it to the kitchen and poured her steaming potion into it. Might as well use my voice in the last minutes I had it.

"It would take a great magic wielder to break her spell completely. As I said, a deity is a possibility, but if not that, then maybe a demon?" She shrugged. "That would cost you your soul for sure. You don't really want to do that. Do you?"

I shook my head as she lowered herself, setting the bowl in front of me. "It won't take effect until tonight. Sundown."

I nodded and paused, thinking of Bebe. She deserved a shot at escaping her body too, and judging by how long she'd been gone, she hadn't met with much success. "I have a friend. She's also been trapped by Petunia—"

"Bebe's case is different than yours," Georgia said, not unkindly but firmly. "Her path out of her current situation will not be the same as yours. Another tale to tell, if you will."

How did she know Bebe? Maybe my friend had already spoken with Georgia, maybe as I was coming here, Bebe was headed home with news of the witch. "You can't help her?"

She paused, slowly lowering herself back into her chair, re-arranging her skirts. "Won't. She is paying the price for something she did do, while you are caught up in others' machinations. None of this was your fault, as far as I can see. Unless you convinced Juniper to seduce the warlock?"

Well, shit. "No, before all of this, I hadn't seen my family in years."

Georgia looked over me. "Then why did you go back?"

"I thought my sister was in trouble," I said softly. "Turns out she's just like the rest of them."

Georgia tsked. "Don't be too sure. Sometimes we do what we have to in order to survive."

I blew out a long sigh, knowing she was right. She also seemed to know an awful lot about my life for someone I'd never met before yesterday, but that was witches for you. The top of the potion rippled, shimmering with that blue liquid I'd seen her pour into the bubbling pot. I couldn't see any of the little waving creatures, thank fuck.

"It reminds me of the water near my home." She smiled down at me. "I do like to add a little pizzaz to my spells, make them a little bit more mine." She winked and sipped her tea. "Drink up. You've already signed the contract, don't let it grow cold."

I lowered my face to the bowl and began to lap up the blue liquid. It was warm but the neon turquoise and streaks of shimmering silver like chunks of ice made it look cold. Tasted like milk and honey, but under those dominating flavors was something else, something that tasted of darkness and fire. That gave me pause, but I was already halfway through.

"I wouldn't do that," Georgia said. "Halfway will leave you a mess, half transformed each day."

Yup, I was not doing that.

I drank it down until I was licking the bottom of the bowl. I was not going to give any part of this a chance to screw up.

Georgia leaned in close to me, her smile less kind and more calculating. "How do you feel? I must know."

My heart was pounding far harder than it should be, and my skin itched. "What did you do to me?"

Her smile widened, and her visage slowly changed, shifting to that of a man dressed in a sweeping long black cloak. A man I knew all too well.

Petunia's husband.

14

WORST. CONTRACT. EVER

"**M**otherfucker. And I mean that in every sense of the word!" I barked out, my voice still operational for now.

Petunia's husband stood in front of me, his body morphed out of Georgia's curvy female form.

He laughed, his green eyes flashing as if this was the best joke in the world.

"Why? Why would you help me? Or did you just kill me?" Horror flooded my body.

"Because you intrigue me, little wolf. Very much so. And I want to see how you handle challenges. You never know. Maybe one day I'll need you to save me. But until then ..."

He reached out with his right hand and curled his fingers.

My throat tightened as if every muscle had contracted at once. He grabbed my jaws and pried them open. From between them he pulled out a shimmering thread and wrapped it around his hand, turning it into a bracelet set with black and gold stones.

I jerked my head out of his hands and barked. *Tried* to bark.

Nothing came out, not even a wheeze.

He crouched next to me and winked. "Now, let's see what you can do without a voice. Those two should be worried, I think. You have enough heart to be a dragon, never mind a golden dog."

I had no idea what he was talking about. What two?

The world spun around me as I collapsed to the floor, legs in every direction, tail silent as the potion ripped through me, fusing with my bones, blood, and muscle.

I closed my eyes, berating myself for believing a witch could be kind. Or helpful. Or honest. I couldn't forget honest.

Then again, he *had* given me two legs during the night.

"Oh, and one more thing, kind of minor in the scheme of it, but I should mention that if your mate finds out that you're also his dog? That starts a countdown, if you will. Three days after he learns what and who you are, you'll die. The only thing I will say is that I had to give you an out—that is something Petunia forgets, but have no fear. I was able to work it in. You'd need a prince. Old school, again, but I can't make it easy. If your man finds out what you are, you need a prince, and voilà, no dying."

I shot to my feet as the room spun—and I don't mean in a metaphorical, feeling woozy sort of deal. This was a Dorothy-in-the-twister kind of spinning.

What? The one-word question rocketed through my mind as I struggled to stand in a house that was suddenly coming apart around me.

"Yes, I know. Kind of shocking, isn't it? I probably should have mentioned it. But you see, I know Han. Quite well, actually. So I need you to not tell him. Don't write to him. Send him a letter. Nothing. He can't know that you're his dog. Got it? It's for his own good. You need to save him, and this is the only way."

The prince thing. What is that?

He tucked a piece of paper under my collar. "Here. All the details of the contract for you to look over."

Shit. I should have done that earlier. I'd been so excited, so full of hope.

He smiled down at me. Not mean. Not nice. The kind of smile that would make you wonder what the fuck he was up to.

I couldn't even scream and rage at this asshole for what he'd just done. Had he helped? Yes, possibly, I could admit that. But seeing as he knew this whole thing wasn't my fault... I was betting he could have turned me all the way back to a werewolf.

"Yes. There is that. You are correct, I could have actually shifted you all the way back."

Fantastic, he could read my thoughts.

"But it's in my best interest to have you in this position, doing my work for me," he continued. He laughed, winked again, and then was gone with a clap of his hands, while the place was ripped to pieces around me as if a tornado had birthed inside of it. I bolted out through the spinning debris as the space behind me exploded.

Thrown through the air, I tumbled across the pavement and landed up against a pair of legs.

Wolf legs.

The blue-eyed wolf stared down at me, lips slowly curling back, baring teeth that were made for ripping flesh. Death, I could see death in his eyes.

Worse than all that, I could smell him now and I knew exactly who it was.

Ice.

A hint of Han.

Han had blue eyes. But this was not him. As my nose rapidly pulled the scents apart, I knew I was very much wrong.

I was staring up at the wolf version of Havoc.

He locked eyes with me and the monster in him, the darkness that lived inside of him, all but pinned me to the ground. The power of an Alpha rolled through him and into me. There was only one thing I could do. I was stuck as a golden, and no true golden would fight a wolf.

I rolled onto my back, showing my belly and offered up my throat in complete submission, too physically weak from ingesting the potion, too frazzled to think of anything else. Hating that I had to submit, tears leaked from my eyes and into the fur of the ruff around my neck.

His growl was a deep rumble. "I should kill you."

I, of course, said nothing.

He stepped over me, and his mouth was on my neck, squeezing, baring down to the point that a few teeth broke through the flesh. I held still. I knew this game, maybe better than anyone else.

A power move, to show me he was superior. Well, I wasn't fucking arguing with his royal assholeness. If I'd been in my wolf form, I'd have fought, or at the very least made it clear that I wouldn't go down without a fight.

A snort chuffed out of him, and he let me go. Was he *laughing* at me?

I didn't understand why he would let me go, not that I was complaining. He stepped back, his eyes sweeping over me, thoughtful. Then he turned and walked away from me, his tail stiff with irritation.

I rolled onto my belly and pushed slowly to my feet. He called over his shoulder, "You'll die soon enough. Everyone who loves Han dies. Remember that when your moment comes to suffer for him. You may be his dog, but that means nothing to him."

Soon enough. But not today.

How did he know that I... no, I didn't love Han. I wasn't that stupid. But he was my mate. I didn't mean nothing to Han, even as a dog. He'd taken me to the vet, gotten me stitched up.

He left you at the murder house too.

I grimaced, there was that, though he'd said he'd thought I'd run away.

I pushed to my feet and stared at Havoc as he strutted away. It wasn't often that a wolf's eyes changed color along with their form. Usually it was the result of some sort of injury. Was that what had caused his color change?

I shook my head and backed up. He hadn't killed me. Did he understand that I was trapped like this? Somehow, I thought he did.

How did I know he wouldn't follow me right

back to Han? Call me crazy, but I suspected he knew exactly where Han was... and yet it was me he had followed. One more question without an answer, but I suspected this might be the most important one of all.

15

FOUR MINUS TWO

I made my way slowly back toward Han's home. There was no hurry at this point. I figured out pretty quickly that if I shifted from four legs to two anywhere in Han's house, it would be noticeable, and I couldn't let him see that I was his dog. If I did, I'd be toast.

There didn't seem to be cameras or anything set up within the beach house. But even if Han didn't notice, I was sure that Sven would. That one was attentive.

My mind wandered as my feet took me back to Han. I'd been gone for over a full day now. Would he be sad that I'd gone missing? Or would there be a new dog in my place already, to help him find Soleil?

That made me pick up my pace some. In fact, I was so focused on my path, I ran right over Bebe.

"Hey! What the hell, you stupid dog?" She rolled and came up spitting at me, her hair fluffed right up. "Oh shit! Cin!"

I stared at her and sighed. I couldn't even tell her what happened.

"What do you mean you can't tell me what happened?" She tipped her head sideways and looked me over. "I don't see an injury."

My jaw dropped. *You're a mind reader?* I didn't expect it from anyone but the wizard. Few and far between, there were some in every species, but most common amongst humans touched with fae blood. Maybe that was why she'd been attracted to the wizard in the first place.

She shrugged. "I don't know, I guess? Didn't you pay attention when we were in the shelter? It's a gift. A curse. I don't always hear thoughts, but your brain is screaming."

A small mercy then, to have a friend who could still understand me in this form.

I met a witch, only it wasn't a witch, it was that fucking warlock who you and my mother fucked, and now he's fucked me over again. He turned me back to a woman, only part time, lost my voice. Proverbially fucked over of course. I wouldn't touch that piece of shit with a ten foot—

"Wait! You mean you're going to look like a woman again?" She set her paws on my face and put her nose to mine. "This is amazing! What about me? I didn't find a witch, I've been searching since I left."

Sundown to sunup. And I asked him to help you. He refused. Said it wasn't your path.

She crinkled up her face. "Imma claw his eyes out, scratch his balls and I don't mean the rough play like he liked, I mean I'm gonna slice them like a ripe peach! What a dick."

Bebe bounced around on her pads, dancing like a prized fighter ready to go ten rounds. I looked past her to the beach. We were almost back to Han's home.

I don't even know if Han will like me... I'm his mate, but what if he prefers round women? Like the vet? And I can't tell him what I am, because if I do that, then I have, like, three days before I'm dead.

Bebe shrugged. "Then I guess you'd better get eating those cookies. Wait... you can't tell him, or you die? That seems extreme."

I looked at her. *And getting turned into a dog and cat isn't extreme?*

"Point made." She nodded.

I shook my head, and a silent sigh slid from my lips. I turned my head to nudge the note tucked into my collar. *I'd better read this, it's the contract. I guess he added a clause about breaking it. Something to do with a prince, but where am I supposed to find a prince?*

Bebe tugged the note out with her teeth and we

smoothed it on the ground. What an image it would have looked to a passerby, a dog and cat reading together.

The first part of the contract was simple. An exchange of my legs from sundown to sunup, for my voice. A few other bits about not being held responsible if I died while drinking the potion, and then the part about the prince. If Han were to find out about me being a dog, my only hope was to find a prince and—

"That wasn't how Disney did it," Bebe said. "You have to fuck a prince? Seriously? Why not just a kiss, or a handshake?"

I didn't have time to answer her. A spasm rippled through me, starting deep in my belly and spreading outward. I looked to the sky. The sun was officially gone, the light fading on the horizon.

"You okay?" Bebe butted her nose against mine, and I shook my head. Shifting didn't hurt like this. Then again, when I'd first shifted into my wolf form, I'd been very young. Maybe that had hurt? Maybe it would until I'd gotten used to this shape?

I stumbled toward Han's house, legs wobbling, feeling like they were being pulled in all directions, muscles and ligaments tearing free from their connection to my bones. Bebe plastered herself against my side as best she could, steadying me.

If I could just get to the side of the house, I could shift there.

"Just breathe. It's like giving birth, right? At the end of this will be a glorious new form. Perfect. Two legs. Big boobs."

My boobs aren't that big.

"Shit. Well. Maybe he won't want you after all. Maybe I still got a chance!" Bebe teased as I flopped down onto my belly. I wasn't going to make it to the side of the house. Seizing and shaking, I fell on the bottom steps, legs splaying in all directions, tongue lolling out of my head. A groan slid out of me, but it was more of a wheeze as the air escaped my lungs. Painful, yes, but what scared me most was my inability to think straight. Always, even in the midst of pain, I could see a way out, or at least be cognizant of the world around me.

Not anymore.

The sun had fully dipped below the horizon, and the world changed from day to night, the last of the light fading. Time seemed to pause. My body crackled and popped as the golden fur sloughed off, and my limbs lengthened at a pace that was stupidly slow.

I gritted my teeth against the pain. Every day like this? Fuck. This was going to cost me time and energy. Suddenly the comment about eating more protein made sense. The warlock had known.

I couldn't let Han see me, or it would mean my death. I forced myself up and Bebe followed, her voice a distant buzz as I got myself around the corner of the house, hidden in the shadows. It took what was the last of my energy, but I made it.

Minutes went by—one by one, until twenty had ticked past. Twenty minutes for the full transformation from golden to woman.

When it was done, I lay on the ground, naked as the day I was born, the concrete cold against my back and legs. The chill against my sweat-slicked skin was almost pleasant. I sighed and ran my shaking hands over my body, checking.

"Oh, you are a beauty. All that dark hair! I was totally expecting you to be blonde, you know considering your doggo coloring." She butted her head against my hip, and I scooped her up, holding her tight under my chin.

I could still understand her. That was good.

Do I smell like a wolf now?

She sniffed under my chin. "Musky, like the forest. And yeah, not a dog anymore—something wild. Yup, wolf. You smell like a wolf now."

Then Han would know me for his mate when he finally scented me. Relief flooded through my body, and with it came confidence. I would be okay. Even if I couldn't speak.

I struggled to my feet and managed to get back to

the steps, but once there my knees gave out. I lifted a hand and banged a fist on the door. There was no way I'd be breaking through all the locks they had in place. Curling up on the stoop, I waited for him to come to the door.

"What are they doing in there?" Bebe grumbled as she lifted herself up and patted the door with her murder mittens. I lifted my fist and slammed it harder. It was all I could do since I couldn't yell or scream for him to come find me.

I closed my eyes and dozed off while my belly rumbled, demanding I find some food. Transformation from four to two had never been so hard on me before. Was it because I wasn't supposed to be a golden, or because I wasn't supposed to have my two-legged form back at any point? Drifting in and out of wakefulness, I latched onto the roar of the surf across the street.

"I don't think he's here, goldilocks." Bebe said, her voice careful. "Let me get up to the bedroom window, okay? Maybe I can see something."

I nodded and she took off, climbing the side of the house like a mountain goat moving up a sheer rock face.

My hair got caught up in the ocean breeze, and I took in a deep breath.

Gagged on the smell that reached me. Nothing dead, nothing rotting, something far more troubling.

Fuck my life inside out, the timing could not have been worse.

Bebe let out a yowl and dropped from the window ledge she was on to the front steps. "We gotta go, we gotta go, *now*."

Yes. They've found me.

The scent was faint, but I knew it to my bones, and every nerve in my body lit up.

At least one of my brothers had found me.

"Yeah, well, I'm more worried about the dead woman in Han's bed," Bebe shrieked, "and Sven looking like an ax murderer! He was standing over her with a literal ax! Like he was going to chop her pretty blonde head off!"

I pushed to my feet. *All the more reason that we need to move. My family is here. Dead bodies in there. No reason to stick around. But I need clothes.*

Bebe shot ahead of me, moving around the side of the house. "This way, come on!"

I wobbled for my first few steps, and then I got my legs under me and started moving in a relatively straight line. So, Sven had killed a woman. Did Han know? Maybe that was why he'd left the house?

Which meant I had to find him. All the toasted fucks in the world were not enough to get me through this day.

Between the two houses we went, and I used the side wall to help balance myself, pushing off, keeping us moving, hating that I had to touch anything. My scent would be everywhere. Fuck my life, why had I chosen this moment to be turned back to two legs? I knew that my brothers would be looking for a golden, but I didn't smell the same in that form, not at all.

I could almost hear the warlock laughing in the distance.

Bebe dodged around garbage cans and junk left out on the side streets. "Here, I think, yes, here."

She'd stopped beside a house, a clothesline hanging off a window twenty feet above us, strung between two buildings. Taking a deep breath, I leapt to the side, using the building as a push-off point to get some height.

My fingers snatched a single T-shirt. I yanked it off the line and landed in a crouch, already pulling it over my head. It barely came to my mid-thigh, but it would have to do. The huff of a canine behind us had me bolting forward.

Whatever instability I had from my transition was gone now, banished by a rush of adrenaline and fear, and I was running full tilt, bare feet slapping the pavement. Too loud, it was too loud, but there was not a lot I could do about it.

"I have an idea. This way!" Bebe shouted and I let her lead me away from the houses and back toward the ocean. "Water will make it harder for anyone to track us, right?" She was right, and salt water was better than anything else at wiping scent clean.

It was a testament to how fucked up the transition had left me that I hadn't thought about this in the first place.

We crossed back toward the water way south of Han's place. The sand was still warm under my feet as I sunk in and raced to the edge of the water. *Bebe, you have my scent on you. You have to come in too, or they'll hurt you.*

"Well good thing I like swimming." She leapt in ahead of me, landing in the ocean with a tiny splash. I was doing my best not to freak out. This was an ocean full of things that would eat you, given the chance. Particularly at night.

I dove in anyway. There was no choice. The devil I didn't know was far better in this case and I was swimming with sharks regardless. At least the ones in the water weren't looking for me.

Swimming out past where I could touch, Bebe trucking along beside me, I moved up the coastline. The urge to go north was strong in me, so I followed it.

Bebe began to slow. "This is hard! When did swimming get so hard?"

It's the current. It's pulling us back.

I grabbed her tiny body and slung her around so

that she was crouched on the back of my shoulders, her claws hanging on for dear life. "I see them back there, they're in the water," she whispered. "Two... no, three of them. One in wolf form. The other two on two legs."

I didn't look back. Couldn't. I was already fighting the currents that were tugging at my limbs, and any distraction would have us swept out to sea in no time. I kept swimming, kicking hard, not imagining any scenes from the *Jaws* franchise. Nope, I was not doing that.

Twenty-five minutes I swam, fatigue eating away at me with each stroke. I needed Han. I needed my mate to save me. Where was my hero in shining armor? Or was he so busy trying to save Soleil that he wouldn't even notice me?

"Nope, we gotta save ourselves," Bebe whispered. "I can't see your brothers anymore. Head to shallows so you can walk, but maybe stay in the deeper part?"

I bobbed my head and got a mouthful of salt water. Slowly, with far more effort than I'd thought it would take, I got us back to shore—or at least back to where I could walk with my head just above water.

Bebe didn't let go of me. Just kind of clung with her front paws and let her body float out behind her. "Least the water is nice. Warm."

I nodded. *Yeah, I'm not freezing my tits off. That's a bonus.*

"Duck," Bebe whispered.

I turned to see a figure lurching along. Staring out at the water. "Here, little sister. Where did you go? Don't worry, just wanna haffa talk, you know."

Richard. A very drunk Richard.

I took a deep breath and ducked down in the water, right under. Bebe clung to me, and we stayed there for as long as I could before breaking the surface as quietly as possible. Just enough to get my nose clear for a breath of air.

Scanning the shore, I found him further up the beach, hollering and throwing shit into the water. I was lucky that it was Richard and not Shipley or Kieran. They'd obviously thought I'd go south and had headed that way.

"Now what?" Bebe whispered.

We wait. Give him time to get farther away.

A full hour ticked by, and I knew we had to get out—with my luck, we were in danger of getting snagged by a hungry shark making the rounds along the shoreline. I made my way all the way out of the water, staying crouched so as not to present a profile against the lights. On the sand again, and a mile or two up the coast from where my smarter brothers were no doubt still looking for me.

I sat and took a deep breath. How long before

Richard came back? I'd bet a good long while. But Kieran and Shipley, they'd figure out that I hadn't gone south. They were not drunk.

As if I weren't screwed enough before, this is so fucking toasted. I don't even know where to start! I'd thought I'd be with Han—

"Banging away, yeah. I figured I'd be listening from downstairs." She shook herself, her fur still plastered to her body. "It's warm enough. We can just stay here until you shift back, then go find Han? Your brothers won't recognize you right away as a golden. That's what you figure, right?"

It wasn't a terrible idea.

I rubbed my hands over my face, bits of sand biting at my cheeks. *Maybe. Let's sit another minute, let me catch my breath. We need food—protein. I'm starving.*

I drew in a quick breath, trying to pick up the smell of a restaurant or someone cooking. But the salt water was all over me, in my nose even, and I couldn't pick up much of anything. I looked south down the shoreline. I didn't see Kieran and Shipley coming—not yet.

Because I couldn't scent anything, that meant I would have to find food the old-fashioned way. Standing, I motioned for Bebe to keep up and hurried up the beach to the road, waited for a lone vehicle to pass, and then hurried across the street.

This was more of a shopping area, less residential. I wasn't sure that would help me, but—

The howl of a wolf cut off every thought running through my head.

That's Kieran. My second oldest brother. He's... I paused in my thoughts, *he's a few miles south of us. That's not good. It won't take him long to pick up my scent.*

"Yeah, but you're still all salty. Your shirt is dripping." Bebe pointed out. I nodded.

I know, but it will dry, and he will *pick up my scent. He was the best our pack had at tracking. I need to get in a vehicle and put some distance between us. It's the only way to drop him at this point.*

But it didn't matter how many car doors I tried, or how many bikes and scooters we saw. They were all locked up tight. There was nothing but my feet, which were leaving a perfect scent trail straight to me.

My luck, such as it was, had officially run out.

16

ENEMY OF MY ENEMY STILL WANTS TO KILL ME

Another few blocks and I knew I was done.

It didn't take long for Kieran to find my scent once I was out of the water; he must have been racing up the beach. Sloppy fucker that he was, he couldn't help the howl that ripped out of him, the excitement of the hunt taking over any better senses.

That gave me a small leg up. He was a mile back, maybe less. He'd cover that distance very quickly. What was more worrisome was that more than two voices answered him. One farther back and one to my left, about the same distance away. Those two I'd expected. It was well-documented that my brothers were dicks. The fourth I hadn't anticipated.

Meghan. She was helping them hunt for me.

My guts lurched and churned, and the urge to

give up, to lie on my back and beg for my life was a sudden and horrifying sensation. Fucking weak dog emotions! I was not going down without a fight. No matter how much it hurt that Meg had turned on me so fully, I was not giving up.

Picking up my pace, I ran. *Bebe, get out of here. They'll tear you to shreds!*

"No, I can help you." She zoomed along next to me, her tail straight up, her ears swiveling. "You got me out of the shelter, I would have died in there. Let me help you now. It was my idea to go to the water. I can be useful."

Arms pumping, I kept up my punishing pace. My shirt was pretty much dry, leaving a sticky salt residue across my skin. Not enough to break my scent up. I found myself back where the warlock had lured me, back where I'd started this day.

I was sucking wind hard, and that's when I caught the smell of something else. *Someone* else.

The heavy layers of another wolf, one who was brutal and vicious beyond measure. I reached up and touched the top of my right ear. Yup, still missing.

Crazy, the idea was utterly insane. But I was betting my life he would not want other males in his territory.

"Wait, are you suggesting we run to that big ass

monster of a man?" Bebe yowled. "Are you crazy? He almost killed us the other day."

You got another idea? I'm all ears. I was already following Havoc's scent as I kept running. She was right—this really was insane—but he'd only seen me as a golden retriever. He wouldn't know who I was, and I could play up the damsel in distress bit. At the very least, I could pretend that I didn't know him. That it was an accident that I'd stumbled into his... house? Lair?

Whatever it was, I could play the part.

If I was wrong, he'd kill me, of course. But at least it would be quick with that ax of his. Unlike my brothers, who would drag me all the way back to Montana, torturing and maiming me along the way, assuming they didn't try for worse things. In the past, Kieran had made it clear that he barely saw me, a half-sister, as being related to him, which meant he wouldn't hesitate to hurt me in other ways...to try and take me as his bitch.

Yeah, quick and brutal was much better in my estimation.

I deliberately touched my hands to the sidewalls of houses as I ran now, leaving my scent behind.

"I hope you're right about this," Bebe said as we ran. "I mean, really?"

I hoped I was right too.

Havoc's scent was growing stronger now, fresher.

I drew it in by the lungful and followed it into a different subdivision. This one had older houses surrounded by big walls with larger, maintained yards.

There was the sound of laughter up ahead, many voices, music, and... the clink of glasses? A party then. And Havoc's scent was leading me straight to it. Fuck, I was about to party crash.

"What do you mean we're crashing a party?" Bebe yelped. "Now, that's going to be epic! I love a good crash!"

There was a solid brick wall in front of us, easily fifteen feet high. I bent and scooped up Bebe, tossing her up so that she landed on the top of the wall, where she immediately poofed up as if she'd French kissed an electrical socket.

"Fucking hell. That's him! This is a bad idea, he's looking straight at me! He knows me!" She screeched as I scrambled up the wall, my fingernails digging deep into the brick, the skin of my toes tearing as I fought my way to the top. I could hear them behind me now. My siblings had caught up to me.

There was hot breath on my heels, the scrape of fingers down my calf as I yanked my way up to the top of the wall and fell over. I hit a table, scattered the occupants, and rolled onto my side curled tight in a fetal position.

It wasn't just Havoc that was here, of course.

His pack surrounded me in a flash.

Bebe leapt down and stood between me and them. I grabbed her and tucked her under my arm.

Be quiet! This is the time to be quiet!

I couldn't look away from the pack from my position on the ground. Eight of them, six men and two women. A figure in the back caught my eye. Not a werewolf.

Sven. He was pulling the hood of his cloak up, but that body that looked like bark was unmistakable. And he'd just finished killing a woman. Fuck. Fuck. Fuck.

He was playing both brothers? Or just playing Han?

"What is this?" Havoc's voice echoed out over the pack, and they made way for him, parting to either side of the back yard. He seemed strangely bigger now that I was on two legs instead of four. I should have looked away; I shouldn't have locked eyes with him—a direct challenge if ever there was one. But I wasn't a golden anymore, and I couldn't stop my attitude from showing up even though I'd buckled under his gaze earlier.

He stared down at me as he slowly strode between the tables, his eyes dark and the one with that strange silver fleck in it, the scar over the one side of his face tightening as his lips pulled up on one side in a sneer.

Look down, idiot, look down!

But I couldn't even obey myself. If I was going to die, I would do it with my chin up, and with what was left of my pride intact. Clutching Bebe, I stumbled upward, my back against the brick wall, calf bleeding, fear and stubborn determination lacing my every move. The scrabble of nails on the other side told me that we were about to be interrupted.

A shiver rolled through me, knowing what I was going to have to do.

The timing was everything. A waft of my brother's scents slid over the wall, just ahead of them, and I pushed off, straight into Havoc's arms.

"What the fuck?" He caught me by the throat, fingers tightening around my neck. I stared up at him, still unable to look down. Fuck me and my wolf, we were going to die tonight.

Three pairs of boots thudded against the ground behind me, and I closed my eyes.

Bebe lay absolutely still in my arms. "Oh, shit," she whispered.

Still holding me by the throat, Havoc spoke softly, "Who the fuck are you three?"

I rolled my eyes to look at them. Kieran stepped forward, a smile on his greasy fucking face. "Kieran, alpha male of the Grayling Pack. Me and my two brothers, we've come to collect our sister. Seems she crashed your party? We'll take her off your hands and out of your territory in short order. No offense was meant, of course. She's a wild one, out of control as you can clearly see."

Smooth, he was so fucking smooth.

I opened my eyes, not realizing that I'd closed them, and found Havoc still staring down at me. I couldn't stop trembling, but I mouthed the two words that would end this.

Kill me.

I reached up slowly and touched his fingers, adding pressure. I could not go back with my brothers. Maybe this was for the best. Han would just have to go on with his life, never knowing how close his true mate had come to him, he'd find his Soleil and live happily ever after. For me, death was better than the short, violent future I would have in the Grayling pack.

Havoc tipped his head ever so slightly to the side, dragged me closer and took a good long sniff at the bottom of my earlobe. His breath was warm, ghosting across my skin and sending a shiver right to my toes. Funny, from the way he smelled, I'd expected him to be cold. But the heat was intense.

He gave a huff, almost... laughing? Was he *laughing* at me?

"I think I'll keep her." He didn't let go of my

throat, just held me to one side while I stared at him in utter shock. Keep me? "You have one hour to leave my territory."

Kieran let out a low growl. "She's ours, and if you don't give her to me, I'll kill you and take your pack. Is that clear you dumb fuck?"

Havoc finally let go of me, tossing me behind him casually, like flinging off a coat. Bebe squeaked as I spun, but I managed to keep my balance. A hand touched my back—big, wide, and with root-like fingers.

"I know you?" Sven asked under his breath.

I cringed and shook my head but didn't look away from the scene unfolding in front of me. I did, however, step away from the murdering bastard who'd put his hand on me.

Kieran squared off against Havoc. Apparently, he thought he could kill the man that I suspected was a demon in disguise. A true monster, pretending to be a werewolf.

I didn't move again, just stood there silently as Kieran took an experimental jab at Havoc. I don't know what he expected, but I already knew that he wasn't going to like how this went down. That jab was the only move he managed to make. Havoc caught his fist, twisted his arm, and forced him to his knees, spinning him so that he faced Shipley and Richard. Without even a pause—hell, there was no monologue coming from this bad guy—he grabbed Kieran's head and twisted hard to the left, snapping his neck. The crack of bones shattering split the air.

There was no chance to beg.

There was no chance for my other two brothers to try and help.

He was alive one second, dead the next. I couldn't help the relief that flowed through me.

Shipley and Richard just stared, maybe as thunderstruck as me. Because Kieran was the strongest of the three boys, I'd thought the fight might go for more than ten seconds. For it to last less than ten...

Havoc let Kieran's body go, the whole thing anticlimactic. "You are down to fifty-five minutes. Unless you wish to join your brother."

Shipley and Richard shot a look at me, at our dead brother, and then they were scrambling for the brick wall and disappearing into the night.

It'll be quick at least. He won't torture me, Bebe. He won't rape me. That's what would have happened if they'd taken me.

Bebe shivered. "I don't want to die."

Nor do I, but I am fully prepared. I don't think he'll hurt you. Just run for it when he snaps my neck.

I wasn't lying either. Havoc turned and stared me down once more. "You smell like my brother. That's an interesting problem to have when you arrive in my territory."

He knew that I was Han's mate. And suddenly I understood why he'd kept me.

A slow smile slid over his face. "This is a new twist. Loki only knows why my brother would be given a mate at this juncture, so close to the end, but I can only assume you are as conniving and sadistic as he is?"

I blinked and screwed up my face.

He stalked toward me until he towered over me. "What, nothing to say?"

Well, that was the fucking understatement of the day, wasn't it?

Bebe shot up and to my shoulder. "Listen you big thug! She can't speak! She gave up her voice—"

Havoc's hand shot toward Bebe, and I reacted without thinking of the cost, matching him for speed. I blocked his arm and kicked out, landing my foot in the groove of his hip, shoving him away from me. A collective gasp went up from the other wolves around us.

"Fuck, she *does* want to die," growled a man to my right. "But she's faster than her brother. I set a fifty on her lasting longer than him."

"I don't think she knows what she's dealing with," Sven said from behind me. "She's just a werewolf, Havoc. She doesn't know. Let her go."

Was he trying to... help me? But was that only so

he could kill me? I couldn't forget what Bebe had seen at Han's house.

Havoc let out a low growl. "The cat is not just a cat. So, I doubt the woman is just a werewolf."

Bebe stuck out her tongue at him. "Bingo, dumbass."

Havoc's eyes shot to me, narrowing, raking over me. "What has Loki sent Han now? He always favored my brother."

I didn't think the ancient Norse god had anything to do with this situation, any more than Jesus Christ or the Dali Llama. But Havoc seemed somewhat intrigued, and that could play in my favor.

"Is she marked?" One of the two women approached me. I backed up, right into Sven, who suddenly felt safer than these other werewolves despite the fact that Bebe had seen him standing over a dead body with an ax. I couldn't fight my way out of this. There were too many of them. Besides. If I left, my brothers would have me in a matter of minutes.

That would mean rape and torture and eventually death.

I'll take option number two, thank you very much.

The woman held her hands up in the universal sign of a truce. "Easy. I'm not going to hurt you unless you give me a reason. I just want to see if you have a tattoo or something like that."

I gave her a quick nod. Good enough. I didn't have anything for her to find.

Her blonde hair was loose around her shoulders in those perfect beach waves that I swear only a true west coast girl can manage on her own. Her eyes were a soft gray with a ring of blue around the edge. I'd put her at about my age, but I wasn't sure. Her hands were careful as she lifted the hair off my neck and touched something.

It stung, as if she were poking at a fresh burn. I flinched but kept my feet still.

She nodded and pointed at the sore spot without touching it again. "It's his mark. You think he sent her to you?"

Havoc looked me over. "Loki is... not as clear in his instructions as he would have anyone believe. He is an agent of chaos, as you know. Nothing is clear here."

The entire pack snickered. The woman stiffened. Maybe she was new here too?

I lifted a hand to touch the side of my neck, tracing the thing that hurt me. An S symbol of some sort. The lines were complicated, but the general shape was an S.

I looked down at Bebe.

Why didn't you say anything?

She put her paws on my chest and sniffed at me. "I didn't know it wasn't a tattoo from before. It's two snakes, kind of twisted around, making a solid S shape."

Right, fair enough. The comments about Loki, the accents...I finally placed them. They were Norse. Finnish. Northern European, in that range. Or at least, Havoc, Han and Sven were.

The woman stepped back. "I'm Claire."

"Don't give her names." The man behind her pulled her away from me. Not roughly, more like he was afraid I'd do something. Like he thought I was infected with something. Other than shitty luck, I wasn't sure what I was bringing to the table.

Through all this, Havoc had not once looked away from me. "She's meant for my brother. We'll be grateful for the boon, and use her as a bargaining chip. Take her inside."

17

INSOMNIA

I turned around and found myself looking right into Sven's face. He squinted at me. "Usually, the reaction I get from people I haven't met before is stronger than this. Your eyes are familiar. Do I know you?"

He looked down at me, then at Bebe. His gnarled brows crinkled. "The cat. I know that cat."

"Fuck you, murdering asshole!" Bebe swatted at Sven, her claw skimming his gnarled skin. I clutched her closer to me.

"What about it?" Havoc strode toward us, catching my arm as he approached, and dragged me into the house.

"I know that cat," Sven said. "Havoc, wait."

Surprising me, Havoc did as the strange tree man asked. "What is it, old one? A new rhyme for me to decipher? A new lead? I want you to go to Han and tell him I have his mate. We will meet tomorrow morning. A truce for a discussion regarding her."

Sven was circling me, though. "Why is that cat in her arms? That cat came with the shelter dog." He shook his finger at Havoc, as if the monstrous man had been naughty. "This woman might very well be his mate, but Han has not been spending time with her. There is no way I wouldn't have noticed a dark beauty. You know she is not his type. He prefers them as pale and fair as the day, not...not like her."

Havoc put his nose to my hair, and I went still, those shivers running through me again in a way I most certainly did not like. He huffed a few times, my hair fluttering under his hot breath as he breathed in deep. "Maybe he hasn't been fucking her when you're around, old one. But his scent is all over her. She's been in his bed, I guarantee it."

Sven stared hard at me. "I know you, somehow. But neither you nor the cat fit. I have been with Han—"

"Except when you are here," Claire said. "Men are sneaky bastards, Sven. He's been cheating on you."

The pack laughed at that, and Sven rolled his eyes.

I, on the other hand, agreed with Claire. Men were sneaky bastards. Sven included.

I had nothing to say to all that. Even if I could talk, would they believe me? I doubted it. They thought I was a werewolf, not a golden retriever.

Havoc shook his head. "You are losing it, old one. Go. Tell Han to meet me on the steps of this house first thing in the morning."

Morning. I'd be a golden again. I reached out for Havoc, wanting to hurry him up, but how.

I touched his arm at the wrist, and he whipped his hand around to grab my forearm. He was like a wild animal, edgy as fuck and ready to kill first and ask questions never. I moved slowly and touched my own wrist with a finger, tapping it.

Sooner, he needed to bring Han sooner.

Havoc's fingers dug harder into my flesh. "I'm not hurrying anything for you or your bastard of a mate." He growled, but he did not let me go.

Fuck.

"You cannot believe he will come," Sven said. "He knows you would kill him in an instant, given the chance, and that would set him back years."

Havoc let out a slow breath. "I give my word on Soleil's immortal soul that he will not be harmed if he comes, not by me and not by my pack. A one-hour conversation. A truce."

Soleil again. Did Havoc have her? Was she some sort of prize between the brothers?

Bebe was silent. There wasn't a lot to say. Because

by the time that Han arrived, I would be back to my golden retriever self. Yep, I was so screwed.

Havoc's hold on my wrist was hard enough to grind the bones together, and I let him lead me along.

"Why aren't you fighting him?" Bebe whispered.

He paused. "You know, Cat. I can hear your words. Can she speak?"

Tell him I have no voice. Don't tell him why.

Bebe snorted. "I know the rules, girlfriend. Listen, you great big prick. She can't speak, not with her mouth. But I can hear her words in my head. Like, magic, motherfucker."

Havoc nodded as if it was the most normal thing in the world to have a woman who couldn't speak but had a mouthy, overconfident cat as her translator.

Right.

He dragged me into and then through the house, down a set of wooden stairs, and into a room that was completely dark. No windows. A single door and a single light bulb hanging in the middle, a bed pushed up against the wall with a single mattress and no blankets. I knew a cell when I saw one. I blinked as he spun me into the space so his back was to the door. "What is your name?"

Bebe sighed. "That's complicated."

His hand tightened on my arm, but I knew this

game with someone bigger than me. I didn't strug-
gle, and he eased off. "Name."

"Her real name, or the nickname Han gave her?"

Bebe! Don't you dare!

"The name Han knows her by," Havoc growled.

"He calls her Princess."

I thought he would laugh, snort, something. But
he just dragged me a little closer to him so that he
was staring straight down into my face. "Princess?
And are you?"

Am I what? Royalty?

Bebe translated quickly.

He didn't look away from my face. "Yes. Are you
royalty?"

I shook my head. *Outcast. You saw my brothers. I
have no pack.*

Bebe translated that too.

Fuck, he would know if I lied. Most alpha wolves
could smell a lie, amongst other strong emotions.
Lust. Hate. Fear. Joy. I blinked once. He didn't pull
back but instead pressed his nose into my hair. "You
smell like him. You've been sleeping with him
recently."

How the fuck could he smell anything after I'd
been in the ocean?

"Yeah, that's a good question. We did a total
skinny dip in the big water, my man, how can you
scent anything on her?" Bebe pushed herself up to

my shoulder and stuffed her face as close to him as she could get.

I reached up and pulled her away. He'd snapped Kieran's neck like it was nothing. She seemed to have forgotten that he'd slaughtered an entire household without blinking and tried to kill both of us with his two-handed ax. I, on the other hand, had not.

"Do you think he'd be bothered if I touched you?" Havoc growled. "You seem...defiant. My brother likes his women submissive. Like a weak-willed dog."

Oh. Fuck. Was he going to rape me? I would say try, but even I could see that I wouldn't be able to get away from him if he wanted to have his way with me.

I forced myself not to move. There was no good answer here, particularly since I couldn't even speak and I suspected a quick move would only have him more on edge.

"Don't you touch her!" Bebe shrieked, puffed up at our feet. She took a swipe at him, her claws slicing right through his pants, the smell of blood in the air instant.

Havoc's body tensed, and I knew that he'd swing a boot at her, something that would hurt, if not kill her. I yanked backward, unbalancing him, rolling myself so that his arm wrapped around me as we fell. I landed elbow point first, right into his sternum, driving the wind out of him.

Bebe, get out of here! Run!

Spinning, I straddled his waist and pressed my free arm across his throat, hard enough that he got the point that I was not the weak-willed bitch he thought I should be, no matter what he thought Han liked.

Bebe picked up for me, speaking my thoughts.

"Don't hurt my friend. Ever. Or I'll kill you myself," Bebe whispered. "Shit, girl, that is badass."

Havoc sucked in a breath. I hoped we were done.

Nope, apparently just getting started.

He threw me off him with a sweep of his arm, but I was not Kieran. I had no doubt this one could kill me, and with a simple twist of his wrist. I stayed on my back, kicking out and catching him in the knees and shins, driving him off balance. I was fast, maybe even faster than Havoc. I didn't think he'd kill me. He needed me to bargain with Han. Which made me bolder than I should have been.

His snarl echoed through the semi-darkness.

"What can I do, what can I do?" Bebe yelled.

Stay out of it!

"Stay out of it, cat!" he growled as he snagged an ankle and dragged me toward him. "If Princess here wants to play, then I'll *play*."

Shivers of fear rippled through me.

Fear, right? Yeah, of course it was just fear. Nothing else.

I let him drag me toward him before I kicked up with my free leg, catching him in the jaw and snapping his head back.

"Yeah, get him again!" Bebe screamed her encouragement. "Bitches be bad ass!"

I slid both my hands around his arms and locked them tight as I snapped my head forward, catching him on the nose. Feeling it break. Blood gushed, and he... laughed.

"Oh, you'll pay for that." He stood up, and I did the only thing I could. I locked my legs around his waist and whipped my one arm around the back of his head, cinching it in a headlock that hopefully would drop him. He slammed us both into the wall, my back hitting first, hard enough to shudder the house.

I clung to him.

Tried not to notice that he was enjoying this fight on a whole other level.

Tried not to notice my own body's reaction, the urge to hold on a little tighter with my legs.

I clenched my teeth and tried to crank on the head lock.

He growled, and the sound...

Fuck, the sound was on par with that damn howl of his. I struggled against the tingle of something I did not want to name as pleasure. Nope. Nope, *I didn't want him.*

My knees started to shake, and he slammed us into the wall again. Pain sparked down my spine, tangling with the heat growing between my legs, but I didn't let go. I was not submitting to him.

Bite me.

The growl rumbling through him intensified, traveling straight into my own chest and driving lower, a wave of need stroking across my—

No. No, I could not do that.

"You will not win." His breath was against my neck, his lips brushing the sensitive skin.

And then he did exactly what I'd told him to do.

He bit me, on the neck, right below my ear.

I sucked a hard breath, hating the fact that my body was reacting to his, that it liked the werewolf dominance game more than a little bit. The orgasm that was building wanted me to press my hips to his, to writhe against him, heat and need building with every second that passed. That bite, and the pain and strange pleasure that came with it, only added fuel to the fire.

My breath hitched as I fought it all. My wolf squirmed and danced under my skin.

I started to let go, I needed space between us to get control of myself, and he twisted around and slammed me into the floor, my legs still around his waist. One hand just behind my head, cradling it.

My body went limp as I lost the ability to

breathe, my spine tingling, nerves going numb. Havoc grabbed both my hands and locked them behind my back in just one of his. The other went to my throat once more, fingers brutally tight, his mouth right against mine as he spoke.

"You think you can beat me? You think you can save Han from me?" His blood dripped down over his lips and across mine as I glared at him. My silence didn't seem to bother him. Mind you, I was fighting the urge to arch up and into him, to dry hump the fuck out of him. His dark eyes didn't so much as flicker as he stared me down. "Does he love you? I don't think he does, Princess. Han is like me, he's not capable of love. No matter what Loki might think of you."

I managed a shaky breath as I stared right back at him, my legs limp around his waist now, my muscles unhappy with what had happened to my spine, my pussy pissed that I hadn't gotten further with Havoc. Traitorous body.

Still, I glared up at him. Defiance might as well have been my middle name.

I think you don't know me. Or what I am capable of. I think you underestimate love and the strength of a mate bond.

I waited for Bebe to translate. Havoc stared at me, his eyes narrowing.

"You aren't capable of stopping me, Princess. No

one is. And love is not real, nor is it worth saving in this world that is about to burn. Mate bonds are for weak-minded fools."

He dropped me to the ground in a heap and was out of the room before I could so much as stutter a response. He'd heard me.

Havoc had heard my voice.

18

CAGED. AGAIN

Bebe trotted over to me where I lay on the floor of my new cage, wondering what had just happened. Havoc had heard my voice clearly.

"What the hell? I can't decide if that was terrifying or hot as sin, Cin. But you were a total badass!" Bebe laughed and butted up against me. "Did you see the size of his cock? Holy shit, he's huge, apparently it runs in the family!"

I groaned and rolled over onto my hands and knees, body trembling because I'd felt that hugeness against my pussy, and my traitorous body had very much wanted to get to know it better, invite it inside for a visit. My fingers went to my lips, where I could taste his blood.

He tasted like snow and ice. I scrubbed the back

of my hand across my mouth as I blew out a long, slow breath of air, trying to find myself again.

Talk about blue balling it, that orgasm was still there, right on the edge of spilling through. Another breath, and I was able to push it back some, gain some control.

I made myself rise to my feet, then wobbled across the room and checked the door. Locked. Not like I'd expected anything else.

"What do we do?"

What I needed was a stiff drink to stifle the memory of Havoc's body against mine. Something was wrong with me that he even caused a single tremor of desire in me. He was a monster, and I had to remember that above all else. I made myself focus on Bebe and the situation we were in.

I don't know. I think we have to wait on Han.

I paced the room slowly and ran my hands over the walls, searching for... something. Another way out. Maybe a weapon? I wasn't sure. *I can't leave like this on two legs. Shipley and Richard will be waiting.*

"Wait, but Brutus just killed the one guy and threatened the other two. You think that they will be stupid enough to stick around?" Bebe leapt up onto the bare mattress and paced around the edges, mimicking me.

I rubbed my neck where Havoc's fingers had held

me tight. Tried not to think about the way it had made me feel.

Yes. There are ways to hide scent, a spell that the pack shaman would have made for them. They will use that spell and continue to search for me. They won't give up now that they are so close to taking me back to Grayling. I ran a hand over my sticky, salt-water-infused hair and began to tug some of the knots free. *But by morning, I'll be a golden again. They won't know me that way—at least not by scent. I don't know how well they'd recognize me in that body. What happens when Havoc sees me as a dog and knows that we bested him at that house? Will he kill me?*

Bebe stood with her feet on the wall, acting for all the world like a normal cat. It made me miss Martin, his solid warmth, his judging eyes. "You mean will he kill us? Because we both fought him." She paused. "Okay, obviously there are no windows. What about vents? Like for air and stuff?"

It was a good idea, and it gave me something to focus on that was not the lingering energy rippling through my body.

It didn't take me long to find the one vent in the wall, behind the bed. I pulled the bed frame out and ran my fingers over the edges. Too small for me, even if we did get it open.

I sat on the edge of the bed and stared at our one possible chance for escape.

"Maybe I could slip out and get help?" Bebe stood on her back legs, rested a front paw on my chest and patted my cheek with the other. "Don't give up now, Cin."

I'm not giving up. It's not in my nature. I forced a smile at her. *I mean, this isn't as bad as being shot with silver and thrown into the river by my brothers. Or being fooled by my younger sister, all so I can take a punishment in the place of my shitty mother. This isn't that bad, Bebe. Han will be here in the morning. And he will want his dog back, right?*

Bebe screwed up her face. "Probably not enough to give Havoc what he wants. But, you know, you could try."

Yeah, that was my fear too. They both seemed obsessed with this Soleil woman. But why?

I looked at the vent and the tiny screws holding it on. One was already loose. How many people had Havoc locked in here? I worked the loose screw free and then used it to loosen the others.

You're right, you should get out if you can. I don't know who you'd go to for help, but maybe you could find a gun and bring it back for me? I smiled at her since I couldn't laugh.

"Yeah, I can just imagine tripping over it and shooting my tail off." Bebe snorted and sat next to me while I worked the screws. Didn't matter if it took me a long time, not like we were going anywhere.

Minutes ticked by, and then I was pulling out the last screw and lifting the vent covering off. The space was about eighteen inches across, big enough to make a person consider trying to escape through it, I suspected. I peered inside and looked around. The vent went to the left and then shot straight up.

Bebe peered into the vent. "Oh, dark and mysterious."

Do you want to check it out?

"Yup, I do." She shot into the smallish space and hadn't gone far before she stopped. I could still see her tail.

"There's another vent opening right here. Hang on, let me see... can you reach?" She moved to the side, and I lay down so I could reach through the duct to the other vent.

My fingers quickly found the back end of the screws, sticking through just enough that I could spin them.

Worrying at them, I got the bottom two loose enough that I could shake the vent cover a little, which loosened them the rest of the way until the bottom flipped open. Like a cat flap.

"Brilliant. We could totally turn into thieves." Bebe was gone in a flash.

Be careful! Don't let them see you.

She didn't answer. I slid my arm out of the ducts and sat waiting for her.

Which gave me time to think.

What the hell was it about Havoc's howl... and his growl? I'd never heard of a werewolf's voice being like a damn tuning fork to an orgasm. Just thinking about it had me clamping my legs together and gritting my teeth against the remembered pleasure washing through me, stroking the edges...

Nope. Nope, I could not go there.

Bebe popped her head back through the open vent. "It's another room about this size. Looks like storage. Do you think you could fit through as a goldie?"

I looked at the opening again, running my hands over it. *It would be tight, but yeah, I think I could.*

"Then that's what we do. We just wait until you shift and then we go." She bobbed her head as if the matter were settled.

I curled up on my side, and Bebe snuggled in close. My thoughts about everything I'd seen, smelled and experienced in the last few weeks sliding into place.

I saw Sven weeks ago, before I ever met him here, as a golden. Seeing him pull the hood up over his face, I finally put it together. I lifted a hand to scratch Bebe on the head. *You mind?*

"You asking if you can pet me?" She laughed. "I'm soft as a fucking feather, you'd better."

I let my hand drift over her head and neck,

taking comfort in her warmth, again, missing my Martin. *He was with a woman, she was scared and running. It had to be Soleil, she smelled like sunshine, and then when I was scenting her in the house it was the same. She was scared, but the same woman. I just didn't put it together. Like the scents I picked up before I was a golden are dulled compared to what I smell now. I didn't realize they were one and the same.*

Sven was trying to keep her from someone, but which brother? Han or Havoc? And would Sven have hurt her?

Bebe began to purr, the vibration going straight through me, lulling me into a doze. She didn't answer my questions. Didn't try to help me figure everything out. But I could clearly see Sven in that deep robe that had mostly concealed him, with the girl and then the black wolf with the blue eyes and the howl that had brought me to a wild ride of an almost orgasm.

That had been Havoc even then. All in Edmonton, same time as me. Coincidence? Somehow I didn't think so. But what had brought us all there? Was it my connection to Han? Because it seemed that wherever Soleil and Havoc were, Han was too. My mate bond could have been bringing me along even then.

"What?" Bebe asked sleepily.

I swallowed hard and held her a little closer as shivers of fear and uncertainty rippled through me. *Nothing. It's nothing.*

"Then you should try to sleep. Big day tomorrow, escaping and all."

I nodded because she was right. Not like I was going to get a chance to show off my legs to Han. I found myself reaching up and touching the mark on my neck as I lay there, questions floating through my brain.

What did the gods have to do with werewolves? Most especially Loki? The trickster, the half ice giant? Father of Fenrir? Yeah, I was a nerd about ancient civilizations. And while I hadn't studied Norse mythology in depth, I knew enough to be concerned.

Because if Loki was involved, I was pretty certain the trouble was only going to keep coming. Even if I refused to allow that for myself.

19

GOOD MORNING, MOTHERFUCKER

I woke up slowly. There was no alarm clock, no sunshine, but I knew it was morning. I stretched out my legs in front of me, golden fur everywhere once more.

"Hey, you're back!" Bebe bounced around my head. "What happened? It didn't hurt this time?"

I snorted and shook my head. I'd finally fallen into a doze near the end of the night and apparently had slept right through my transformation back into a golden retriever. I wagged my tail as I thought about how pissed off Havoc was going to be that I was no longer the captive he'd assumed he had.

Yup, I was grinning like a fool—or like a golden, I guess you could say. I hopped off the bed and went and sat in front of the door, waiting, tail thumping away. We were getting out of here today, one way or another.

Footsteps had my ears twitching, and then the door opened and the woman from the night before stepped in. Claire.

Her soft gray eyes shot to me, combed the room, and then whipped back to me, widening just before she spun away. "Shit! HAVOC!"

She was gone, the door slamming behind her.

Bebe giggled and came and sat next to me. "Oh my God, this is going to be the best! I was hoping we could escape through the vents, but maybe this is better. I can't wait to see the look of shock on his face!"

You know, when you're backed into a corner, it's the little things in life that make it sweet. I bunted my nose against hers, practically a fist bump, but we didn't have long to celebrate.

A second set of footsteps, heavier than the first. He was not even trying to be quiet.

I stepped back so that when the door flung open... the edge swung past my face, just missing me.

Havoc stood in the doorway, his eyes locked on mine once more. I perked my ears and made sure to wiggle the one he'd cut the tip off of. Motherfucker, how you like this good morning?

Bebe leapt from my side and perched on the bed behind us. "Surprise!"

"Feed her, Claire." His voice didn't so much as raise in volume a single decibel.

Well, shit. He didn't seem surprised at all. How was that possible?

Claire slid a plate into the room, two eggs, bacon, toast, and a fruit bowl. I carefully reached out and tugged the plate toward myself with my paw, eating the toast and half the eggs and bacon. *Bebe, come eat.*

Did I need the protein? You bet. But I was pretty sure Bebe hadn't eaten anything in like two days.

She slipped forward and sucked back her portions as if we were in an eating contest. "Thanks, girlfriend."

I nodded at her and then gave the plate one last lick, my stomach rumbling hard.

"She likes coffee, two cream, two sugar," Sven said softly from behind Havoc. "Are you sure it's the girl from last night?"

I blinked up at him. What was he still doing here? He was supposed to be getting Han.

If Sven had put two and two together...

Han could not know that his dog was his mate. Toasted shits and fuck damns, this was bad. Terrible.

I was in trouble. I started to slink back, thinking about that open vent again.

Havoc was fast, I'll give him that. He shot forward

and grabbed my muzzle, clamping it shut while the other hand went to my neck. Big bastard had a thing for throat grabbing. I writhed to get away from him, but he wasn't trying to choke me.

Nope, he was just lifting the fur up to get a look at my skin. "The mark is still here." He let me go. "But Han won't believe she is his mate, not as a dog." He let me go, and I hunched up, unable to keep from cringing away from him. Oh, I hoped he was right. If Han didn't believe, did that still count against me? I was banking on it not counting.

"Shift back to two legs, now."

I shook my head. *I can't.*

Before I could get Bebe to tell him it was useless, he held out a hand toward me and crooked a single finger. "Come. Shift now."

Havoc's alpha power was…brutal was the only word I had for it. Like being slammed headfirst into a mountain. I lost all thought as he tried to force me to do something I literally could not do no matter how much he wanted it.

Pain, yes, there was pain, but also a strange sense of defiance. Even he could not make me shift.

Over and over the waves of his power hit me, like being shoved back and forth between prize fighters. I finally just went limp and lay on the floor, panting, grunting as the invisible blows rocked me.

"Stop it, you're hurting her!" Bebe launched over me and took yet another swing at Havoc's legs.

He dropped his hand, and his power slid away from me. I was flat on the floor, tongue hanging out, vision blurry.

"When will Han be here?" Havoc asked.

"He wouldn't listen to me," Sven said quietly. "He knows. He refused to even speak with me."

"*Gargan!*" Havoc slammed a fist into the wall, shattering the plaster. If I could have whimpered, I would have, but as it was, I stumbled away, stuffing myself under the bed before I could stop my legs from moving.

The two men turned and looked at me. Or I assumed they did as I could only see their feet now.

"What will you do with her?" Sven asked, and did I detect a note of concern in his voice? Maybe he was still working for Han, but fooling Havoc? That was possible. And if that was the case, he would want to help me. Unless, of course, he wanted to kill me like he had that other woman.

I inched out a bit so my nose emerged from the T-shirt that hung off the bed.

"Give her to her three idiot brothers. They think they hid themselves, but they've holed up a couple of streets over, watching for her, no doubt."

I scrambled out from under the bed, my stupid

tail wagging along. *Kill me yourself then, you big bastard.*

Havoc's eyebrows lifted ever so slightly. "You wish to die?"

No. But my brothers will do worse than kill me. I didn't know how to explain to him all the things that had happened in my family, how much torment lay in wait for me if I were to be captured by Shipley and Richard. Wait, he'd said three. Kieran was still alive?

Even worse.

He looked at me. "His neck healed. He must be wearing a charm of some sort."

I thought of all the things they'd do if they caught me. Hell, even if all three of them died, Juniper would still hunt me down.

Havoc laughed. "You think me merciful?"

No.

"Yet you ask for mercy?"

I shrugged, understanding quickly that he would do what he would do, and I would have to deal with the fall out. I said nothing, kept my mind quiet, and stared up at him. The golden I was did not like making eye contact with him, and I struggled to stand still and not start quaking or, worse, pee myself.

"Leave her locked in here for the day. See if she will shift again. I doubt Han knows she's a mutt,"

Sven said softly. "Or that the mutt's a woman. You could try again tonight."

Havoc grunted. "You're getting soft, old man. You like her."

Sven sighed. "I am tired of all the things that follow you and your brother, Havoc."

The things? What things?

Havoc looked at Sven and just shook his head before walking away and heading back up the stairs.

Without another word, Claire slid a bowl of water in to me, and the door was shut tight behind them, leaving us in the windowless room with nothing more than a single bulb hanging from the ceiling.

Bebe paced the floor. "Well, this is a damn mess."

I nodded. *Worse than that rescue place we started at?*

She paused. "An easy tie for first of the worst. You want to go out the vent now? Wait, let me check it out."

Before I could say yes or no, she was gone in a flash of gray.

I trotted over and stuck my nose into the vent, trying it out for size. If I squirmed, I could probably push my way through.

"Fuck, the door is locked." Bebe slipped back into the ducts. "And no window in the other room either. Goddamn."

I nodded and stepped back.

We just have to wait for an opportunity. That's all.

The morning was slow. No one came to check on us, which meant no opportunities presented itself. Bebe slept most of the time. I lay on the floor, my mind racing despite the stillness of my body.

What in the name of all the stars in the sky was I going to do? I had to get back to Han. That was the only option, the only way for me to stay alive long enough to figure out this mess. But he didn't know I was anything but a dog. A heavy blow of air slid out of me, flapping my lips.

Footsteps coming down the stairs had me lifting my head. His scent hit me before he even opened the door. Ice and death.

"Han." Havoc spoke into a phone as he opened my door. He crouched down and showed me the phone. I saw the name he'd tagged Han with: Gargan. That same word he'd yelled in frustration. "I have something of yours."

"I told you I am not coming to your house. You think I'm a fool? You must have lost your mind somewhere in the last five hundred years." Han's voice, full of irritation, echoed through the room.

Then his words hit me. Shit, they were old. The oldest werewolves that I knew of topped out in the three hundreds.

Havoc slid his thumb over the screen and

sneered down into it. His scar pulled a little, which only increased the sneer. Then turned the phone around, and I was looking at Han. I couldn't help myself. I leapt up and tried to grab the phone with my mouth.

Havoc shoved me back, sending me tumbling across the room with hardly any effort.

Han laughed. "You have my dog? You think I'd bother to come and get her? There are a thousand—"

"She's your mate, asshole," Havoc growled. "And if you don't come and get her, I'll claim her as my own."

Sprawled on the floor, I stared up at Havoc in disbelief as he smiled into the camera of his phone. He couldn't be serious. Could he? And then it all clicked, truly clicked.

Havoc had told Han I was his mate. That I, a dog, was his mate.

"Oh no," Bebe squeaked.

If Han believed him, then I only had three days left to... to what? Make my peace with the world? Because finding a prince, making him fuck me...that was impossible. I could try, of course I could try but...I started to pant, breathing fast enough that I was sure I was going to hyperventilate.

"You'd fuck a dog?" Han laughed again, his voice

seemingly far away in that moment. "Not that I'm surprised—"

"She shifted to her human form last night," Havoc said. "And smells like a wolf from the icy fields. Dark hair, hazel eyes, built for fighting and fucking. Interestingly enough, she does carry some of your scent. Of course, I could just kill her. I suppose that's an option."

If there was any doubt that the curse had kicked into high gear, it was in that moment when Havoc pretty much spelled it out for Han.

There was the softest intake of breath from Han. "I know what she is. I knew it the moment I brought her in from the shelter, so you aren't telling me anything new. She reeked of black magic, even then."

I stared up at the phone. He knew?

Havoc nodded. "That's what I thought. Even you couldn't deny her. Come and claim your mate, Han. Let us make a trade."

I closed my eyes. He wouldn't let me die. Well, not on purpose. I'd obviously have to tell him about my deal with that fucking witch, who was really a warlock. That I had three days to find a prince, or else lights out.

Would he be okay with me fucking another man? Probably not, but I had to hear him fuck the vet so fair was fair.

This was not going to go well.

The silence went on for so long, I found myself looking up and then creeping forward. Havoc turned the phone around so I could see Han, just as he spoke.

"Let her die then. She is not my issue." He shrugged as he noticed me and then winked. "Sorry, Princess. I don't do the mate thing."

But he'd known? He'd known what I was all along and had just let me suffer? Called me into his bed and held me. Jacked off in front of me and then fucked another woman knowing I could hear. Left me in that murder house, with his fucking monstrous brother to die? In that moment I'd have bet he didn't think I'd run away. He'd run, leaving me behind.

For maybe the first time since I'd become a golden, my tail stopped wagging as the tiny specks of hope that had been sprouting in me withered, the future I'd conjured in my mind shattering. A shiver ran through me.

Bebe butted her head against my side. "Goat fucking tiny pricked dick. He doesn't know what he's missing out on. I'd be your mate in a hot second, girl. But we have bigger problems than Han right now."

She was right.

The world around me fuzzed, though, white

noise filling my ears as I blinked through watering eyes.

I stared at the screen as Han shrugged and waved at me. Fucking *waved*.

Just like Mars, the only father I had ever known, had waved the last time I'd seen him. Like he was going away on a day trip, not leaving my life forever.

Han was abandoning me to a fate that I could not escape except through death—which would happen in three short days if I didn't figure something out. Havoc glanced at me, his mouth moving, but I couldn't hear his words.

A mate was supposed to fight for you, protect you. I wanted to scream and rage, and all I could do was sit there, like a medusa-made statue.

He'd done all those things despite knowing I was his mate.

Why?

To hurt me? I struggled to make sense of it.

An ache started low in my belly, spreading like a toxin. Han was rejecting me because I was a dog, I was sure of it.

His murderous brother would have no reason to keep me alive if I was not a bargaining chip—assuming he didn't just keep me his prisoner until the curse took me.

I was well and royally fucked up shit creek with a

god damn straw for an oar if I didn't figure something out, and fast.

Havoc turned the phone off and looked at me.
His eyes swept over me, and all he did was shake his
head before he left the room, locking the door
behind him once more.

For a few minutes, I just sat there, my mind
looping over and over what had happened.

Han had known from the moment he'd found
me that I was his mate.

I thought back to the rescue center.

*Bebe. Han knew I was his mate before he even picked
me. He touched my head. He... was willing to leave me
there.*

"Oh, fuck. You mean, before...when he was going
to pick the other dog?" Bebe's eyes were wide.
"You're sure?"

I thought back to that moment, the feeling, the
sensation. I'd thought it had just been me, but....

*He apologized to me as he walked away. He knew
then. He doesn't want a mate. He is not going to help or
protect me even if we get out of here.*

Maybe he didn't want a mate for this very reason
—because a mate could be used against him.

I shivered. I wanted to blame Han for this, but
the truth was I'd sought Havoc out when I was on
the run from my brothers. I'd gone to the witch for
help too. I'd done it to be with Han, but he hadn't

asked that of me. He'd only asked that I help him find this Soleil woman that both he and Havoc were searching for.

Or maybe Havoc already knew where she was?

Time was ticking. Three days. End of the third day, and I'd be breathing my last if I didn't figure something out. Which meant I had to get out of this house. There were no princes here ready for a good romp. Certainly not with a golden.

"I see it in your face, you're thinking about a plan to escape, right?" Bebe sat right in front of me, leaning back on her haunches, and put her front paws on my chest. "Tell me you have a plan to get us out of here?"

Maybe. I couldn't let this rejection from Han derail me, or my life—even if it was just three short days. He didn't know me. He didn't know what I was capable of surviving.

Bebe, there is a chance my brothers won't recognize me as a golden. They may know what I am, but my scent is different in this form. You heard what Havoc said.

"And?" She tipped her head to one side. "What good does that do us?"

If we can get out of the house, I think I can find Han before dark. That's what we need to do. He may not want me as a mate, and I understand why he won't make a trade, but I need help. He's all I've got. Or I'm going to die in three days.

Besides, part of me wanted him to tell it to my face that he didn't want me.

"But what if he's the bad guy?" Bebe looked at me. "That body could have been from him. She was in *his* bed. What if Sven was just getting rid of it?"

I hadn't forgotten about the body that Bebe had seen through the window, the one that Sven had stood over. I scrunched up my eyes. *I know. Listen, I'm open to ideas. Who else do we have for help then?*

She stared at me. "Um, yeah, so here's the thing. Han can't hear you or me. How are you going to explain all of this?"

I'll shift tonight, I reminded her. *I'll explain then. And then he'll help. I can write it all down.*

Bebe didn't ease off on the stare. "You think that the same guy who put you in danger within hours of taking you home, knowing full well you were his mate, will help you? Did you ever see the vet after he fucked her? No? Me neither, and I was watching to see her leave because I wanted to see the look of satisfaction on her face. And where has he been for the last couple of days? Looking for you? Putting up posters? No, he isn't worried about you, and you've been gone days at this point. He just fucking rejected you! Going back to him is stupid!"

I sat on my haunches and just stared at her, swallowing every last bit of my pride.

I'm not going back to him. I'm going to him for help,

Bebe. I don't expect a sudden resurgence of feelings on his part. I'm going to die in three days because of this fucking curse. Unless, of course, you think Havoc is going to suddenly turn into a kind man? You think we have a chance if we stay here?

Bebe blinked up at me. "You really don't think Han could be as bad as his brother? Because let's be honest, Havoc is a monster. Han could be a monster too. Maybe he just hides it better. One woman went missing after being with him, and another turned up dead in his bed. The more I think about it, the less certain I am that Sven is the problem here."

Her words were digging into me, forcing me to see the situation for what it was, not through my bond to Han. She was right. I couldn't go back to Han. He was obsessed with Soleil, and the chances of him helping me were no better than Havoc or my brothers.

Thank you, Bebe.

"That's what friends do, smack you upside the head when you start letting your hormones get the better of you. I wish I'd had someone to keep me away from that wizard. So what's the plan then?" She looked around the room. "We can't stay here."

Let's try the other room. Maybe we can get the door open. Once we're out, then we'll take it from there.

Bebe ran over to the air vent and slid through the small opening.

I put my head into the opening and turned to the left. Shimmying forward, turning my shoulders so that I was at a bit more of an angle, I managed to get inside the duct. Scrabbling with my back feet, I shoved myself the small distance between the two vents.

"Shhh." Bebe kicked me in the nose with a back foot.

There were no voices coming from the adjoining room. Bebe moved aside so we could both peer through the vent. "I can't believe it. The door is open! We could slip in here and then work the house over? See if we can find a way out?"

I took a deep breath as we peered out of the vent. *The room doesn't belong to anyone in particular. It has all sorts of scents. I think maybe storage, like you said.*

That was good. The door was open, that was better.

Bebe pushed her head against the vent, and again it popped open. It had almost been too easy. Of course, not many people would consider the possibility of anything traveling through the vents. Probably most people they kept in that cell-like room were werewolves, far too big to slide into a house's vents in either form. She slid out and I crawled out after her, shaking my fur so it fluffed up again. Boxes and a few bookcases were pressed up against the walls.

I crouched and went straight to the door, but my nose twitched at all the smells.

Turning, I looked back over the room. I sniffed at a few of the boxes and found one heavy with Havoc's scent. An idea formed, slowly at first and then faster, like an avalanche gaining speed. He'd been around for five hundred years—at least. Any one supernatural being that had lived that long had developed a breadth of knowledge, and he'd spoken of Loki as if he were a friend.

Maybe I could find some information here that would help me?

Yes, I know, I was grasping at straws.

Bebe, you scout the house, be careful. I'm going to move some of these. I grabbed the edge of the box with my mouth and tore it open. Nothing here.

I kept on working through the boxes, using my nose as much as my teeth. What was I looking for? Couldn't really tell you, I only knew that my nose in particular was being drawn through the different boxes.

Four or five deep, I paused, nose twitching.

Yup. This one. I yanked the edge of it open and peered in.

A bunch of books that looked handmade had been stuffed into the box. They had leather covers and smelled musty. I pulled one out and nosed it open. It was handwritten—Havoc's writing, it had to be—full of a mixture of English and something else. Maybe Norse? But there was enough English I'd be able to read it.

Havoc's handwriting was smooth, and it didn't waste space—economical, that's what Denna would have called it.

Soleil is running hard. Has been for months. If I could kill her and end this—

Soleil, it always came back to her. I stared at the words. Havoc wanted to kill her and end what? The chase? The next bit was in another language, the handwriting curvier with little pictures drawn in. Doodles. I couldn't read it. I skimmed the page to find something more written in English, and boy did I find it.

I dream of blood. Of death. I crave it. If it were up to me, I would bathe the world in death and destruction and laugh as those too weak to survive begged for a mercy that will never appear.

Shivers rolled through me. I shoved the book away. I did not need to see on paper what I already knew. Havoc was a true monster. Nosing my way around the room, I felt drawn toward a small box, behind the door.

A tickle of something darker, of magic and pain swept up my nose. The faintest whisper, but that was what I'd been following.

It smelled a bit like the warlock.

Without another thought, I dove for the box and came out with a single small book with blood splattered on it. Havoc's blood by the taste. Leather like the others, only this one had an S etched onto the cover. An S that looked like two snakes.

Loki's mark. The same mark that I had on my neck.

Bebe came sliding back into the room and ducked behind the door.

Did you find a way out?

Her tail twitched. "All the doors are guarded. There aren't any windows on the basement floor, which I'm pretty sure violates housing codes, and the windows on the first floor are all barred. This house is all about keeping people in and keeping them out."

What about a second floor? Any better?

"Well, those windows aren't guarded. But last I checked neither of us can fly."

She wasn't wrong on either count, but I healed fast, and she was a cat. Surely, she could land on her feet?

"Oh no, I don't like that look in your eye." Bebe shook her head. "No, we aren't jumping!"

I put my nose to hers and spoke quickly. *This is our chance. We need to get out while we can and run as far as we can before I shift again to two feet! Bebe, we have to go now.*

I could feel the time slipping away.

Han wasn't coming for me, and Havoc was going to kill me once he realized what I had come to accept —Han truly did not give a shit about the mate bond. There would be no negotiation, no deal made. I was just another burden.

Bebe, I have three days to try and break this curse, or I'm dead.

She scrunched her eyes shut. "I know. I know, there just has to be another way."

I looked at the book at my feet. Blood stains and the mark of Loki. Maybe it would prove useful, maybe it would just be a good fire starter. Acting on instinct, I scooped it up off the floor, held it lightly in my mouth, and then motioned at Bebe with my head.

Time to break out.

20

OUT OF THE FRYING PAN

"**Y**ou can't be serious about jumping out a window!" Bebe hissed as we crept out of the storeroom. "That's really not an option, we'll break our legs!"

What choices are there at this point? You want to stay and beg for mercy from Havoc? I just read his journal, and the man is a fucking psycho. Worse than we even realized.

She crinkled up her nose. I bobbed my head. *Exactly. We'll use one of the upstairs windows. Jump out. You can land on me if you want.*

"You'll break *your* fucking legs!" she hissed.

I'll heal if that happens. Fast too. Just... let's go, we're wasting time.

She scrunched her face up again and shook her head before she let out a sigh. "Fine."

Bebe led the way out of the room and up the first flight of stairs. There were voices floating through the house, but they weren't close. The other members of the pack were the most likely candidates for those voices which meant we had to be quiet and fast.

Bebe motioned with her head to follow her. Moving in a crouch, I slunk up the first set of stairs that took us from the basement to the first floor. The first floor was covered in tile, not concrete like the basement. My nails would click if I weren't absolutely precise with each step.

I placed one foot in front of the other, and a burst of words from the other room made me freeze mid stride.

"What the fuck is Havoc going to do with her? A shifter that turns into a golden retriever? I'd fucking kill myself, curse or not." The speaker was a man. A *loud* man. Maybe he was hoping I'd hear him all the way down in my room.

"She's in trouble, that's for sure," Claire said. Her voice had some kindness to it at least. "I don't think Havoc cares. She's tied to Han, but Han doesn't want her, so she has no value. If he can't figure out what to do with her, he'll probably give her back to her pack for some deal. Maybe he'll get them to help us?"

They weren't saying anything I didn't already know.

Bebe patted my face with her paw, her claw tips out just enough to get my attention. She was right, we had to go. No more eavesdropping.

Creeping across the landing, we turned the corner to go up to the second floor. All wooden flooring, only slightly less clicky than tile. Werewolves had excellent hearing, which meant that I only had to plant one foot wrong, and the entire pack would be on us.

Fuck.

Halfway up the stairs, I was struggling not to pant. At least the book I held clenched between my teeth was helping me keep my tongue in place.

At the top of the stairs, I took a deep breath and once more followed Bebe. She led the way down the hall to a room that was blessedly carpeted.

Scents rolled through me as we crept along. Havoc, his smell was everywhere. But the rest of the pack too, and...was that Soleil I could smell?

I drew in a deep breath. Faint but unmistakeable, I picked up her scent. Sunshine and summer wind, wildflowers.

What in the hell had she been doing here? And if she had been here long ago, why was she still alive if Havoc wanted to kill her?

Maybe it was a game to him, and he wanted to end it but didn't, because he'd miss playing with people.

I crept along, belly nearly dragging on the carpet, tail wagging softly again as I followed Bebe into the room. A massive bed dominated the middle of the space, the four poster wooden spires dark, cut with jagged lines. Bebe hurried across the space to sit underneath an open window. Open, as in the curtains were fluttering, and the breeze floating in was cool and fresh.

Someone was confident.

A groan from the bed turned my head to the occupant.

I should have known it wouldn't be that easy to get out.

Havoc lay on the mattress, tangled in his sheets. Thrashing.

Moaning.

Cursing in another tongue and speaking softly in English.

"No. Do not hurt her," he mumbled. "Mine."

I lifted my head and stared. His sheet lay just across his hips, leaving chest and legs bare. Fuck, he was built like a brick shit house.

Scars ran across his chest, along with a series of tattoos that I couldn't quite make out—tattoos that wound their way up and over his left shoulder and down his arm. There seemed to be another tat on his right thigh, but I was trying very hard not to stare.

Monster, he was a monster, not eye candy.

Bebe wacked me hard this time, her claws digging into the soft flesh of my floppy lips.

"Quit staring!"

His eyes opened—he'd heard her. "Cat?"

I dropped to the floor and scooted a little under the bed. Bebe joined me, and we held our breath.

He swung his legs off the side of the bed, so I was staring at his calves. "Fuck," he whispered, and it sounded like he rubbed his hand over his stubble.

I hadn't expected a big, long villain monologue out of him, and I didn't get one. Havoc stood and walked toward the adjoining bathroom. Naked.

Neither Bebe nor I said a word, but I did glance at her. Her eyes were wide.

Yeah, it felt a bit like déjà vu to me too.

The difference being that he slammed the door behind himself.

"Damn, I was kinda hoping," Bebe muttered, and I stared at her, horror filling me. She just couldn't keep her mouth shut.

The door was yanked open and Havoc, towel held in front of his family pride, stared straight at us. "I fucking knew I heard you."

Thanks, but we'll be leaving now. I made a fake lunge as if going for the door, and he followed, creating just enough space for me to make my move.

I spun off my haunches and bolted for the window. Bebe leapt and landed on my back as I jumped for the fluttering curtains, paws straight out, fully expecting to feel hands on my back paws or tail.

I really didn't think about anything else until we were freefalling out toward a front yard that had no fence, thank fuck.

From the window, Havoc yelled something at me.

I hit the ground, grateful it was lawn and not concrete. The impact shuddered up through me, but nothing snapped—lady luck was on my side for the moment. I didn't pause, I just took off running.

Bebe let out a yowl. "We did it!"

She clung to my back, and I let her, not caring that people were probably staring at the strange combination of a cat riding a dog, who held a book in her mouth.

I'd bet that Californians had seen stranger.

I ran for at least an hour, though not in a straight line. I stopped to soak myself in every water barrel and ditch along the way and took a dip in the ocean for good measure as I slowly made my way north, feeling the pull of that direction.

Home. If I was going to die, then I wanted to do it at home. In Skagway, in my bookstore, surrounded by familiar people and...maybe I could get a message to Denna? Maybe she could bring Martin home. Bob could make me his infamous cookies.

Martin and Denna would take care of each other, Grant would make sure they were safe.

The question was how long did I look for a prince? I was no child; I didn't believe in fairy tales or happy ever afters. That's what made the mate bond so hard for me to fully dig into. I could admit I felt something but I couldn't let myself be blindly led.

So what did I want for my last few days on this earth? I wanted people I knew as my friends around me.

"You don't think that Havoc will come after you, do you?" Bebe asked as I began to slow. I had no idea where I was, or how far I'd run, only that I needed a break.

No. I think he'll be grateful I'm gone. I mean, I was just a tool to him too, one that wouldn't work because I don't mean shit to Han.

"Oh, tell me you're done with believing Han is the good one? You've got it into your head that they are both monsters, right?" Bebe trotted alongside me now. I turned down a street that looked solidly like suburbia, down to perfectly manicured lawns and cookie cutter houses. I slowed and turned up the driveway of the next house before making my way around the back. The yard gate wasn't very high, and after a quick sniff to make sure there were no other dogs, I jumped it.

In the shadow of the house, I lay down and nosed open the journal. Just because I knew I was dying, didn't mean I couldn't still...what, try and figure out what the game was?

Maybe Mars was right, maybe I was part cat. My curiosity was flowing hot.

Fuck, this one was *all* Norse. I pawed it shut. So much for finding anything useful from the book—fire starter it was.

I can't read it.

"Why did you even bring it?" Bebe sat beside me, her tail twitching. "Man, I'm hungry. You think we can break in and get something to eat?"

First, I brought it because I feel like understanding Havoc might help me understand... everything. And an enemy who just so happens to be your mate's brother is in a unique position to help you see them clearly. As for the food question, I doubt that anything was left unlocked.

Bebe left me there, muttering about finding a way into the house.

Me, I just couldn't fathom the weirdness that had brought me to this moment. And how in the actual fucking hell was I going to get out of it? I had few friends left. Most were in Skagway still.

My family was a shit show.

My mate didn't give a fuck about me.

I had Bebe, but she was pretty much in the same boat as me—only not on a countdown. I needed someone who could pretend to be my owner while we figured this out. My jaw hit the ground, and if I could have woofed, I would have. Why hadn't I thought of this sooner?

Bebe! I've got an idea!

She poked her head out of a window she'd pushed her way into. "Yeah, and I've got us food! Come on!"

21

CALLING IN THE RESERVES

An hour later, after helping ourselves to the house's inhabitants' store of food and water, we were on the move again. "So, explain this to me again? Who is this and why is she going to help us?"

Denna's a ghoul, so she doesn't really have to follow the same kind of rules as you and I do. And there is a huge connection of ghouls across the country. Maybe even the world. They get information to each other some-how. Like playing telephone.

"But we have to go to a graveyard?"

That's the most common place to find them. Denna was unusual because she stayed in the bookstore. And she doesn't have the same kind of diet most ghouls do. She doesn't like what ghouls are supposed to eat.

The day was starting to slide toward darkness.

You'd think that finding a graveyard would be no big deal, but it wasn't like I could use a phone and there was no major signage to direct me. I was relying on my nose, looking for the smell of death and decay. Sadly, this took us on a few side trips that led to people's houses.

Fucking monsters were everywhere.

"So you haven't given up? Because I didn't mean to, but I totally heard your thoughts about going home to be with your people to die."

I grimaced. *If we can find a prince on the way, I'm totally in for shagging him. But I have to be brutally honest about what I'm up against. I'm not a child, Bebe, neither are you. Women have to make hard decisions all the time. This is one of those where the reality is unpleasant, but that doesn't change that it is my reality.*

She sniffed. "God, I hate that you're right about that."

We reached the graveyard with barely an hour left of daylight. Good enough. I still had the book that had belonged to Havoc. I clung to some small hope that there would be something within it that would help me understand everything. Why Han didn't want me. Why he'd left me to be killed by Havoc. Why Soleil was so important to them both.

Maybe it would have a listing for a prince hidden in its depths. One could hope.

I grimaced and began to scent my way through

the graveyard, looking for something that smelled like Denna—aged flesh, grave dirt, magic. Different than a witch, but on the same lines too.

Old fears and wounds nipped at me, but it would be dangerous to give them more power. I needed to focus on getting away from all of this, away from my brothers and Han and Havoc. And do it all in three days before I kicked the big one.

"What should I be looking for?" Bebe asked. "A ghost? A zombie?"

I took a deep breath and headed across the middle of the graveyard. *Honestly, I'm not sure. Denna was very long limbed after she changed, like her body had thinned out and she moved more like an animal than a human. Her mind was mostly intact, and she had a distinct smell.*

"Mostly?" Bebe squeaked. "You mean we might run into one that isn't intact in the head?"

A possibility.

Up ahead there was the sound of a woman crying. My ears perked, but I flipped them back. I did not need to get in between a person and their grief. I had enough of my own shit to deal with, thank you very much.

I turned from the sound and went deeper into the graveyard. A whiff of magic trickled through the air, and I tipped my head just in time to see something skittering across the graves. I ran toward it, the smell of magic and old flesh growing stronger.

The creature moved like Denna. All limbs, scurrying along like a big insect. But it was trying to get away from us.

"That thing?" Bebe gasped. "It looks like it crawled out of a horror flick!"

Tell them we need to get a message to Denna! Let her know that I'm in trouble, and she needs to come here to this graveyard. Say we'll keep checking for her.

We were racing toward the ghoul, who'd turned to face us, raising himself up to his full height, like some sort of dark praying mantis.

Bebe slid to a stop, and the words poured out of her. "We need to get a message to Denna. Cin's in trouble. We'll be here checking for her, but fuck, I hope we aren't staying here, because I don't think this guy is the guy, man. I don't!"

The ghoul spread his arms wide, and his eye holes swiveled to me. "Who are you?"

Gaunt face, bones poking out from under thin, blue-tinged skin. It was always a wonder to me that humans didn't see ghouls. They often felt them, but that was it. The dark pits of his eyes were facing me. I think.

Can you get a message to Denna? She was a bookstore manager in Alaska, but she could be in Edmonton or even in Montana right now, near Grayling if she followed me. Tell her that Cin is in trouble, that's me. She needs to come here as fast as she can, she needs to bring Martin too. I'll check every night.

The ghoul slowly retracted its limbs until it sat squat on the headstone, more like a gargoyle than a ghoul. "Yeah, I can do that."

Thank you. I bobbed my head and took a step back.

"You aren't going to ask the cost?" he asked.

I shrugged. *We'll discuss cost when Denna gets here.* That was one thing I knew well—ghouls didn't take payment until the transaction was complete.

The ghoul sighed, shrugged, and then gave a nod. "Fine. I'll send out the telegram."

He slipped over the back of the gravestone and was gone without a sound, his scent disappearing.

I looked down at Bebe, who was totally puffed up, making her body twice her normal size. "I don't like that. I don't like that at all. And if your Denna is like that, how can she help?"

Ghouls aren't actually bad, Bebe. They just kinda get stuck after death. Maybe unfinished business, like a ghost, only...more. I didn't know Denna before she became a ghoul, and she doesn't talk about what brought her to that point. But she has opposable thumbs, and while humans can't always see her, she can help. I looked up at the sky. Thirty minutes until I shifted to two legs. Not that it was going to do me much good.

Once I was back on two legs, my brothers would find me faster.

I started back across the graveyard and found we were getting close to the crier again. I sighed and made to turn away from her.

Only I got a waft of her scent, just a hint, and that was enough to stop me. Sunshine. Summer breezes.

Soleil.

22

WHEN THE SUN SHINES ON
YOUR ASS

Once more, I was running. This time toward the crying woman whom everyone and their dog—me included —was looking for. I came flying around a couple of headstones to see her lying flat on the ground, silvery blonde hair tied into a ponytail, her head pillowed in her arms as she sobbed over a grave.

Relatively fresh too, by the look of it, not even a marker of a name yet, just a number on a stick.

I couldn't believe it was her, but the nose of a goldie did not lie.

I approached slowly, but she didn't notice me.

"What are you doing?" Bebe whispered as she caught up to me.

This is the woman they are looking for! Holy shit,

how had this happened? Was this my chance to somehow make it past the next three days?

I shook my head. No, I was likely going to bite the big one, but that didn't mean I couldn't fuck with Havoc and Han before I died.

I found myself grinning. Yeah, that was the way to go out. Sure, going home to Alaska held some merit too, but revenge had its own flavor worth tasting.

By keeping her alive and getting her away from the two men who had quite literally ruined what was left of my life, I'd be making their lives difficult.

I nosed the woman's hand, and she gasped and scrambled back away from me. As if she expected... well...a werewolf. When her tear-filled eyes finally saw me, she reached out a trembling hand and touched my head. "Oh. Hello, sunshine."

My tail thumped the ground, idiot thing. But she smiled and stroked her hand over my head, and I found myself closing my eyes. My goldy self-reveled in being patted, in the affection of any human.

Idiot.

"Where did you come from? What's this?" She took the journal out of my mouth. She flipped it open, and her long lashes fluttered against her cheeks, a gasp escaped her. "Did Havoc send you?"

I shook my head. No, the motherfucker sure as hell had not.

She reached out and circled an arm around my neck, hugging me. She was warm, so warm, as if the sun had made her its namesake. I sighed and leaned into her. "You want to come with me?"

I bobbed my head. Han was looking for her. Havoc was looking for her. And I'd found her first.

Go me. Go us. Team cat and dog to the fucking rescue.

Bebe let out a meow and jumped up onto my back, forcing her way into Soleil's arms. Soleil laughed and scooped her up. "Okay, I guess you can both come with me. I could use a friend or two."

"I don't think she can hear me," Bebe said. "Not like Havoc."

She's as good a place as any to hole up for the night. But we need to hurry. I'm going to shift soon.

As it turned out, Soleil didn't live too far from the graveyard. Only a few blocks. Her home was in an apartment building. She took us all the way to the top floor, which to me seemed like a terrible idea for someone who was being hunted. How had she survived this long? Years, that's what it seemed like Havoc and Han had been going after her for.

Her keys jangled as she opened the main door to her apartment. I noticed there was only the one lock. So, either she was very confident about her place here or she was not afraid of the men searching for her.

Or was she just done with being chased, ready to die?

Was it some sort of game? I thought back to Havoc's words and decided it wasn't—at least not for him.

"Here, you can stay here with me. If you want to." She turned and looked me in the eye. "Do you have a name?"

She was talking to me as if...as if she knew I'd understand. My thoughts fled rather suddenly.

A pain in my middle doubled me over, and I grunted as I fell to the floor, the change to two legs overtaking me in a breathtaking shot.

"Oh shit!" Bebe yelled. "Is it as bad as last time? What do I do?"

Make sure the door is shut.

Bebe scrambled behind me and karate-kicked the door, much to Soleil's surprise, if her wide eyes were any indication.

I shook my head as my body crackled and danced between forms. It wasn't as bad as the first time, quicker but still painful. The entire thing took less than three minutes, but it again left me panting on the floor, naked and aching all over. And ravenous.

A blanket settled across my shoulders, and then Soleil was helping me to my feet. "Here, Jesus in a blanket, I'm guessing that was not pleasant? It sounded awful. I've seen werewolves shift, and it's much quicker."

She was guessing? I blinked down at her, raising an eyebrow. She wasn't very big, petite even. She didn't seem to recognize me from our brief interaction in Edmonton. Mind you she didn't smell me then, and she'd been in tears.

She helped me to the couch and wrapped me in several more blankets. "I'm Soleil, my friends call me Solly."

I mimicked writing something. Her eyes widened—that was definitely her schtick—and she went and got me a pen and paper.

I gave her my name.

"Cin, nice to meet you. Do you know sign language?"

I shook my head and wrote *recent development*.

"Gotcha. Okay, so...do you know who this belongs to?" She held up the journal.

Havoc.

She smiled and touched the name on the paper. Stroking it. "He's been looking out for me. There's another one, his brother. He's trying to kill me."

Nope, that could not be right. I couldn't be hearing her correctly. I stared at her. Then wrote quickly: *You sure about that?*

She smiled and her face lit up. "Absolutely. It's...complicated."

Yeah, and I somehow got dropped into the middle of it.

She smiled as she read my words. "You sure did. Let's get you some clothes."

And that is how I ended up meeting Soleil, the object of everyone's desire. Wearing a pair of her shorts and a tank top, I sat across the table from her, and we got 'talking,' each of us with a glass of wine. A plate of snacks sat between us.

I explained that I was a werewolf—figured that wouldn't be a shock to her—that I'd been cursed to be a golden retriever during the day, and that Han had scooped me out of the rescue place.

That Havoc had tried to kill me.

That Han had left me to die.

That I didn't much like either of them at this point.

I didn't tell her that I had two and a half days left to get my curse figured out. I was just going to ignore that. What were the chances of finding a prince in that time frame? The only ones I'd heard about lived a long plane ride away, and my passport was in Canada.

"Preaching to the choir, girlfriend," Soleil said. "Preaching to the choir." She sighed and took a sip of her wine. "Havoc doesn't like me, not really, but I'm...I guess you'd say I'm useful because Han wants me. Wants to kill me, to be clear. But no one will tell me why." She frowned. "I've been running for the last year. Havoc won't take me in—he says it would be too dangerous because it's what Han expects. So he kind of just ghosts along behind me, and I try to live something of a life. He gets me money when I need it, so I don't have to work."

I scribbled fast. She read.

"You were in Edmonton? Yes. I was there! I was speaking to Sven—he's been trying to help too. But he's no better than Havoc when it comes to telling me what's going on. Why I'm so freaking important, excuse my French." She sighed and slumped in her chair, the light around her seeming to dim a little. She fiddled with a few bracelets on her left hand. Beaded, they made a soft tinkling sound.

You shouldn't wear those. The noise probably gives you away. I tapped my hand on the bracelet.

"Oh, well, they're supposed to be for protection. This one is from my friend—she passed right around the time she gave it to me. This one is from Havoc." She touched the solid black beads. No, not solid, they seemed to swirl with a silver, not unlike the mark in his eye. Her fingers moved to a third set of beads. "And this one was from a woman named Gina. Said she was a seer and that I would need this. They change color depending on the temperature."

"Maybe she could tie them together?" Bebe said as she cracked a large yawn.

It was a good suggestion, and a moment later Soleil and I tied the three bracelets with some thin string. "You're so smart," she whispered. "I wish we'd met sooner."

I smiled and patted her hand. She seemed sweet and totally unsuited to being stalked by two large, centuries-old werewolves.

I began to chew the inside of my lip, still thinking about screwing over both Havoc and Han and messing up their plans for Soleil. I started another page on the paper. *What if we work together, you and me? What if I help you? I understand were-wolves, we have this journal, and maybe it could tell us why you're so important?*

She read the paper. "How? I mean, I like you and all, but how will us working together do any good? Can you fight them?"

I looked at Bebe, who had curled up on the couch and was sound asleep. *We're trapped in bodies that aren't our own. Cursed. You're trapped here, because every time you move, Han has a chance of finding you. Fighting them is not a good idea. At least not face to face. They're big, fast, and mean. I'm fast, but that isn't enough. We have to be smart.*

She nodded. "I hate him. I hate him so f-ing much, again, excuse my language. I want my darn life back."

I grimaced. I didn't love him, but the urge to

defend him as my mate was still there, which made me feel slimy and gross. Stupid mate bonds. *I don't know what the answer is. But surely, we're stronger together? Smarter together?*

"And what about your family? They still want to kill you." She pointed out as she poured us both another glass of wine. Yup, I'd even scribbled that bit down during our 'conversation'. I kept stuffing in the bit of food she'd put out, trying to get enough calories into me.

I stood and paced the room. I found myself standing in front of the main door that led to the elevator. I frowned and tipped my head closer to the door, pressing my ear up against it. Footsteps. I pointed at Soleil and lifted a finger to my mouth, then pointed at the door.

Someone had found us. But which one of us were they here for?

Soleil had a backpack on in a flash, and I scooped up a snoozing Bebe and followed my new friend out of a side window and onto a fire escape.

"She's here!" boomed a voice from the street below.

I didn't recognize it. But the man who stepped into the light cast by the streetlamp was one I knew.

"Han," Soleil breathed out. I nodded and dragged her upward, to the roof top. If Han wanted to kill her, then we had to get her the hell out of here.

I was going to fuck Han over, at least in this.

We clattered our way to the roof. Bebe woke up. "What's going on?"

Han has found her. We have to get her out of here, Bebe.

I searched the rooftop, finding only a few loose pipes and another ladder that led down. Men were racing up it, dressed in fatigues and carrying cattle prods.

"I can't fight, I freeze up! I'm not good at this," Soleil cried. "We're trapped!"

I tapped her shoulder and shook my head. I scooped up one of the pipes and strode toward the far side of the roof. I was going to get us out of here.

If there was one thing I was good at, it was protecting others.

These weren't werewolves Han had helping him. He was a lone wolf in every sense of the word. They were hired thugs, humans, which meant I could deal with them.

The first one popped his head up above the roof, and I swung like I was aiming for a home run.

His neck cracked and he fell backward, taking the two men below him out.

Three for the price of one. Pulling Soleil after me, I headed to the ladder and went down first, clattering my way to the first open window and letting myself in. Bebe was right with me. The family eating dinner was rather surprised as we burst through the window. First me and Bebe, then Soleil.

"What in the hell?" The gray-haired man stood, his pot belly pushing his TV tray dinner over onto the floor. I gave them a wave and a shrug as I dragged Soleil through their apartment and out the front door.

We ran to the elevator and saw that it was already binging its way up to us.

Stairs, Bebe!

"I'm on it! Girl power!" She streaked down the hallway ahead of us, and Soleil kept up as we slammed through the EXIT ONLY door at the far end of the hallway. We were through, and I jammed the piece of pipe I'd been carrying through the handles, blocking it, before we raced down the stairs.

I held out a hand to Soleil, and she gave me her pack. That wasn't what I was asking for, but it would do.

I slung it over my back and kept on going until we hit the basement level. I pushed the exit open and peered outside. Nothing.

Taking Soleil by the hand, I led the way, barefoot, out into the night. We ran full tilt toward the grave-yard, Bebe racing alongside me. There were lots of scents there, lots of places to hide if you knew what you were doing.

Han would have something of a nose on him, even on two legs, but this would help hide us for a few minutes.

I tugged her down next to a large gravestone to catch her breath. I wasn't winded, not yet.

Soleil stared at me, her eyes dimming a little. "I wouldn't have made it out without you."

I squeezed her hand and gave her a wink. It was the best I could do without my slip of paper.

Bebe, do you see them?

She was perched on my shoulder, peering over the top of the stone. "Yes, they're coming. Not Han though, just three of the thugs. Not the ones you took out, other ones."

I handed Soleil her pack back to her and motioned for her to stay. I grabbed Bebe and set her into Soleil's arms.

Stay with her. I'll deal with them, then we'll make a run for it.

"You got it, badass. Kick them in the balls for me!"

I motioned again for Soleil to wait, and she nodded. "Okay, I'll wait. Are you going to fight them?"

Again, I nodded and winked, and then I slid out from behind the tombstone and made my way far to the right before I stood and let them see me. Then I sprinted further yet to the right, and they followed, only seeing a woman. Idiots. They were looking for a woman, and they didn't even take into account that I was the wrong shade of blonde. You know, being raven haired as I was.

Ducking down behind a gravestone, I held my breath, waiting on the sound of feet. There it was. I spun out to my left and shot upright, driving my fist into the soft underside of a jaw. The man's eyes rolled, and he dropped without a sound. His two buddies surrounded me. One of them touched the walkie-talkie attached to his shoulder. "We got her, boss."

Han's voice scratched through. "Good. Keep her there. I'm on my way."

I didn't like thinking ill of the man who was supposed to be my mate, because what did it say about me? But talk about being a lazy fucker. Was that why he'd gotten a dog from a shelter? Just so he wouldn't have to do the hard work?

It was a good thing I was going to die in three days. I did not want to have to admit to anyone Han was my mate.

I engaged with the two men—thugs indeed. Taking out a knee on the first and the throat on the second, I had them flat out in a matter of less than a minute. I stripped the first of his flak jacket and emergency bag, paused and then took his head set too.

I knew enough about the game of war to know how to fuck with Han's head. I smiled to myself as I raced back to where Soleil and Bebe waited. I motioned with my head, and the three of us ran hard, leaving the graveyard behind.

But not before one last thing....

Ghoul! There is a blond man coming through who looks like a Greek god. Feel free to rough him up!

The ghoul popped his head out of the grave he'd been resting in. "What do you mean, rough him up? Can I eat him?"

Feel free to try. He's a mean fucker!

The ghoul ghosted away from us. At the very least, he'd slow Han down, and that was what we needed.

Finally, we were getting a break. Just not the one I would have liked.

23

GIRL GANGS RULE

Soleil was laughing as we ran down the street. "I saw you! You totally kicked their behinds, and it was like you weren't even trying! Where did you learn to fight like that?"

"I taught her," Bebe yelled as she ran alongside us.

I rolled my eyes. We needed a place to hole up for the night. And I had an idea. *Bebe, what if we got on a boat? Moored it way out so that we'd see people coming? Or used it to move up the coast?*

"That is fucking brilliant!"

Bebe seemed to have some sort of compass locked in her head, and she turned, taking us toward the ocean.

"No, wait, that's toward Han's house!" Soleil began to dig her heels in.

I shook my head and made a wave motion with my hand.

"Water?"

I nodded. Moon goddess above, this not being able to talk was a real pain in my tail feathers.

"Okay, you think we'd be safe on the water? I haven't tried that yet, I guess it's worth a go."

I nodded again, tugging her along with me. Once more she handed me the pack and I took the weight from her. It was the least I could do seeing as she was as far as I could see and smell, totally human. Her scent off her bag would help keep me hidden from my stupid werewolf brothers.

I really needed to know the story here when it came to Soleil, and yes, I was using that distraction to keep from worrying about not finding a prince. What was she, and why did they want her so bad?

As we made our way to the water, I was gratified to see she wasn't completely lacking in street smarts. She flagged us a cab, had it take us partway to the docks, then we got out, flagged another cab, then another. Four cabs later, we were at a series of docks that were quiet at that time of the night.

"Do we just steal a boat?" Soleil whispered as we walked along, the ocean slapping against the wooden pilings.

The answer to that was yes and no. We did need to steal a boat, but it had to be the right boat—one that wasn't used often. I made my way along until I found one that I liked. The rope had been left tied for a long time, the layer of dirt and ash from the fires and lack of rain was thick and the boat itself was not overly fancy. There was a small cabin and simple living quarters. I hopped aboard and flipped the moorings off.

Soleil and Bebe followed me, carefully.

"You sure know a lot about a lot of things," Soleil whispered. "Like you could survive anything."

I snorted, thinking about how many times I'd almost been killed in my short fifty years. The engine of the boat was slow to turn over, but it was fueled up. Getting us out of the marina would be no problem, but where to go from there?

Digging around, I fumbled through the papers inside the cabin. *We need a map of the area. Bebe, see what you can find.* Some of my old confidence was sliding back to me. Funny how taking care of someone else had helped change my outlook. That was being a werewolf for you. It was all about family, all about pack.

I didn't like thinking that I'd spent the last ten years doing nothing but floating along. Looking back, though, it was true. Without a pack, I'd been wallowing in mediocrity and uncertainty. I'd told myself that I did better without a pack, but maybe it had just been the wrong pack...

Bebe scrounged around, chasing papers, and Soleil seemed to catch on to what she was looking for. "Here, a map of the ocean?"

I nodded and spread it out as I took note of the few landmarks we had. Putting the boat into gear, I started us up the coast, headed north.

On a piece of paper, I wrote swiftly.

If we can get to another marina, or maybe even two or three up the coast, we will be harder to find. Then we can either travel by land or keep going by boat.

"That's a good idea." Soleil sank down into a chair beside me. "Are you sure you want to come with me? Because Han is going to keep coming. Every time I get close to someone, make a friend, he kills them." She bit her lower lip. "That's what I was doing in the graveyard, saying goodbye to my friend. Terrence. I...never told him that I loved him. And he'd worked so hard to protect me." Tears slid down her face. Bebe snuggled up to her, purring, and she clung to the cat. I remembered her saying that name, back in Edmonton, when she had the conversation with Sven, her worry over her friend. "I don't want you two to get hurt. It would gut me to be the cause of more pain."

I scribbled a note. *We aren't leaving you. In a few hours, I'm going to be a golden retriever again. We need you too.*

No, I didn't write that I'd be dead soon anyway. Maybe I felt a little bad about that, but there you go.

She read what I'd written. "And this happens every day? For how long? What's your time limit?"

I frowned at her and shook my head. Nope, was not going to tell her.

"Well, every curse that I've ever heard of has a time limit. You know, like, you have to make a prince kiss you before the full moon or something like that." Damn, she'd hit the nail on the head.

I smiled and shook my head. Then I wrote another note, lying my ass off.

As far as I know, there is no time limit. Mind you, the person who did this to me is a right rotten bitch, so who knows?

We boated along, passing two different marinas before docking at the third. There we got off the boat, keeping an eye for anyone watching. I moored the boat as fast as I could, doing just enough to ensure it didn't look abandoned. Then we ran for it.

Once more, Soleil proved herself invaluable, getting us two Ubers and then a cab before we stopped at a rather dingy hotel.

"Seriously, it's too bad we couldn't stay at the Ritz Carlton. They have security, you know." She sighed. "But I've tried that too. Han knows I like the nicer things."

I grabbed the notebook that had been Havoc's

and flipped to an empty page. *Second floor room. Nothing higher.*

Soleil gave me a smile and a thumbs up. She looked incredibly young in that moment, and I was hit with the realization that some of my compulsion to help her was because she reminded me of Meghan. Sad. Young. Terrified.

She got our room key, and we smuggled Bebe in Soleil's backpack to the room assigned to us.

"Sorry, it's not much, but it's all I could afford. I always keep cash in my bag, but...."

I motioned for her to pay attention, then I scribbled down my bank account. The passcodes. Everything. I wasn't going to need it.

Take all the money out.

She stared at me. "We can't do that. Your brothers—"

Will not know you. They won't hurt you.

"Are you sure?"

I gave her a quick nod and checked the time. We only had a few hours left before I was going to shift back to four legs. I tapped my wrist, then wiggled my fingers, then tapped my palm. It was best that I went and got food. No one knew me here, and my brothers were a long way off. The chances of them finding me was slim to none.

In a pair of her flip flops, I headed out to find us some food. Okay, mostly me some food. Soleil didn't seem to want to eat, but I was starving. Typically, I didn't shift more than once or twice a month. Shifting every day was going to be brutal. I mean, if I kept it up, it could...kill me.

I paused between steps and looked down at my body, at the way my belly sunk in and the visibility of my ribs. I'd always been thick with muscle. That muscle was fading fast.

Shit. Fuck. Damn. *There* was the time limit outside of the three days. If Han hadn't found out that I was his mate, I would have died in a matter of weeks anyway. Soleil had been right. I could slow down the process, but that would mean consuming huge quantities of food.

I found a gas station with a grocery section and picked out the highest calorie protein foods I could. Pepperoni, those shitty already soggy sandwiches, a stack of hot dogs minus the buns, a few cans of tuna for Bebe, and a stack of chocolate bars. There is nothing like drowning your sorrows in chocolate, I don't care what anyone says.

I hurried back to the hotel to find Soleil on the phone.

"Claire, we're safe. A woman named Cin helped me. She beat the shit out of Han's men and...oh, she's back."

Claire. Havoc's pack member. Fuck. I shook my

head and dropped the food so I could scribble a note.

If Havoc comes to where you are, Han will follow. He needs to fuck off somewhere else.

Her eyes went wide, along with her mouth. "I can't...tell you, Claire. Han follows you."

Claire's voice was as clear to me as if I were standing right next to her. "We can't protect you if we don't know where you are. You have to tell us, Soleil. You know this. I don't know who that woman is, but she can't protect you from Han."

I kept on writing, and Soleil kept on speaking my words. "But you don't know the line isn't bugged. You don't know that there isn't a Sven in your pack working for Han...wait, what does that mean?"

Soleil looked at me and I tapped the paper. She gasped. "Sven is a double agent?" I nodded.

Claire disappeared and someone else came on the line. "Soleil. That woman will get you killed. She's cursed," Havoc said. "We saw you leave the apartment with her. We know her."

"I know she's cursed," Soleil said. "She told me. Which is more than you've ever done. You won't tell me why Han wants to kill me."

"I can't," he growled.

"Or why you can't just let me stay with you."

"Because I can't." He sounded beyond frustrated.

I stepped back. This had to be her decision, or

she would forever believe that I was the bad guy. I glanced at Bebe, who was looking up at me.

"Are we really taking on a gang of werewolves to protect her?"

I looked at Soleil, at the hunch of her shoulders and the fear shuddering through her. I slowly nodded.

Yeah. Yeah I am. Because who is protecting her now? Havoc? He's doing a piss-poor job. If we hadn't been there, Bebe, Han would've had her. And Bebe... I'm going to be dead in three days. Less than three now. I... if I can help her, it fucks with them. She can have my money, I don't need it. Certainly not by Friday.

Bebe frowned up at me. "You aren't going to die. I won't let you. We'll find you a prince to shag, I just know it."

I scooped her up. *I hope you're right, but I'm preparing for the worst. Okay?*

Bebe sniffed. "Well, we are incredibly bad ass. And I agree, making Han suffer will be fun in the interim."

I grinned and turned as a sound on the window caught my ear. A sound I recognized. Our badass girl tribe had just increased by one. I went to the window and opened it, letting Denna in. She flung her arms around my neck, sobbing.

"I knew you'd be okay, I knew it!"

I patted her back and set her down.

Can you hear me? Where is Martin?

"Of course I can... wait, why is your voice in my head?"

"That's a long story, I'm Bebe. Used to be a woman, now stuck as a pussy... cat." She reached up and bopped a paw to Denna's hand. Denna looked down at her. Bebe cringed and her fur fluffed up a little, but she managed to control whatever fear had her by the tail.

"Cool. I used to be a bookstore manager, and now I'm a ghoul. I got a message to Copper, she flew back, took Martin with her to London. I told her I'd find you and bring you along."

How did you find me so fast? We only sent the ghoul like eight hours ago. And I didn't tell him we'd be here.

Denna smiled. "I was already on my way to the west coast. I went to Montana after you, and found out from the ghoul near the pack, Sherry, what had happened and where you'd been sent. Using the ghoul network, it didn't take long. I knew you were a golden, so I was checking all the shelters. That's when Franklin reached out to me. I got to the graveyard as you were leaving. I followed you up the coastline."

I hugged her again. *You're a good friend, Denna. Thank you. And thank you for making sure Martin was okay.*

"Well, he was pretty pissed I didn't bring him

with me. He made me promise when we first met that I wouldn't tell you that he can talk. I think maybe he was cursed too?"

Holy shit. As bombshell dropping as that was, I had other matters to deal with right at that exact moment.

I turned, my ears still listening in as Havoc tried to convince Soleil to tell him where she was. As if he was trying to keep her on the line. Walking across the small space to where she stood in the small kitchen, I took the phone from her and held it to my ear.

His breathing changed.

Can you hear me?

His growl was answer enough.

Because of you, I'll be dead in three days. Let me be clear. In those three days, I will make sure that you will wish you'd never met me.

His snarl hit me in the middle of my chest and spun outward so fast I had to grab the countertop to keep from falling over.

"No one is killing you, or Soleil. That's a pleasure I'll take myself—"

I hung up on him in mid-sentence. Mostly because I didn't much feel like fighting off an orgasm in front of my friends.

"What?" Soleil stared at the phone.

They were tracing the call, I wrote, underlining the words. *That's what I would do.*

"Oh. I...didn't think of that." She sagged. "I'm so stupid. I'm sorry."

No, you're not. I'm used to thinking everyone is hunting for me. I smiled at her, but I'm not sure it really softened the blow that the people she saw as friends and protectors maybe weren't what she'd thought.

I made introductions between her and Denna. Who she could see. Interesting. I looked Soleil over, took in an experimental breath, trying to find a scent that would tell me if she was something more than what she seemed. Nope, just human. So why could she see a ghoul? I had all the questions, like how Soleil ended up tangled with the two monsters, if it had only been a year that they'd been trying to kill her, but I was exhausted and I could see that same fatigue on the other's faces.

Denna, will you keep watch tonight? Wake me up if anyone so much as farts in our direction?

Denna nodded, and then it wasn't long before everyone was asleep. Except for me. I lay there, my mind working through the problem at hand. Trying to find a way out—not only for Soleil, but for my sorry ass too.

How was I supposed to find a prince? And what

the hell, Martin was cursed too? That explained his human like behavior, but why didn't I ever hear him?

Getting up, I scooped the journal off the table and went to sit with Denna. She glanced at me but said nothing for a few minutes.

I already knew what she'd want to know. *Yes, two days now. The curse on me was expedited by the stupidity of...wait for it...a man crashing through my life.*

Denna covered her face with her thin fingers as I explained what had happened. "This is terrible. Just the worst!"

I nodded and flipped slowly through the book, hoping to find something. A clue. Anything at all. The pages were again a mixture of that economical writing, hard and blocky, and the softer, more refined cursive. I slid my fingers over both styles but could read none of it, no matter how hard I stared. No, that wasn't quite true. There were a few words.

Names were familiar. Havoc. Soleil. Han. I found Loki too. Fenrir.

Denna did you read much on Norse mythology or history?

I kept tracing the words over and over, as if that would somehow show me what I wanted to know.

"A little," she said quietly. "But not enough to read that." She reached across and brushed a long skinny finger across the journal. "You think it might help you break your curse?"

I shook my head. *No. But maybe it can help us help Soleil. That will make life miserable for both Havoc and Han. Least I can do for them.*

Denna slung a spindly arm over my shoulder as we sat in the window and stared out at the dark street. I didn't want to sleep.

I had two days left of my life, and for what it was worth, I would live them as best I could and go out in the most spectacular fashion I could.

I WOKE up to sunlight streaming across my muzzle, warming me and waking me at the same time. I yawned and stretched, tail wagging. Denna was crouched beside the window.

"No farts in this direction. I like the new look. Not really you, but you know, it's cool. Fluffy."

I huffed at her. It was the closest thing to a laugh I had in my arsenal.

Soleil and Bebe were still sleeping. I let myself dig into the gas station food, chowing down on everything without really tasting any of it. I didn't care about the taste, I just needed to take in as many calories as possible, as often as possible.

When Soleil woke a half an hour later, she was much more chipper, singing away as she made her way to the shower. Like a damn Disney princess.

"Fucking morning people," Bebe grumbled and stretched as she made her way over to me.

I'm worried, Bebe. There's something in the back of my head that I feel like I need to remember, but I can't. Something crucial.

Bebe blinked sleepily up at me. "Like something that could get us killed, or more like hey, I forgot my contacts and can't see quite as good as I'd like to?"

I wrinkled up my nose. *I think it's something serious. Something about Han. But for the life of me I can't think of what it is.*

I moved over to the window and jumped my front legs up onto the ledge so I could look out. There were lots of people moving around here. Tourists, maybe? Hard to say from my perch. Worrying at the inside of my lip, I let my mind wander in the hope that I could figure out just what was bothering me.

Nothing came to me.

Fuck. I hated when that happened.

"It'll be, like, three in the morning," Bebe said around a mouthful of pepperoni. "And you'll shit your pants when it hits you."

Or shit my fur. I pointed at myself with my nose.

"Nope, pants at night," Bebe said around a chunk of pepperoni.

"Where are we going from here?" Denna asked. Then she gasped and scuttled across the room, yanking the journal away from me. "None of us can read this."

Bebe and I shared a look. I knew we were both thinking the same thing—sometimes Denna's mind slipped. It was part of being a ghoul.

"Yeah, we know," Bebe said. "You tried last night. Remember?"

"It's...this is old, Cin. Very old." Denna held up a long skeletal finger, just as Soleil came back into the room, freshly clean and smelling like roses. "But I just thought of someone who could help us. Grant. He's old too. If he can't read it, he'll know someone who can. Right? And he said he'd help you if you needed help."

Grant. Shit, it hadn't occurred to me that he might be able to help. *Does he speak Norse?*

Denna shook her head. "I don't know, but like I said, if he doesn't then he might know someone who does. And that has to be worth a phone call, right? I mean, he's half in love with you, so make him work for it."

I bobbed my head.

Soleil picked up on the conversation quickly. "So this Grant might be able to help us figure out that book, and then we would have some clues about why I'm being stalked by Han?"

Wagging my tail, I grinned up at her. *Bingo.*

Denna borrowed Soleil's phone and dialed up

Grant. I wasn't sure he'd be awake, but he was an hour or two behind us in Alaska. It wouldn't be dawn there yet.

"Hello?" His voice was groggy as he answered. "Who is this? I don't recognize the number."

"It's me, Denna. Cin asked me to call. She can't speak anymore. I think her voice got lost with a curse or something." Vague, that was good.

"Holy gods of the night. Did her family do this?" he whispered, the sound of sheets and another body being shuffled around, the sound of a woman's sighing voice. "Hang on, let me get somewhere private."

Denna looked at me. "He sure didn't waste any time grieving you, did he?" she asked in an undertone.

We were never an item, Denna. You know that.

Soleil shot me a look. "An old boyfriend?"

I shook my head as Grant came back on the line. "What can I do to help?"

Denna got right to it. "Who do you know on the west coast who can speak and read Norse? Assuming you can't?" Grant was silent long enough that Denna shook the phone. "Hello, Grant? Did I lose you? Are you dead?"

"You know I'm dead, Denna. No, I'm still here. There is only one person that I know that might be able to help you. He's kind of a miserable fuck though, and his payment will be steep in a weird way." Grant sighed. "Do you want me to set up a meeting?"

Where is he?

Denna asked my question.

Grant rustled some papers. "Outside of Portland, when can you get there? Cin, are you all right?"

I nodded, touched that he was so concerned. *Tell him I'm fine. Soleil will get the money today from my bank account, and we'll get there tonight at the latest. We can give this guy a good chunk of money. See if that works.*

Grant sighed. "His name is Theodore; he's a very old vampire who is incredibly set in his ways. I doubt Theodore is even his name, but I know he was born in northern Europe and speaks several Scandinavian languages. Fluently. But he can be...odd. Grumpy. Strange. Unpredictable. You name it."

Soleil scribbled down the information inside of Havoc's book. "Got it."

I wish I could say that was the start of a fun girls' trip, but alas, life is not that kind.

24

WHEN MEETING VAMPIRES, DON'T SHOW UP BLOODY

Soleil had no trouble getting half of the money out of my account. Twenty-five thousand and we would be good for a bit. Interesting, Soleil didn't so much as blink at that amount, and thoughts of Havoc helping her repeatedly made me wonder again at their relationship.

She was lovely, don't get me wrong, but there had to be more to this than just a lovely woman tied between two men.

Renting a car under one of her many false names was also no problem. Driving up the coast, I stuck my head out the window and let the wind rush over me, blowing away all the worries of the night before. No problem.

For a while, it seemed like things were going

great, which is usually exactly what happens before everything implodes.

"Okay, so let's go over the plan again," Bebe said. Denna translated for us, so Soleil wasn't left out. "We're going to find this Theo dude, get him to read the journal, and then what? What if it's, like, old family recipes? Or like a list of all the ladies Havoc has fucked or, worse, where he's buried bodies! It could literally be for nothing. You know that, right?"

Soleil looked across to me. I sat in the passenger seat, my golden hair ruffled by the blowing wind. "What do you think, Cin? You know this world of werewolves better than me. I got thrown into it last year. My best friend for my whole life died in my arms, and then I was suddenly being chased by the man who'd fucked and killed her."

I scrunched my face up and looked at Bebe. That was likely what happened to the sweet, beautiful eyed vet who'd stitched me up. Fucked and then killed. My brain just kinda skipped over that for right now and latched onto the fact that Soleil was saying she'd only been on the run for a year. How was that possible? *Havoc and Han, they said they'd been searching for you for the last several hundred years. The timelines don't add up. How old are you?*

Soleil shook her head. "I'm twenty-nine. Thirty next month. I don't know, maybe like re-incarnation?

My friend Vicky met Havoc first, a few months before Han started chasing me. He wouldn't sleep with her, so when she met Han, she totally went for it out of spite I think. I met him too. We shared an apartment, Vicky and me." I looked over at her. She was gripping the steering wheel, worrying at it. Bebe shot me a look, her furry eyebrows high. "I don't think Han realized that Vicky wasn't...all the way...dead when he left. He was happy. Celebrating and talking in another language on the phone. He completely ignored me."

All the way dead. I reached over and put a paw on her arm, doing what I could to comfort her. Seeing someone you loved and cared for die, that was hard. Especially if it was violent.

"What happened next?" Denna whispered the question we were all thinking.

Soleil's eyes fluttered closed as tears leaked down her cheeks, tiny diamonds catching the light. She opened them again quickly, eyes back on the road. "I held her close, begged her not to go. It was like she was someone else though... she wasn't my friend in those last few seconds. She gave me the first two bracelets—the black and red ones—and said I needed to wear them. That they would protect me, that one was from Havoc for protection, one from her. The third one, I got just a few days ago."

She dangled her arm up, shaking the beads.

"Then she died for real," Soleil whispered. "One

last breath, and she was gone. After that, Havoc found me, told me that Han would come for me next, and I needed to hide. He said he'd be watching over me."

Bebe clicked her teeth together. "None of this makes sense. Unless Han is just a serial killer? But if that's the case, why doesn't Havoc put an end to him?"

Soleil nodded as Denna translated. "I asked him that once. Why he didn't kill Han. He said it was in the rules. They could hurt each other, even maim each other, but it wasn't *possible* for him to kill his brother."

I frowned and tipped my head to the side. *Not possible is different than not allowed. It's almost like... Han is immortal? Because Havoc said something about killing Han, but that it would just put him back a few years.*

Soleil shuddered. "I hope not. But I don't know."

Why for the love of all the moon and stars had I ended up with a psycho fated mate who was quite possibly immortal? I was beginning to believe that he was worse than Juniper, which was saying something.

"Yeah, but only for two more days," Bebe bit out.

Denna unfortunately translated that bit right away.

"What do you mean?" Soleil asked. "Why only two days?"

Bebe shook her head and promptly spilled the beans. "Because the curse on Cin is going to end her life at sundown. Not tonight. Not tomorrow, but the next day. So two days left."

Soleil jerked the wheel and pulled us off the road. The car shuddered into park. "What? No, that can't happen! What do you mean?"

I scooted closer to her and put a paw on her arm. *Listen to me. My life has been a shit show from the beginning. I have my brothers, who are still hunting for me. A mother who hates me with the passion of a thousand suns, and while I do have* amazing *friends, the way my family is hunting me puts them in danger. If the last thing I can do is thwart Han and Havoc and help you survive, then that is what I want to do with my last two days. There's no way to break this curse on me.*

Soleil just stared at me, a slow tremor rolling through her as Denna spoke.

"I think we should try and fix your curse," she said.

Bebe grunted. "I agree."

I huffed. *There is no way to fix it. Bebe, you know that.*

Soleil slipped off her bracelets and slid them over my front right leg. She slid them up until they were above my elbow and tight enough to stay in place. My long fur covered them completely. "There. Now you will have the protection that Vicky, Havoc and the seer gave to me."

I doubted her pretty baubles were going to break the curse, but I gave her a cold nose to the cheek. *Thank you. But we still need to protect you, Soleil. And that means understanding what the game is. We figure that out, and we can find a way to win it for you.*

Bebe batted my face with a paw, getting my attention. "But a vampire? You can't be serious. I mean, I know you're used to dealing with that sort of thing, but I feel like it might be a bad idea."

Denna tapped her fingers on the back of the seat. "Honestly, vampires are not all that bad. They get a reputation, same as ghouls, for the few that are the bad appleholes."

Soleil pulled back out into traffic. "I'm game for anything at this point."

I'll be back to two legs. I'll deal with the vampire. Denna is right, they aren't all bad. Yup, speak with confidence, and fortitude will find you. That's what I was I hoping, anyway. Because Denna was incorrect. Grant was the exception, a vampire with some kindness and desire to be part of a community. Most were solitary creatures, coming out only to feed and fuck and cause mayhem when they were bored.

Soleil turned up the radio and began to sing along to some pop song I didn't know. I set my head on the edge of the window, muzzle out, and closed my eyes. *We need food too. Burgers. Something with lots of protein.*

"I'm sure there will be some fast-food places," Soleil said.

My stomach grumbled and I tried not to think about how much the shifting tonight would take out of me if I didn't eat enough today. Fuck, what a mess. Even if I did manage to somehow not die from the first portion of the curse—because Han knew what I was—then I would surely die because of the second portion of the curse, my body eating itself away.

With my eyes closed, the fatigue from staying up all night caught me, and I floated in and out of sleep. My dreams were strange, ghost like. I was sure I could see Han, and he was pissed. His face was twisted in a way I wouldn't have thought possible, making him ugly and monstrous. When he swiveled around, his eyes locked on me. "There you are. Bitch. I've got you now."

I jerked awake, panting, my body overheating as if I'd been running hard through the desert for days.

I wasn't naïve enough to think the dream was not real on some level. Han was looking for us. I was his mate.

Which meant...

Fuck, Han can track us through me.

I hadn't even thought of that until now, but we

were connected. That's what had been tickling at the back of my head. We were fated mates.

Again, it only pointed out that when I'd been missing, he could have found me at any time. Gods above, I was a fool for thinking that a mate bond could be anything but a fucking weight around my neck.

I looked across at Soleil as Denna swiftly spoke my words about the mate bond, and Han tracking me.

Soleil's eyes crinkled with worry. "What, like he put some sort of tracer on your phone? How can he find you?"

I shook my head and spun on my seat. *I'm his mate. Mates have bonds. It allows them to find each other. Or at least get the general direction and distance.*

Soleil grinned. "That's amazing! I would have loved to have that with Eric. He...he was the one...he died last week."

Bebe choked. "Are you insane? That means she is leading him straight to you! Straight to us!"

Soleil waved a hand. "Yeah, but it also means Cin should be able to tell where Han is, right? How far back is he? How much time do we have?"

Smart girl, she was right. I squinted my eyes and carefully felt for the mate bond. Because we weren't totally tied together—aka we hadn't fucked—it wasn't as clear as it would have been otherwise.

But there was a foggy sensation of him behind us, to the south. *I think still a long way off. It's not clear, which means it won't be clear for him either. He'll have a general sense. North, south, east, west. That sort of thing.*

"There, see? It's not that bad. And even helpful." Soleil grinned across at me. Her sunny disposition matched her name. She took up singing again, and Bebe climbed over the seat to sit next to me.

"Denna, do not translate this, I don't want Soleil to know," Bebe said.

Denna gave a quick nod and a tiny thumbs up. She clung to the edge of the seat, staring out the front window from her position in the back seat.

What is it?

"This feels like a set up," Bebe said softly. "I can't shake the feeling that we might be about to walk into a trap. Which I know isn't a big deal because you're ready to die, but I think for Soleil and me and Denna, we need to be careful."

Her words stung a little. Okay, a lot. *I'm not ready to die, Bebe. I'm not. I'm trying to do what I can to help her. Then you and Denna can stay with her. Have something of a life.* I shook my head and veered away from the I'm-about-to-die part. *Grant wouldn't send us into a trap, and no one else knows where we're headed. There's no way that they would have a clue that we're going to see Theodore. We're driving up the coast, headed north. That's all that Han can tell from me.* I looked down at her, but she wasn't looking at me. She was staring at Soleil. *What is it really?*

Bebe glanced quickly over her shoulder at Soleil. "I can't put my paw on it. I feel like she's just *too* happy. Like...how is she this happy when she's been hunted for the last year of her life? Her best friend killed by Han? Something is off to me. Especially since she gave you the bracelets. Like shouldn't she be sweating, at least a little? I am. Denna is. You're calm as a giant cucumber, but you've accepted your death is coming."

I frowned as best I could as a golden and thought for a minute. *I'm not disregarding what you're saying. You have good instincts. I think we just have to keep an eye on her. If she's not stable—which is what I think you are trying to say—then that's even more reason to look out for her. She needs us, Bebe. Maybe more than we need her at this point. Maybe she's like me, and she's accepted that she's going to die at some point.*

Bebe sighed. "And you want to protect her."

I screwed up my face. *She reminds me of my little sister. I couldn't save Meghan. Maybe I can help Soleil make it through this.*

Bebe said nothing else, just curled up next to me and went to sleep. Even so, I felt her worry clearly.

Soleil stopped twice for burgers, and I stuffed myself to the point of being ill—nearly. Even so, I knew it would be just enough to keep me going through the next shift from four to two.

We hit Portland with only two hours to go until dark, Soleil working on her falsetto as she sang along with Celine and Whitney.

"Okay, so do we keep driving out to this middle-of-nowhere place?" Soleil asked. We'd pulled off near a park, and we were all out stretching our legs, except for Denna, who'd stayed in the car, hunched under a blanket.

Denna could handle sunlight to a degree, but she didn't like it. Made her feel gross, which was why she'd stayed under her blanket for most of the drive, or tucked way down in the foot area of the back seat.

I nodded. Without Denna to translate, the best we could do was a yes and no back and forth.

"And when we get there, you're going to deal with the vampire, I'll stay in the car?"

Another nod.

She dry washed her hands, over and over, the skin around her eyes tight, and not nearly as happy as she'd been earlier. "What happens if Han shows up? Shoot, you can't answer that. If Han shows up, should I come in the house?"

Shit. Yeah. I nodded.

"Same thing if Havoc shows up?"

Bebe snorted. "She's going to kill you with a thousand questions. All of which are speculative, and you have no way of knowing what'll be necessary in the moment—"

She's scared, Bebe. Maybe her happiness earlier was just a cover. I nodded for a third time to Soleil as she kept on asking me about various scenarios.

Bebe shook her head. "But you can't possibly have all the answers. She must know that."

I shrugged at Bebe and Soleil nodded. I must have inadvertently answered another question. Turning at the far end of the field, I started back toward the car. Saw a man standing near the trunk ball cap pulled low. Shoulders hunched. Worse than that was the whiff of his scent I caught on the breeze.

Werewolf.

25

TWICE CURSED

S *hit. Bebe. You see that guy? He's a werewolf. I'm* *sure of it.*

"Bad guy?"

Wasn't that the question of the day. I narrowed my eyes and caught a whiff of ogre beer. Fuck me, how had my half-brothers found me so quickly?

And where were the rest of them?

Go with Soleil, to the benches on the other side of the park. Just go and sit.

"And what are *you* going to do?" Bebe tried to block me, but I stepped over her. "Seriously?"

Go. He's looking at us.

I trotted forward as Bebe bounced up into Soleil's arms and patted her face away from the car.

As I drew closer to Richard, my hackles began to lift. Look at me go, getting tough as a golden. The whiff of ogre beer got stronger as I approached him, and he swayed slightly on his feet. Did he even realize who I was? I was banking on no. Praying for it.

I reached the front of the car and bared my teeth at him, forcing my lips to pull up.

"Easy, dog. Just wondering what I'm smelling in here." There was a drunken drawl to his words as he put his hand on the car to peer in the back. "Smells like dog, but also something nasty. Something dead. Something about to be real dead."

I snapped my teeth at him, and he raised a hand to me. I flinched and stepped back, cringing from him. Old habits were hard to fight, even here.

"Fucking mutt. Protecting something, are you?"

Denna, he's going to hurt you. Get out of there!

Denna scrambled out of the window on the far side, blanket wrapped around her spindly body as she ran for the cover of the trees and bush. Richard started after her. "Fun times. Killing ghouls is always good."

I didn't even think about it, I just launched myself at him, the need to protect overriding my fear. Sinking my teeth into his calf, I yanked him sideways, pulling him off balance and down to one knee.

"Fucking dog!"

His other foot swung toward me, and I managed

to duck so that the full impact of the blow skimmed off my side. I kept on yanking him backward, biting down as hard as I could. His blood was hot as I tore a chunk of flesh off. How long had I wished I could beat the shit out of one of my brothers? Too long.

I might have been enjoying this more than I should have.

His howl of pain was immediate, and I let go and took off, knowing he'd follow me.

Denna, get Soleil back to the car and get out of here. I'll meet you on the road to Theodore's.

I could only hope that Bebe or Denna could hear me. I wasn't sure.

Richard's heavy breathing and thumping footsteps were right behind me, and I let him *just* keep up as I ran across the field and straight for the bushes on the far side. If I could cut through, then I'd be able to—

Shipley stood in my way, his eyes hard, though there was a tremor in his cheek. He was the softest of my three brothers. The one I'd once mistaken for my friend. "You dumb bitch, you didn't think you could get away, did you? You didn't think Mom wouldn't have a way to find you? Kieran is going to wreck you now for going to that other wolf."

Was he sorry? He almost sounded it.

Yeah, I *did* think I'd get away, and fuck Juniper and her fucking games. I bared my teeth at him the same way I'd done to Richard. I couldn't beat them both, certainly not as a golden, and if they were here, Kieran wouldn't be far, which meant Meg was around too. I spun and ran to my right, out toward the road. I mean, I had nothing to lose at that point, other than my life, and that was rapidly coming to an end.

I burst out of the bushes as the rental car drove toward me. Bebe, hanging halfway out the window, saw me and screeched to high heavens. A moment later I was leaping into the car, and Soleil was taking off.

I climbed over the back seat, Denna helping me.

"What happened?"

My brothers apparently have a way to track me too. I'm a fucking nightmare. At this rate, I might be more help if I go somewhere else. Away from you three.

All three were shaking their heads before I was even finished speaking.

"No, we can't do that!" Soleil said. "We're a team!"

"What she said," Bebe added. "We aren't splitting up now."

My brothers are as bad or worse than Han. I don't know him well enough to know for sure. But I know what Richard, Ship, and Kieran are capable of, and they won't stop at hurting me. Dick was going to go hurt Denna just because she was near me. No other reason.

Silence met my 'words' as Denna spoke them.

Bebe scrunched her face up. "What about the journal? And the vampire?"

"What about me?" Soleil whispered. "I thought... we were going to find out what Han wants with me."

I blinked and the light around us dimmed. Maybe it was just clouds going over the last of the sun, but either way, my body started to shift to two legs. It was quicker than last time but still brutal.

Sweaty and exhausted, I managed to pull Denna's blanket up and around my shoulders. She patted me on the head.

The thing was, my brothers weren't familiar with vampires, our pack didn't have any near us as far as I knew. So, continuing to Theodore *might* work in our favor. If the vampire was big, bad, and mean enough, maybe we could convince him to kill a few werewolves?

Though how we'd keep him from killing us... that's where we were banking on Grant's connection.

Okay, we'll keep on going to Theodore. But as soon as we have answers for you, Soleil, I will go on without you, and take Han and my brothers away. Understand?

Soleil let out a shuddering sob. "I don't like this. I don't like it at all."

I took her hand and gave it a squeeze, then wrote quickly. *You'll have information. You'll have Denna and Bebe. You can take out the rest of my money and not worry about Havoc providing for you. And I'll be drawing all the monsters away from you. You three will have a solid day's head start.*

Her lower lip trembled and she brushed away her tears. "Where will we go?"

"I could take her back to Grant," Denna said. "He likes playing the white knight."

It wasn't a terrible idea. *Yes, take her to Grant. He's a good one. He'll be kind to her. Maybe he will be able to figure out what to do next.*

"I'm coming with you," Bebe said shaking her head. "Come hell or high water, I'm sticking it out. We started out in that shelter together, on the cusp of death, I'm seeing you through this."

I scooped her up and hugged her tight. *I wish we'd met years ago, Bebe.*

She sniffed. "Me too, girlfriend, me too."

Soleil navigated the roads we were on easily, using the map from the car dashboard. "I had to learn how to use maps. Phones can be traced, as you pointed out."

Her words were...odd. Bebe shot a look at me and I nodded.

I *had* pointed that out, but she'd seemed to be unaware of the possibility when she was talking to Havoc. Maybe because she trusted him?

Bebe whispered to me. "See? That's what I mean. Happy weird. Now she knows maps because phones can be traced, but you told her that?"

Agreed, it's odd for sure, but it doesn't mean that she's doing anything wrong. I like her.

"So do I. But people do weird, dangerous things when their lives are on the line. Maybe she's breaking under the pressure?"

That makes sense. Even so...she'd learned to use maps...but she'd still been using her phone? Super happy when lives were so close to being lost? Trusting Havoc?

I didn't have a lot of time to wonder about those connections.

Less than twenty minutes later, we were rolling down a tree-lined drive, the ruts in the road bouncing us hard in our seats and testing the resilience of the rental car. This was the last turn off the main road, and we'd nearly missed it, the turn was so covered by bush and trees.

"Wheeee!" Denna yelled as she bounced with the bumps.

I had pulled on my shorts and tank top once more, but had also stayed wrapped in my blanket. I was cold, and my ribs were even more prominent than the night before. My belly was so empty it hurt. To make it through, I was going to have to find a steakhouse and finish off half a cow if I wanted to get through my last couple of shifts.

"Maybe the vampire was a prince?" Bebe offered. "You know, like olden times?"

Denna didn't translate, and I realized she'd been staying quiet since the discussion about Soleil.

Not a terrible idea. Fucking a vampire? I wondered if that ever ended well for the fuckee, aka me in this situation.

Soleil slowed the car as we pulled up to a massive house, four stories tall, that looked like it would collapse in a stiff breeze. The structure tilted madly to the left, as if a giant had given it a shove but hadn't quite finished the job. Shakes were missing off the cedar lined roof, windows were cracked and so dirty it would be difficult to see anyone at all inside, even with lights on. Which wasn't exactly happening anyway.

Around us, the world was incredibly dark, no moon or stars peeked through the heavy canopy of trees. No light came from the dilapidated structure. No, that wasn't quite true. I pointed to the top window of a turret. A single candle burned up there, flickering. Looking like a hand beckoning us in.

"Do all vampires live like this?" Soleil whispered.

"No," Denna said. "Grant has a really nice house with a wraparound deck and a pond in the back. And nice gardens. This looks like no one even lives here. Except for that candle."

I stepped out of the car first, bare feet on the fallen leaves that were strewn everywhere. I walked forward, Havoc's journal clutched in one hand. Bebe trotted along with me. I looked over my shoulder. Denna hadn't moved and neither had Soleil. I motioned for them to stay where they were.

But they took a few steps anyway.

"This feels like the start of a B-grade horror flick," Soleil whispered from behind us.

"You've been living that B-grade horror flick for a while," Bebe muttered.

Denna didn't translate, which was probably for the best.

I navigated my way up the half-rotten stairs to the front door and knocked. The sound reverberated through the air, and the door slowly opened.

"Not creepy at all," Denna said. "And that's coming from me. The queen of creep."

"ENTER," a voice boomed out of the open door-way. "OR FUCK OFF WITH YOU."

Grumpy vampire indeed. I stepped across the threshold first, Bebe entering with me. Soleil and Denna hesitated and, as such, they were shut out when the door slammed and locked behind us, apparently forgetting that they were supposed to stay in the car.

"Oh shit!" Bebe screeched as she leapt straight up and into my arms. I caught her and held her in the crook of one arm.

Tell them to hide if anyone comes.

Bebe yelled her orders, but there was no

response. Maybe they couldn't hear us through the walls? That was possible.

I thought for a minute that I heard the car start, but that was probably just my anxiety kicking in. Being left in the forest, trapped without a ride to escape at high speed was not my idea of a fun night.

I trust Grant. He wouldn't put me in danger. I said that as much to remind myself as to soothe a shaking Bebe.

I took one step, then another, as my eyes adjusted to the dim space. There was some light inside, but it came from flickering old bulbs that were either nearly dead or incredibly low wattage.

I had no way of calling out to Theodore, so I drew a deep breath and followed the strongest scent lines of a vampire. Blood, old linens, some sort of cologne, a hint of death. That was our guy. The smell took me through the house, to a set of stairs that led up toward that turret I'd seen from outside, where the candle had flickered. Hurrying, I jogged up the stairs while Bebe shivered under my one arm.

"This is awful. It smells like death."

I know. In and out. We'll get the information, pay him what he wants, and get us all out of here.

Oh, how foolish the unwary are; I had no idea what I was truly getting into.

The stairs led to a second floor, then a third. That was where the scent of Theodore—assuming he was the only vampire present—was the strongest. I walked silently across the plush but filthy carpet to a door that was ajar. I could see the candle in the window.

"I can hear your heartbeat. Come in," Theodore said, his voice thick with an accent reminiscent of Han and Havoc. "I am bored. Entertain me."

Hope flared. This had to work. If we understood the game that the brothers were playing, it would help us beat them at it. Surely that in itself would prove a form of entertainment. Games were fun, right?

I pushed the door open and stepped into a room that was nothing like the rest of the house. Stark white walls, white painted floor covered with thick cream-colored rugs, and a massive bed—also all in shades of white and cream, from the draperies around the four posters to the frame itself.

Looking up, I saw the ceiling was painted black, with tiny lights embedded in it so it looked like the night sky. I could pick out a few constellations that were set into the plaster, glowing with a low light all their own.

"You like it? I miss my homeland, and this space reminds me of the winter and the endless nights in that season." A man stepped out of seemingly nowhere. He was dressed in white as well. Long white-blond hair floated around a pale face with nearly white eyes. Yup, all sorts of creepy-as-fuck going on here. If I were to age him, I'd say early twenties, like Grant. But of course, he wasn't in his early twenties, no matter how soft his face looked.

"The weirdness continues," Bebe whispered from under my arm. "Does he realize this is the worst possible color for a vampire to be infatuated with? Take my money, Tide, I'm going to need some stocks."

His pale eyes shot to Bebe. "A talking cat? Unusual, but not unheard of. Cursed, I suppose? Unless it is a terribly bad reincarnation. And you? Who are you?"

He was being very polite for such a supposed grumpy fuck, especially since we'd essentially barged in. But Grant had said he was unpredictable.

Let's see if he could hear my 'voice.'

My name is Cin. I lost my voice in a gamble to not be stuck as a golden retriever. But the shifts are slowly killing me. And the curse has now sped up and I'll be dead by tomorrow at sunset. Give or take a few minutes. Unless you are a prince by chance?

His dusty pale eyebrows slowly climbed to his hairline. "Grant said you were interesting. What is it that you need help with, interesting one? And no, I am not a prince. Not even a lordling."

Bebe let out a sad mew, and I felt that tiny last hope blow out like that candle in the window.

I held out the small journal, diving right into the real reason we'd come to him. *This could hold the key to understanding why a friend is being hunted by a pair of Norse boys. Assholes, both of them. Werewolves, but... maybe not?* I finally said that bit that I'd been mulling over. *They are very old, so maybe they are part vampire?*

"Good, I'm glad you've finally put them in the same category—deuces of assholeness." Bebe squirmed, and I shifted her around so that I cradled her in both arms as Theodore stepped closer, gliding like he was on skates and not in pristine white shoes, as he took the journal.

He fanned it open, his eyes softening. "Ah, it has been a long time since I've seen my mother tongue written like this. Beautiful script work. You two have brought me more entertainment than I have had in years. Lovely."

I stood quietly. Something tugged at my mind, and I turned inward. What was that....

Fuck. Han, that was what I was feeling. He was drawing closer, catching up to us.

We don't have much time. One of the Norse boys is closing in.

Theodore smiled, showing off his fangs. "*You* don't have time, that may be true. I, on the other hand, have all the time in the world. Your two friends that were outside, you are worried about them? You shouldn't be. They are gone."

The ones who would hurt them are getting closer. Wait, what? What do you mean they're gone? I stared at him. That couldn't be right.

He bobbed his head and flicked through the pages of the journal as if I hadn't just asked a rather important question. "This is...unexpected. Very, very interesting. I would like to keep this, as payment. Once I have given you what you need from it."

That's fine, but what do you mean my friends are gone? Like...are they hiding?

Bebe strained in my arms. "What? Denna and Soleil have left?"

He ignored me and flipped through the book like a speed demon. "Quite the situation, from what I can see. The goal, of course, is to kill the sun and the moon. But...that would bring about the end. There can be a transfer to keep it from happening." He began to pace the room, his finger tracing the pages as he flicked through them even faster. "A transfer, yes. So, whoever the sun is, she can transfer what she has that makes her special to another. On her dying breath. Very interesting. Such a twist. But also, if given as a gift? That's interesting. And yes, your two friends are gone. They left as soon as the door shut."

Soleil's story about her friend dying...I looked down at Bebe. Her chartreuse eyes were wide with the same horror I was sure was in mine. I looked down at the bracelet on my left hand. Three sets of beads winked at me. Mocking. A gift from Soleil. Had she known?

She said her friend was killed, but she held her in her arms as she died and then—

"And then she became the target?" Theodore nodded. "Yes, that fits. It does not say why this is happening, or what the end goal is, but I could likely guess with…" He glanced down and tilted his head. "…a bit more…fascinating…oh, now that's unexpected…." He flicked a few more pages. A boom on a lower floor in the house shook the structure, but Theodore didn't seem to be overly bothered. He was engrossed in the little journal.

I'm going to go check on that. In case it's the bad guys. And also because I needed a word with Bebe.

He waved a hand at me. "Fine, whatever, do as you must."

Bebe tucked tight under my arm as I headed back out into the main portion of the house.

Bebe, you were right not to trust Soleil. I think she set me up. I'm wearing these bracelets. What do you want to bet these were what marked her for Han? For Havoc? She left as soon as we got here. Like she knew they wouldn't follow.

"Oh my God, oh my God, oh my God!" Bebe danced around at my feet. "Are you serious?"

Another boom on the door. The wood crackled

and bent but didn't give. *So now they are hunting me for real, I think. I'm...the new mark.*

"But...what about the curse? Does that mean you aren't going to die?" Bebe whispered.

Another boom.

Looking over the railing, I smelled the fresh outside air before I saw the now-open door and the huge figure blocking the little light that the night gave. All thoughts of the curse fled.

From the shadows, dark eyes, one slashed with silver stared up at me, scar tightening as Havoc let out a low growl that went straight through me, right to my pussy, and I do not mean Bebe.

He put a hand to the door and slowly shut it. As if that mattered now.

As long as he didn't howl, I would be fine. That's what I told myself. Just. Don't. Howl.

He tipped his head back and opened his mouth.

Well, fuck.

26

GOOD VIBRATIONS, THANK YOU VERY MUCH

With all the energy I had, I threw my voice. Only, it didn't throw.

"No, don't howl! My brothers aren't far, and Han isn't far either!" I clapped my hands over my mouth. I'd spoken. How?

The best I got from Havoc, even with me shouting at him, was a pause, a mere hesitation.

"You gotta shut his mouth!" Bebe yelled, but I was already running full tilt down the stairs, using the railing to propel myself along faster.

Havoc spun to face me as I all but threw myself at him, slapping my hand over his mouth.

"You'll get Soleil killed, you idiot!" She had to still be close, and if Han didn't know yet that the mark had been exchanged, then neither would he.

He glared at me and whipped his head to the

side. "If anyone gets her killed, it will be you! Han can track you. You're the fool, not me!"

"I know that!" I snapped at him. "We're using it to our advantage. I'm going another direction after this!" Gods. The glory that was my voice, even as a whisper, was amazing. Perfect. I could truly give him the tongue lashing he deserved.

Not that kind, head out of the gutter, my friends.

He tipped his head again, and I scrambled to keep my hand over his stupid, stubborn face.

Toasted fucks. I tried to slap my hand across his mouth, but he grabbed my wrist, forcing my fingers away from his lips.

"Don't make me resort to measures we will both regret!" I glared at him, fighting to get my hands free so I could choke the life out of him.

The sound of his howl bubbled up his throat, leaving me with no choice.

I hopped up, wrapped my legs around his waist and locked my arms around his neck in a choke-hold. Yeah, I know what you all thought I was going to do.

He snarled and snaked a hand between us, up through the hold, and flung one of my arms off. I wasn't giving up. "Soleil is gone already. She left to put space between me and her because we knew Han would come after me. I'm buying her time, and you're going to bring them down on us!" I whisper-hissed at him at a rapid pace. Still somewhat trying to stay quiet.

"You don't understand anything!" he growled.

My body reacted like a damn tuning fork to the deep rumble. I gritted my teeth and fought to get another hold on him, slapping my hand across his face while alternately trying to choke the life out of him. It wasn't easy, but a girl's gotta do, what a girl's gotta do.

We spun around the main floor like a couple of drunken dancers, wobbling left and right.

Without warning, Havoc stumbled and went to one knee. Bebe shot out from under him, laughing. "Got him this time! Fucker is bleeding now!"

I wasn't sure that was true, but I used the moment of unbalance, flipping us both over so that he was on his back, and I was across his chest, pressing my forearm to his throat.

His eyes flicked to me. "How long do you think to hold me here?"

"Just long enough that your brain will kick in and you'll hear me. Soleil is gone. Han is going to chase me, and I'm going to lead him away. You'll have until tomorrow at sunset."

The intensity of his gaze unnerved me, but I couldn't look away. My wolf wouldn't allow it—she was pissed enough that the golden in me let her lead.

"Why tomorrow at sunset? Why not lead him on for weeks?"

"None of your business," I said at the same time Bebe said, "The curse will kill her. She's dead tomorrow. Unless you happen to know a prince that can give her a royal fucking?"

I growled at her, and he responded as if I were growling at him.

"Stop that," he said, his voice rough and gravelly, "and drop your damn gaze."

"You first." Man, I was LOVING having my voice back. Maybe this was because I was on my last twenty-four hours?

I don't know how it happened, except I was distracted by my thoughts, but in a blink I was suddenly the one on my back, his weight crushing me, his one hand pinning both of mine above my head. I tried to get a knee between us, but I was flattened to the floorboards.

"Stay." He growled the single word before another howl ripped out of him.

Yup, same howl as before. Same effect—no, worse effect than before.

My entire world narrowed to the sound and feel of the reverberations rippling through me, being in direct contact with him only heightened every sensation. This close, I couldn't even think to stop the oncoming orgasm, the deep rumble of his howl thrumming at my center like a harpist plucking strings. I tried to stop it, honest. I tried to think about anything but the weight of his body, the delicious smell of his skin, the vibrations of his howl cutting through any control that I had left, wave after wave, growing in pressure and intensity.

This was not the place. Or the time.

Yet, there I was, my body shaking, climbing that mountain that I hadn't found in, I don't even want to guess how long it had been.

I knew he was looking down at me. The howl had ended, but I couldn't stop this. Panting, I shook my head. "Stop it."

"Stop what?" His voice, it felt like he was right at the sensitive spot under the lobe of my ear. My nipples were pebbled against my thin shirt as I whimpered, writhing to get away.

He adjusted his weight, which slid his body up mine, and that meant his cock was suddenly pressing against my already throbbing clit through our clothes. I had a split second to wonder if he even knew he had a hard-on.

Then it was all over for me. I arched back, pressing my hips up and into that perfect hardness —would have screamed as the orgasm took me but I could barely breathe, panting and moaning as my big O shook me to the core, rippling out in wave after wave that all I could do was hang on. He growled in my ear, which only sent further vibrations straight to my pussy. Goddess of the moon, I hated that he could do this to me.

Worse, as I came out of the fog that was an orgasm of epic proportions—considering we both had clothes on—Havoc was still on top of me. Staring at me. Like I'd sprouted another set of eyes.

"What the fuck was that?"

Bebe answered for me. "That would be an orgasm, guessing you don't give the girls those on a regular basis?"

"Get off me! Get off me now!" Yup, there was panic in my voice. Surprising the shit out of me, he lifted himself off and slid back to a crouch, dark eyes watching me closely. Bebe ran to my side, her head pushing against my knuckles.

"You okay? 'Cause it looked to me like you just came hard underneath that asshole. Like, epically."

Leave it to her to cut to the chase.

I nodded and wobbled to my bare feet. A snap of fingers turned me around. Theodore stood at the top of the stairs.

"You want the short version of what's happening?" he asked. "It'll cost you less."

I nodded.

"Tell her nothing, blood sucker, or you'll be next on the platter."

Theodore laughed. "It's simple. If your friend

who is named for the sun dies, the entire world falls into mass destruction, until everyone is dead. The Norse, we like to call it Ragnarok."

That was not what I'd been expecting. I mean, to be fair, the furthest I'd gotten with the 'what's happening, why is Soleil so important?' question had something to do with bloodlines. Bloodlines were super important to werewolves—hence my own predicament with my family. I'd wrongly assumed that Soleil was in the same kind of boat. That the boys were thinking she'd make perfect little babies. Not everyone who had good bloodlines for breeding were already werewolves.

I did a slow turn to look at Havoc.

"If she dies..." I whispered.

"The world as we know it dies. She is the last stone between life and death." His jaw was tight as he glared at me, then he whipped his head around. "My pack has found her."

I took a wobbling step, my brain still mushy from the orgasm. "Wait, you don't understand, things have changed—"

"You are a menace. You have ties to Han. And your brothers are still hunting you. Soleil does not need a friend like you."

He spun away from me and strode out the door, slamming it behind him before I could tell him about the bracelets. That maybe I was the one Han and him were hunting now.

All I could do was stand there and stare after him.

"Holy shit, did you see the hard-on he had for you? Like...girl, if he wasn't so damn scary I'd tell you to take him for a ride!" Bebe patted my bare legs. "What are we going to do?"

It was a good question. I didn't know the answer. "Theodore, what do I owe you? Is the book enough?"

Theodore tipped his head. "Oh, watching you orgasm under that lovely piece of a man, that was an added bonus. I'll even give you some more information for the scene. That bracelet there?" He pointed at my wrist and then quickly showed me a page in the book that looked a hell of a lot like two bracelets. "I'm quite sure it has seven beads on each strand?"

I looked down at the item wrapping my wrist and counted quickly. "Yes. I think that...this has me marked now, doesn't it?"

He gave me a sad nod. "That woman is not your friend. She gifted you the curse that she has been carrying. You, my new young, foolish friend, have the future of the world on your shoulders."

27

TALK ABOUT BEING FUCKED

I sat there on the bottom step of the stairs in a shitty, rundown house, as Theodore the vampire wandered back up to his turret room and shut the door, muttering in Norse excitedly as he went through the book.

Bebe sat next to me and batted her paw at the bracelets. "Well, this is a bit of a turn."

I mimicked her and brushed a finger across them. "Bebe, I'm going to die tomorrow. So if this is for real...we have another problem." I trailed off because my heart and mind were racing. If it was for real, then the whole world would go down in flames with me.

Did I care?

I looked at my friend, her yellow-green eyes were wide.

"Well, I suppose that's one way to go out with a bang," she said softly. "Not like living as a cat for the rest of my life was going to be a long life. I think...I'm good with it. Maybe we can get ice cream?"

I smiled down at her, my lips a little wobbly. "Yeah, we can get ice cream. I'd like to get some steak too. A really good cut."

Weren't people who were in charge of saving the world supposed to give a shit about it?

Like weren't all the heroes and heroines in books fighting for the people they loved, for their family?

If my family was on fire, I wouldn't waste a spit trying to put any of them out. Even Meghan had turned on me. I didn't even have a mate worth fighting for.

I sucked in a sharp breath, fighting back the tears that threatened.

"We'll be like Thelma and Louise!" Bebe yelled suddenly. "I like this. Ice cream...and maybe we can catch a strip show?"

I laughed through the ache in my chest. "Why not?"

A reverberation down my spine had me shivering. Han was getting closer. Which meant we needed to move, but I found myself hesitating. Did it matter if I died tonight, or tomorrow?

It did to Bebe and that was enough for me. "We should get going. If we can get back to Portland, we can totally get ice cream. I'm sure we can find some naked men too."

I rubbed the one bracelet as I stood, the most recent one added to Soleil's collection. The one she'd claimed a woman named Gina had given her. A bit of dirt fell off it, revealing a golden bead. I frowned and rubbed the next bead. Black. Then gold. Then black. The bracelet that held my voice, the one that the warlock had taken from me and then...had he given it to Soleil? Why?

Someone cleared their throat in front of me. I looked up. The warlock in question stood leaning against the wall, boots crossed in front of him. "This was not how I planned for things to go, you know. Like, really, things went sideways."

"Oh my god," Bebe whispered. "That's him. That's the guy I...hey, can you hear me? I want my two legs back!"

He glanced at Bebe. "I can hear you, but I need to talk to Cin."

I glared at him. "What, setting me up to die wasn't enough, so you decided I should take the whole world with me?"

"Well, everyone dies," he pushed off the wall, his dark green cloak floating out behind him. "That's a given. But I wasn't expecting Havoc would throw you under the bus the way he did. Unfortunate. You were supposed to teach Han to love, and then he would want to save this world. And then I would be the hero. That was the plan."

I stood up and strode over to him. "You can change this. Make it better. Take the fucking curse off!" Then the rest of his words sunk in, and I glared at him. "Han is a fucking murdering bastard! How could you think that he'd learn to love? Or that I'd want to spend my life with a psycho?"

He spread his hands to the sides, palms up. "Very sorry on all counts. I can't take the curse off anymore, and yes, I know he's a murdering bastard. That's why I was trying to get through to him. Now. On to current business. You need to find a way not to die, or Ragnarok is going to start tomorrow at sundown. The world will be destroyed, people will be tortured and die horrible deaths. Blah, blah, blah. I lose my place in the world, and I don't get to be the hero, I'd be the zero. I don't want that."

I snorted. "And what makes you think I give a shit about anyone here, with the exception of a few friends? Have you met my family? If you're telling me that by tomorrow night, they're going to roast on a spit, I'm not really inclined to stop that."

Seeing as I was about to die anyway.

He winced as if I'd hit him. "Yes, well, I have. Quite a treat, all of them. Including, of course, your rapey sadistic brothers, who have now joined forces with your mate. Really, that was not in the plan, they only feed each other's animosities. I don't understand why it's all going topsy-turvy on me? Truly, I had this all laid out."

My stomach tumbled into the pit of my body so fast I swayed. Han and Kieran working together? "Well, that does it. I'll just run until tomorrow and then die. Bebe, let's go."

The warlock gave a sad smile, stopping me. "If you do that, then Han wins."

I blinked at him. "What?"

A sigh from him, then he walked further into the house, beckoning me to follow. "Han wins. When Ragnarok begins, Han will become a god. Little g of course. But still a god. Havoc will perish a final death, as will I, and the world will be remade with Han's help."

I die.

Han wins.

Bebe patted my leg. "Would revenge be enough of a reason to live? Because I gotta be honest. The idea of Han winning at anything really grabs my tail and yanks it."

Was revenge enough of a reason to fight to live? If love didn't truly exist the way I'd believed as a child, was revenge a strong enough motivator?

The warlock came around in front of me, holding his hands out to me like we were going to dance.

"Here's the thing, you need a prince to break this curse I set on you, we all know this. I happen to know a prince. You don't like him much, but if I tell him he has to do it, he'll do it."

"Do. What." I stared at the warlock through narrowed eyes. He squirmed and looked somewhat abashed.

"Well, of course I thought that you and Han would be mating, so when I told you a prince would break the spell, what I really meant was that you would need to be um...intimate with the prince. You did read the contract, right?" He flashed me a wicked smile that made my heart drop.

I just stared at him. Not that the fucking of the prince was a surprise, but that he knew one.

"And the prince?" I whispered the question, because if I didn't whisper it, I was going to start screaming at this lunatic. What had I done to deserve this? It all came back to Juniper.

Maybe revenge *was* enough to keep me alive, because the thought of strangling the life out of my mother with my bare hands was becoming more and more appealing. And I would need to live long enough to do that.

The pause was long.

"Well, Havoc of course. Both he and Han are of royal blood." He smiled. "I do realize that you and Havoc have a different kind of history. But if you don't want to die, and he most certainly does not want you to die because he also does not want Han to win, then the most logical explanation is that you are going to have to—"

"Fuck him," Bebe breathed out. "Oh man. Oh man. I don't know, Cin. I don't know if I like this at all. He choked you! Even if he does have a huge—"

The base of my spine tingled hot, like an ember was glowing there, growing hotter by the second. "Han's close. We have to move either way." I pointed a finger at the warlock. "You are going to help me get out of this place. Right now."

He smiled. "Of course, that's why I'm here. To take you to Havoc."

With a clap of his hands, the air filled with green streaks of light that wrapped around me, tightening like vines until I couldn't breathe.

"Bebe," I whispered her name.

"Oh, right, I'll bring her too," the warlock said.

The door to the house burst open, and Han strode in. "NO!"

He lurched toward me, reaching, but the magic swept us away as his fingers began to close over my wrist.

"Loki's ass!" he roared, and that was the last I heard from him as the world spun and danced around us. Upside down, I couldn't make heads or tails of what was going on.

I couldn't breathe, but I could feel Bebe under my right hand. Then the pressure on my ribs was gone, and I was standing upright. Upright in the middle of the fucking highway.

Horns blared, tires screeched, and an SUV spun to the right, narrowly missing me. I flung myself off the road as a semi went barreling through where I'd been standing only a second before. I hit the grass, rolled several times, and then sat up.

"What the actual fuck?" I screamed the words. But the only person to hear them was Bebe.

"I can't breathe, I can't!" She was screeching and obviously could breathe. "Why did I ever sleep with that asshole? Kill me if I ever look at another asshole like that and want to bang them again!"

I got to my feet and looked around. And just where the hell was Havoc supposed to be? And...did this...was I really going to have to make him...sleep with me? No, not sleep. Fuck.

I put a hand to my head.

"Bebe, what are the chances of us finding a prince at a strip club? Tell me they're good." I looked down at her as she cringed. People were getting out of their cars now, yelling. Freaking out.

"Probably the worst odds you could find, even if a guy was dressed as a prince," she said. "And just where is Havoc in all this? Didn't the magic guy say he was taking you to Havoc?"

Havoc had left with Soleil and his pack.

I looked around at the carnage of vehicles I'd caused. A car was on fire, smoke spilled out of it, spreading everywhere. People were screaming, crying. What in the name of every star above had that warlock been thinking? This was chaos!

Through the smoke, a figure walked toward me, moving like the predator he was.

I stood still, waiting for him. Dark eyes swept over my body. "How are you here?"

"Warlock. Havoc...Soleil gave me the bracelets."

He jerked as if I'd punched him in the balls. "What?"

Speak fast, girl, get it all out before you stall.

"Here's the thing. The curse that's on me? Part of it was that Han couldn't know that me, I mean the golden me, was his mate. You told him. Which put me on a countdown to my death."

I hadn't thought that would bother him, but he paled.

I rushed on. "I have until tomorrow night to break the curse, Havoc. Tomorrow at sundown. And honestly, really only until morning." Because I was not going to go looking for a princely dog to fuck me on four legs.

He closed his eyes. "How do you break the curse?"

"I didn't make the rules," I said. "The warlock did. He thought I'd be with Han and already—"

"How?"

Bebe saved the day. "She needs to get fucked by a prince, and the warlock said you'd do it to keep her alive and make sure Han doesn't win, because you are a royal. He said you wouldn't like it, but you'd do it to keep Han from winning."

Yup, that's how that conversation went.

"I don't like this either, Havoc. I didn't ask for any of this." I was shaking now. Not that it was terribly cold out, but *everything* rode on this conversation. Life. Death. The world.

I touched the beads on my wrist. "I could give these to someone else, I suppose."

"That only works if the person is genuine in their desire to help you, at the expense of their own life," he growled, his eyes opening as he stared at me. "You were willing to die for Soleil. It wouldn't have been a true exchange otherwise."

I gave him a nod. "I was."

His jaw ticked and then he was striding across the space between us. I didn't move. Couldn't breathe. It was as if that magic had curled around me again.

He moved fast, had his hand around my waist in a flash and jerked me close. I ended up with my hands flat against his chest, staring up into his face. His eyes were hard, and I couldn't read him. My eyes fell to his lips as he spoke.

"Then we'd better get to fucking, hadn't we?"

ALSO BY SHANNON MAYER

The Forty Proof Series

MIDLIFE BOUNTY HUNTER

MIDLIFE FAIRY HUNTER

MIDLIFE DEMON HUNTER

MIDLIFE GHOST HUNTER

MIDLIFE ZOMBIE HUNTER

MIDLIFE WITCH HUNTER

MIDLIFE MAGIC HUNTER

MIDLIFE SOUL HUNTER

MIDLIFE VAMPIRE HUNTER (2024)

The Alpha Territories

TAKEN BY FATE

HUNTED BY FATE

CLAIMED BY FATE

The Golden Wolf

GOLDEN

GLITTER

FOR A COMPLETE BOOK LIST VISIT

www.shannonmayer.com

DON'T MISS WHAT'S COMING NEXT

Want an Art Print of Chapter 16?
Submit proof of pre-order and I'll mail you one
(offer only valid until the release of Glitter)

BUY GLITTER NOW!

Sign up for a release day email from
www.shannonmayer.com

Need more shifters while you wait? Turn the page
for a preview of Witch's Reign.

WITCH'S REIGN

Chapter 1

The thing about giants is that while they *are* dumb as a bag of rocks, they're fast and mean, and don't like giving up on prey. Especially prey that is running flat out, prey who just stole a prized possession from them that they believed kept their power at its peak, prey that may or may not have flipped them off as it ran away.

I smiled to myself and dropped my hands. What could I say? The giants deserved at least a one-finger salute.

I bent low over my horse's neck, urging him to greater speed, even though the ground was rock hard, covered in a thin sheen of ice in some places, and bubbling toxic waste in others. No problem.

A pool spewed to my left and we veered to the right to avoid splash back from the stinking green fluid that could burn through flesh and bone if so much as a drop landed on us. I glanced over my shoulder, then let out a low growl at the big-ass creatures charging down the gorge after us.

Weighing in at five tons per giant, they literally thundered along behind, their feet slamming mini craters with each step.

"Nasty shit eaters," I grumbled, doing what I could to squash the fear. Really, it was nothing new. Steal the jewel, run from those we stole from. Simple, yet not really. The giants let out a cacophony of roars that made the hair on the back of my neck stand. The sound was like a wicked choir singing for our destruction.

"Zam, distract them!" Steve shouted from ahead of me, panic lacing his words.

I turned my attention to doing just that. Balder, my horse, could outrun Steve's bigger war horse, no problem, but I couldn't leave him behind. My job was to get the idiot, and the jewel he carried, back to the Stockyards—preferably in one piece.

I glanced back again at the giants. "Shit." I whispered the word and Balder tried to turn on the speed, picking up on the tension that raced through me, but the ice below us made traction for that kind of speed impossible and dangerous. If we fell, that would be bad, worse if we tumbled into one of the toxic pits. Even my shifter healing metabolism wouldn't save me then.

I held Balder back even as the giants closed in around us. He fought and shook his head, knowing as well as I that we were very much the prey of the day.

Seven giants drove us from behind, and that would have been bad enough. But the gorge we galloped through had fifty-foot-high sides blocking any easy escape. But wait, it got better.

On those walls were five more giants, two on the left, three on the right. They used their clawed toes and fingers as if they were enormous, maw-gaping spiders, leaping and working their way toward us on all fours, horizontal. As in sideways. Like gravity somehow no longer existed for the oversized dumbs that they were. Then again, they weren't so dumb that we'd been able to slip in and out without being noticed.

"Steve," I growled. He'd just had to try and get all the glory of the theft.

Now, though, I had work to do. I dropped the reins, giving Balder his head despite the danger of added speed. I needed both hands for dealing with our retreat. I reached for the weapon tucked behind my leg. An over-under shotgun with a grenade launcher, one of the few toys of my father's I still had. And one that I used sparingly. Coming by ammunition was not a small task.

"Please work," I whispered to the weapon. It was finicky at the best of times in perfect conditions. Of which we were not in, with the cold and ice frosting every damn thing around us.

I pulled my feet out of the stirrups and twisted so I sat backward in the saddle, facing the oncoming horde. Goddess of the desert and all she held holy, they were ugly creatures. You'd think they'd be just upsized versions of the average human. But not so much.

Some of them had two heads or multiple arms. Or two arms on one side, and no arms on the other. They all had disfigured faces thick with teeth, noses, and eyes. Like everything was just larger in terms of their senses to make up for their lack of brains, but nothing was really in the traditional place. Like a mouth on the forehead, eyes on the chin, and that sort of shit.

The giant in the middle was the queen, or what passed for their queen. She was the biggest of the brutes and had three tits that hung almost to her waist. As I watched, two of them swung so hard that they hit the giant next to her, knocking him backward onto his ass.

For once, I was grateful I hadn't been so blessed in the boob department. A smile twitched over my lips as I lifted the gun. "Steady, Balder, this is going to be loud."

I aimed for the wall to my right, tucked the butt of the gun against my shoulder as I tightened my legs on my horse, drew a breath and slowly let it out as I pulled the trigger for the grenade launcher.

It blew out with a roar that echoed through the canyon. Before it hit, I spun around to the front of the saddle and jammed the gun into its holster under my leg. Behind me, the explosion of the grenade hitting rocked the air, sending out a shock wave that rumbled through my back.

The reverberation continued through the stones and the ground under our feet. That shouldn't be happening. What the hell had gone wrong now? I had to dare a look back.

The air was filled with dust and shards of rock, and for just a moment, I thought we'd escaped the big assholes—check that, *I'd* gotten us clear of them. Steve, as always, was too busy saving himself to bother thinking about anyone else. I frowned as I stared in the direction we'd come. Something was off, my senses twitched and I turned to face the direction we were running.

The scrabble of rocks ahead of me was the only warning we had and Balder saved us both. A giant leapt off the side wall—how the fuck he'd gotten so far ahead in stealth mode was beyond me—and came at us with a wide mouth and three grasping hands.

Balder zigged to the right, turning on the speed, slipping only once as his iron shoes somehow miraculously took hold on the ice. The giant landed where we'd been only a second before, a three-fingered hand that would engulf us both snaking toward us, closing the gap Balder had created. I grabbed the shotgun, yanked it out and twisted around, shooting before I even sighted properly. I pulled the trigger and the gun bucked against my shoulder, unbalancing me. I hit the giant's middle finger, blowing the tip off. He roared and snapped his hand back but I knew it wouldn't stop him.

Basically, I'd just pissed him off and given him even more reason to come after me long beyond the edge of his territory.

Good fucking job, Zamira.

I straightened and tucked the gun away, looking for Steve.

His horse was a black bay and stood out against the browns of the gorge walls, which meant I should have spotted him right away.

"STEVE?" I yelled for him. Where was that camel's asshole anyway?

There was a low roll of laughter from behind me and my heart sank. I spun Balder around and he slid and slipped to a stop.

Behind us was the queen of the giants and at her feet were Steve and his horse. The horse—Batman by name—seemed stunned, but was still standing, if shaking like a leaf. One of the spiderlike giants grinned back at us, preening. They'd gotten ahead of me in the mess and snagged Steve.

The giant I'd just blown a hole in scurried back to his queen, whimpering and whining, holding up his bleeding finger. She grabbed it and shoved it in her mouth, biting the whole hand off. He howled as she chewed as if she'd gotten a wad of tobacco and then spit the mangled limb to the side.

Steve was alive, his eyes about as big as I'd ever seen them, and I'd seen him caught red-handed cheating on his wife. No small thing that was either. I suspected he'd preferred being caught by the giants than by his now ex-wife.

The queen held him up by one leg, dangling him as though she would bring him to her mouth and bite his head off. I sighed. I should probably let her do it as it would solve so many of my current gripes about life.

Steve's death would make my life a lot easier, yes, but what if she swallowed the jewel? Then I'd have to wait around and dig through her shit to get it. That possibility was not cool; I had no interest in digging through a literal giant pile of shit and body parts for a jewel the size of my fist.

The queen shook him from side to side, her tits jiggling with the movement. "You wanna wanna your mate back? You gimme gimme my jewel." She smiled—though I use that term loosely with the size of her teeth and the twist of her face and mouth. Blood trickled over her lower lip and she slid an overly thick tongue out to lap at it. I grimaced. Disgusting creatures. How the hell they'd found a jewel and understood it gave them power was beyond me. Perhaps it was the emperor's way of making a joke. He'd stolen all the jewels from my mentor, Ish a hundred years before and handed them out to others to make her weak. Giving a jewel to creatures like the giants in front of me was a slap in the face.

"He's not my mate. And no, I'd rather not have him back." I grinned up at her, knowing I was playing a dangerous, reckless game. But what was new about that?

Nothing. Reckless was my middle name. No, really it was. Zamira Reckless Wilson. That's what you get when your ex-marine dad gave you your name. My mother chose my first name, and that had been good enough for her.

The giant queen frowned and I reached slowly to the left side where I'd stashed one of the other things I'd taken from the giants' hoard.

Steve had grabbed the jewel, and I'd taken two

other items. A black jewel that was flashy as hell, and the flail with my family's crest etched into the wooden handle. The face of a lion in mid-roar, its mane a mass of hair, and eyes studded with tiny green emeralds. Coincidence that I should find it there, only a few hundred miles from my homeland? I think not. Anything with my family crest was rightfully mine, so I didn't consider it stealing, just taking back my birthright. The black jewel I'd taken, well, that was prep work for the next hunting trip for Ish. I was, if nothing else, prepared.

At least, that's what I liked to tell myself.

I let the flail slide through my hand until I was holding just the end of it, and the eyes of every giant followed the movement. A tingle started in my palm and rose along my arm, which I noticed, but ignored. So far so good. Lighter than any other weapon I had on me, I had no illusions about it. This weapon was not made for fighting; this show was to draw the giants to me—they were almost as bad as dragons when it came to guarding their treasures and what they believed was theirs. I swung it once, the two spiked balls hanging at the end of three-foot-long chains clicking, the chains holding them to the wood creating a nice patterned staccato of a rhythm. The tingle on my skin intensified.

"I have the jewel," I said. "So . . . what are you gonna gonna do about it?"

Steve groaned as the giant queen tightened her hold on him, lifting him as if to put him in her mouth. "I kill kill him. Eat eat him."

"He likes to be eaten. Don't you, Steve?" I laughed and he glared at me.

"Ish is going to hear about this," he yelled.

"Not if you're dead." I shrugged and turned Balder around with my legs, giving my horse silent cues. "No loss to me. He's a right bastard, that one. Nobody likes him back at home."

"Zam, don't leave me!" he howled. I lifted a hand, waving at him while I stared forward, my heart clambering up my throat. I didn't really want him to die. I just . . . didn't care like I had once if he lived. Bad spot for him to be, really. I'd trusted him at one time. I'd trusted so many people and they'd all shown me that trust was stupidity.

Trust would break your heart and get you killed all in one fell swoop.

I gave Balder a gentle nudge, urging him into a slow gallop. Fast enough that the giants would think I was running, not so fast that we used up everything Balder had left in his reserves. The sweat on his gray hide was still slick and he glistened in the light of the dying sun even in the cold of the northern desert. While he had amazing stamina, I knew we were pushing it if we had to go hard for very long.

This was a gamble and if I was wrong, I'd

sentenced Steve to death and lost the jewel we'd come so far to find. His death would be bad, the loss of the jewel . . . worse. The closest thing I had left to family was depending on us to get that jewel. I took a quick look under my arm like a jockey on the race-track. Steve was falling to the ground, dropped like the useless piece of shit he was. Perfect. One problem down, one more to deal with.

My jaw tightened with each stride of the horse beneath me. The rumble of heavy feet reached my ears as the giants once more gave chase. I leaned over Balder's neck. "Time to go, my friend."

He plunged forward and once more we streaked down the gorge, drawing the heaving mass of giants after us. They were slow to get going, like a boulder rolling downhill. But once they were moving they were fucking hard to stop just like that same big-ass boulder.

I dared a look back to see them gaining on us once more, but the giants were not what I was looking for. No, I was checking to see if Steve was still alive after his fall.

I squinted, finally picking him out in the distance beyond the tree-trunk legs that hammered their way toward us. His golden hair and eyes seemed to catch the dying light as he turned his face toward me. He stood next to his horse and lifted a hand in a salute, then flipped me off.

That was about right for our current working relationship.

Saving him, keeping him alive was part of my job —and I hadn't failed yet, nor did I plan to. I might have screwed up everything else in my life, but keeping Steve alive was not on that list. My pride alone would never let me just give up. The taste of failure was not something I needed to have coating my mouth.

I put my boot heels against Balder's ribs, giving him the ignition spark he needed to finally unleash the remaining portion of his speed. He gave a grunt and then leapt forward as if I'd cracked him with a riding crop, when in reality . . . he just loved to run. I held my breath as he picked up speed, taking off as if we'd been standing still.

The giants behind us roared, the fury coming through clear along with a waft of horrible rotting teeth and soured stomach acid. I scrunched my nose, wishing not for the first time that I didn't have such a strong sense of smell.

The gorge widened in front of us, branching off to the left which would take us home, and to the right which would take us to a dead end. I urged Balder to the right. The only way Steve was going to make it by them now and get the jewel back to Ish was if I kept the giants busy long enough for him to make a clean getaway.

"Good thing I did my homework," I muttered. I'd scouted the gorge the night before, knowing we would likely need a quick escape and knowing there was a chance we'd be forced to the dead end.

I blew out a slow breath and once more dropped the reins so I had my hands free. This was going to be tight, there was no other way to look at it other than as a Hail Mary. I grabbed the shotgun from its holster under my leg once more. I only had two grenades left in the launcher, and they would have to be enough if we were making it out of this alive. The thing was, death didn't scare me anymore. It hadn't for years, which made me perfect for hunting the jewels in some ways. But it also meant that whoever I was working with was constantly put in situations far more dangerous than they needed to be. I couldn't seem to help it. But maybe if I could trust the partner I worked with, that would be different. As it was, Steve proved again and again that trusting others was not a good idea. End of story.

I didn't turn all the way around in my saddle but instead held the gun out to the side and pulled the trigger, shooting straight at the wall to my right. Before the recoil had even completed, I twisted to the left and repeated the shot.

Balder's speed got us out of the explosions' ranges, but just barely. The blowback from the rock wall sent shards of stone slicing through the air. One cut across my cheek, opening the flesh like a razor blade, and Balder stumbled, hit somewhere on his back end by the feel of the change in his stride.

He began to slow, his smooth gallop turning into a lurching leap.

Shit, this was not good. I looked back.

The rock wall had come down on either side, blocking the giants. For the moment.

But already they pulled at the boulders, throwing them out of the way, screaming at me.

"Pulling pulling her head off."

"Eating eating her horse."

"Take take our jewel back."

"Spray spray her face."

That last one made me shudder. Far worse than the others, spray was a term used for a giant's mating so I didn't want to think too much about it. Not when I was in the middle of seeing if we were even going to survive this race to the end of a dead-end gorge.

I let Balder slow, feeling the limp start to really set in on his right hind leg. I hopped off and ran beside him. There was a gash over the thickest part of his rump, deep enough that it was bad, but not so bad that it wouldn't heal. Assuming we got out of here, that was.

"Just keep moving," I said. "Keep moving, Balder. That wall over there? It doesn't look like much, but there's a goat trail winding up. If we can get on it, we can get out of here. No problem, right? We've been in tighter spots. You remember the jewel we took from the murder of griffins? That was rougher. And the coven of witches in India, that was no small thing either."

He snorted as if he didn't believe me any more than I believed me. I hurried our pace and then suddenly we stood at the bottom of the "goat trail." I'm not sure I'd even call it that. When I'd seen it the night before it had looked bigger, wider somehow. The narrow twisting path was barely a foot wide, and in many spaces crumbled into nothing. A true switchback trail, it wove its way to the top of the fifty-foot cliff. The giants were fifty feet tall at least. Which meant we had to be all the way to the top before they got through the barrier I'd made.

Staring down at us from the top were several goats, brown and white with tiny nubs for horns. And then one of them grinned at me.

Not goats, or not only goats.

A satyr waved at me from the top.

Fucking hell, the last thing I needed was a bunch of randy goat men leaping around us. They liked to cause trouble just because they could. I grabbed at the necklace with the thick man's ring on it, the only true talisman I carried. We could do this, we had to.

I put one foot on the bottom of the path and from behind us there was a massive crack and a boom as if a rock had been split and tossed out of the way. I didn't look, I didn't need to. I could feel the rumble of the giants' feet as they pounded toward us.

This was going to be tight.

Chapter 2

Merlin leaned back and steepled his hands under his chin as he stared into the crystal ball. They'd been watching Steve and Zamira steal from the giants, watched now as Zamira fought for her life. He itched to help, but they had to see if the young woman would be able to save herself.

"Flora, what do you think?" He touched a finger to the glass of the ball and the image tightened on Zamira's face, the green eyes and swath of dark hair tipped in auburn as it swept around her.

His companion, a young voluptuous woman with stunning raven-black hair and bright green eyes, snorted at him in a most unladylike fashion. "You can't be serious about her? That . . . girl is barely a shapeshifter. She's a runt, Merlin. She has no power, so to speak; how exactly do you think she's going to bring down the western wall exactly? Not to mention that curse she's carrying. If *that* gets loose, there will be no helping her then."

He ran a hand over the spinning ball in front of them again. The girl was trying to push her horse up a trail that had very little footing. From the angle he looked, he could see the flash of fire in her eyes. "Reckless, determined. I like her."

"You would. We need someone who actually has a chance at the task at hand. Someone who could face the challenges and has the potential to survive. That other one, the one who has the jewel in hand would be better to help, I think." Flora leaned forward and tapped a finger on the sphere, changing the image to show the blond man and his horse, racing down the left branch of the gorge. "He has a strong sense of survival."

Merlin's eyebrows shot up. "You can't be serious? He's out for himself, he just left his partner there to deal with the giants on her own after she saved him." This turn of decisions was a surprise. Flora had been a champion of any underdog she could be in the past; now, though . . . it seemed that gaining back her youthful visage had made her a bit more ruthless.

"I know. But if we give him a reason to go after Maggi and her three guardians, then I think he could be persuaded." Flora leaned back, her green eyes thoughtful. "Why don't we each help our champion of choice?"

He sighed. This was the side of Flora he'd hoped was gone, but as it was, he would deal with it. She loved to win, at any cost. "A challenge then?" he asked.

She smiled, and there wasn't an ounce of malice in it, nothing but excitement which made it easier to accept that this was fun for her.

"Exactly. We need to see this through. You can't directly be involved, and I will hold myself back too. We can be like fairy godmothers to our chosen champions."

His lips turned up in a slow smile. That did sound like a bit of fun. After all, as serious as this was, he wouldn't turn down a challenge like that, especially if it got him something he'd wanted for a good period of time now—well, the last week if he was truly counting.

The bigger issue that Flora was unaware of concerned the emperor. The emperor was still alive and well and was one of the few people Merlin couldn't outright stop, which were two rather problematic points. The emperor was the reason he couldn't take care of the Ice Witch himself. The reason Merlin was trying to figure out this mess. He sighed.

If Flora knew about that side note, she'd be gone faster than a snowflake disappearing in the desert. He had to make her think this was nothing more than a silly game with only a hint of danger. Not enough to scare her, just enough to intrigue her.

"And if I win?" He leaned forward and caught the edge of one loose raven-colored lock off her shoulder and wound it around a finger. "What will you give me, Flora?"

She smacked his hand away. "Get over yourself, Merlin. I'm too old for that shit."

He laughed. "Please, you're Greek, and you've been returned to your youth. You've probably got so much pent-up sexual energy you're ready to take on a satyr just to release some of it."

Her jaw dropped. "I may be a priestess of Zeus but that does not mean I'm *like* him!"

Merlin winked. "Too bad. I always liked you, Flora."

Color swept over her high, pale cheeks, and her green eyes glittered. Perhaps he was not so far off the mark after all. This would work in his favor if he could keep her eyes on him, and not on what was out there behind the wall.

She looked away from him and to the sphere. "Fine. We will each choose a champion. You want the little girl?"

He nodded, trying not to breathe a sigh of relief. "Yes. We can help them, but not directly influence. If we do that, we'll draw the attention of the Desert Guardians, and we do not want that." Worse, they'd draw the attention of the emperor. They did not need him showing up, not until they were ready for him.

She snorted. "No, we don't want that."

"We could have them work together," he paused,

"like we are doing. Burying their differences and learning to love perhaps?"

"She'll never go for it. She hates him." Flora's eyes softened. "Worse, she doesn't trust him—or anyone for that matter. That much I understand."

In that he *did* agree, but it had to be offered on the off chance they could make the two desert shifters work together. They would be stronger together, and the oracle had pointed out that it would take two from the desert to tackle Maggi and her guardians.

Flora frowned. "Perhaps in their journey, they will learn to work together."

"I'm with you on your initial assessment. I doubt it." He leaned back, but his eyes were not on the sphere. "I mean, look at us. Together, but not working together."

She rolled her eyes. "That's because you're a donkey."

"But a handsome donkey, with much power and a great need to feel your lips on mine." He grinned as she blushed once more. Yes, there was something between them. He just needed the time to make her see it too. Apparently, he was losing his touch; normally a week was plenty of time to bring the ladies to him.

Of course, taking down the Western European Wall would elevate him in her eyes. He wasn't entirely sure she realized he'd been the one who built it. At the time, it had seemed prudent to keep the emperor contained. To put the supernaturals inside a very, very large cage, and keep the humans out. Only it hadn't worked that way. The supernaturals were already too far spread to be contained properly. Which had only meant more walls.

More divisiveness.

Now, the emperor was building his power again. And Merlin was the only one who seemed to realize the danger they were all in. Which meant he had to move fast, and with great discretion to get someone else to do the work for the job he should have done if not for problems he was dealing with. He rubbed the back of his neck. If there was so much as a hint of his magic on the wind, the emperor would sniff it out. He'd have to be damn crafty to help Zamira without using magic. Zamira's life would be on the line and he wasn't sure he could so much as light a fire for her without drawing unwanted attention.

Flora would have no such constraints in helping Steve.

Maybe we should switch was his last thought.

Green eyes flicked to him as Flora arched a delicate swoosh of an eyebrow, as if she knew something of what he was thinking. "Then we are agreed? I help Steve, and you help Zamira?"

Merlin held his hand out to her and she set her

tiny, warm hand in his palm. He tightened his fingers over her hand before he brought it to his lips. He spoke against her skin as he raised his eyes to hers, seeing the flush of desire spread up her neck. "Agreed. Let the games begin, Flora."

Chapter 3

The winding goat path beckoned and I didn't hesitate another second. Couldn't hesitate, to be honest, not if I wanted to live a second longer. With a rush of giants behind me, and safety at the top of the path, there was no reason to hold back. I mean, other than the chance that Balder or I could be snatched off the wall like some sort of fast-moving food if we dawdled.

I pulled Balder forward but he refused to take a step up the slope. I spun around and stared at him. "Not the time to act like a jackass, Balder!"

He grunted and I yanked on the reins, something I never did, but panic made me harder on him than I liked. The rumble of the earth increased as the giants once more picked up speed, seeing us standing there as if we were waiting on them. I ran around behind Balder and pulled my leather belt off from around my waist.

"Sorry," I said as I raised it and brought it down hard on the left side of his ass, the crack resounding in the air. He dove forward and I kept at him, driving him up the hill. This was not the time for being careful despite the shitty footing. This was the time for running for our lives and praying to the desert goddess that we survived.

"Fucking Steve. Fucking idiot. Flipping me the fuck off instead of helping me get us out of here like the fucking douchecake camel's dick that he is. Shit and smegma for brains, only ever thinking with his tiny, useless cock, goddess damn him and his stupid, frigging lying face . . ." Somewhere in my tirade, about halfway up the path, I realized the giants had reached us and were not doing anything.

I didn't dare look at them. And in a flash, I knew why they'd stopped. Steve had said the reason, last night as we solidified our plans.

"You know, if you get stuck, just start swearing." He leaned back against his saddle across the fire from me.

I curled up by my own saddle and ignored him. That was best. If I said anything, we'd be fighting in a matter of seconds and be loud enough that no amount of stealth would help us.

"Kiara told me she read about giants. They love new curse words and people losing their shit in a rant. Or the potential of learning new words. It's nice to have someone who's smart and beautiful."

I hunched further against my saddle, wanting nothing more than to strangle him.

Okay, so they liked learning new curse words. They loved to hear someone get cussed out, and especially if it was a tirade. We were halfway up the path and now Balder didn't need me to push him.

He fought to get to the top, his back leg working hard not to give out under his weight.

Anger spurred through me, anger at myself along with a tentative hope that we would make it. My bestie Darcy would be howling with laughter at me, seeing me here now while I cussed out Steve to the entertainment of a rush of giants who'd only moments before been bent on pulling my head from my shoulders.

"I should never have trusted that cockwomble, cheating camel's stinking rotten asshole who thought no one would notice he was playing around, no one would notice because he thought he was smarter, but in truth, he was as always dumb as a sack of hammers that have their handles on backward. Useless, no good for anything—not even *sex*. Fucker couldn't even seem to figure out that the woman should *enjoy* it, too, but what does he care? He'll just damn well go onto the next one and then the next, not bothering with anything other than what he wants . . ." I let the words pour through me and out my mouth, the pent-up anger and hurt that stemmed from my relationship with Steve and having to work with him after said relationship had broken into a thousand pieces.

And people wondered why I had trust issues.

We were ten feet from the top and I didn't slow my feet or my mouth. The giants obviously liked foul language, and a good sordid story, but I had no idea that it could be so effective. Or mesmerizing. There was no way I was telling Steve *he'd* actually helped me.

"I hope the rest of his life he spends with a woman covered in warts and yeast infections, that even a whore wouldn't sleep with his infected tiny, smaller than a worm, limper than an overcooked noodle for a manhood..."

Balder reached the top and bolted away from the edge, away from the giants. I stumbled forward, and the words stopped as I took a deep breath.

From behind me came a screech that ended in a bellow. I felt the air swoop around me as a giant hand swept my way. I spun and fell backward as I pulled a blade from my side. The curved kukri knife was sharper than any razor, and I gave everything I had in that swing as I fell. The three fingers that came for me were curved, grasping, and I saw the queen's eyes at the edge of the cliff.

The knife cut through her palm, opening it like a ripe peach in a perfect line. Dark blue blood poured from the wound, spilling on the ground, leaching toward me like a floodgate opened. She yanked her hand back and I pushed my way farther from the cliff's edge as fast as I could, scrabbling while keeping my eyes on the tops of the giants' heads. The sway of their scraggly strands of hair was like some weird floating forest of dying trees.

A pair of hands caught me under the arms and I jerked away from them, fear making me clumsy. I spun with my knife up, still dripping with the giantess's blood.

Above me stood a young satyr, the same one I'd seen grinning at me from the top of the hill. His legs curved backward and were covered in hair, and on his head peeking between dark brown curls were two nubby horns, which meant he was young, mid-twenties at best. He grinned at me. "That was amazing. Really, I don't think I've ever seen anything quite like it. Or heard anything quite like it." He laughed. "I wish I had something to record it with."

"Thanks?" I pulled a little farther from him.

"I meant the story mostly; fighting I've seen before. Were you really cheated on by some guy with a tiny dick? I mean, wouldn't you be glad that he cheated, because I thought women didn't like small . . . packages?"

I snorted and pushed to my feet, wanting more space between me and the cliff edge. For all I knew, the giants would start lifting each other up and over to get to me and the treasures I'd stolen.

The satyr settled into a tight trot beside me as I strode away, following Balder's hoof prints. Scrub brush grew here and there, and smaller stunted trees, but I couldn't see my horse anywhere. No doubt he was pissed that I'd smacked him.

I grimaced. He wasn't like a normal horse—but to be fair, most animals on this side of the wall were not normal. They'd been around the supernatural creatures here for generations, locked in with us, and with that, had learned some tricks of their own, making them smarter than their domesticated cousins, and better survivors all the way around. At least, that's what my father had always said. I sighed. I would be paying for this for weeks if I didn't treat Balder right, if I didn't apologize. Oats, carrots, a nice warm mash at the very least would be the start of my apologizing.

"You can slow down. They won't climb up here," the satyr said. I glanced at him.

"Thanks . . ."

"Name is Marcel." He smiled and I felt the flush in my belly spread upward. Satyrs had sex magic and that could make it very hard to keep your clothes on. I gritted my teeth and closed myself to his magic.

"Knock that shit off," I growled as the shiver ran through me right to my middle and then lower, curling across parts of me that hadn't been touched in a long time.

"Oh, come on. From that story, if even half of it is true, you could use a good flouncing." He got in front of me and jogged backward, showing off, contracting his pecs and even going so far as to flex his arms.

Flouncing . . . that was a new one to me. "Yeah, no flouncing for me. That shit gets old fast."

"Not if it's done right. In fact, I bet if you had a *really good* flouncing, you'd enjoy it for weeks on end. At least." He winked at me. "I didn't catch your name, pretty lady."

"Zam." I looked past him, seeing Balder under a couple of trees, his head low and his back leg cocked, favoring it.

"Well, Zam, you escaped the queen of the giants, which in and of itself is impressive. But I have to ask, did you know they would stop and listen to your story?" Marcel did a little half-step, a hop and kick as if a bug had landed on him. I raised an eyebrow.

"No. I'd forgotten that part of the information pack I read until the last minute."

"Information pack?" He let out a noise that I suppose was a laugh, but to be honest, it sounded like a goat being strangled. Which made my lips twitch upward.

"Dude, you cannot laugh like that." I shook my head.

"Can't help it." He did that same braying, strangling goat scream and I had to stop walking.

"Sweet baby goddess, stop it!" I took a half-hearted swing at him. "Every predator within a ten-mile radius will hear that and think you're being tortured and then come looking for what's left of you!"

He slowed his horrifying laugh to a low-end chuckle that was at least not so friggin' loud. I shook my head. "Go on, get out of here."

"You don't want my help?" His face fell as if we were best friends and I'd just told him I hated his goaty little guts.

I tried to push past him but he moved with me. "What are you going to help me with exactly? I already turned down the flouncing."

"I could help your horse over there, stitch him up, make him good as new."

I sighed and tried again to go around him to get to Balder, but Marcel kept himself between us. I flicked an ascending eyebrow and held up the kukri blade I'd not yet put away. "Seriously, get the fuck out of my way."

He held up both hands as if surrendering. "I also saw your buddy, the big blond dude on the black horse. I can tell you what direction he went." Marcel waggled his eyebrows and fingers at me at the same time. "And for all that, just a quick flouncing. Twenty minutes, tops."

I stared hard at him, his words slowly sinking in. "You saw Steve? When?"

"Oh, right about as your horse crested the hill. He took one look at you coming over the top and the queen's hand coming for you, and took off fast as he could go. Not real brave, is he?"

Any gratefulness for keeping Steve alive, saving his ass—again—fled in a flurry of anger so hot, I thought my clothes would burst into flames. Not that I had that kind of magic, but in that moment, I could almost feel it under my skin, like a phoenix rising with a fury as scorching as any blaze.

Marcel's eyes widened. "You okay?"

I put a hand out to him, palm against his chest, and shoved him out of my way. I didn't think I could handle speaking right then for fear of what would come flooding out of my mouth. As it was, my mind raced, dancing forward with just what Steve was up to.

He'd take the jewel back to Ish, show her that he'd gotten it all on his own, hoping I was killed by the giants. Thinking I was dead, he could take all the glory. Again.

"Satyr-flouncing face-sprayer, I'm going to kick his ass all the way to the desert and back."

Marcel laughed behind me. "I'm going to steal that one. If you don't mind."

I reached Balder and he gave me a dirty look, his ears pinned to his head. I held up both hands. "I'm sorry, my friend. But you had to get up that hill or end up inside a giant's belly."

He snorted and one ear flicked forward. I reached out and touched his uninjured hip and he leaned into my hand. I had to let my anger with Steve go while I worked on Balder. The horse was far too sensitive to my emotions to give him that anger when he didn't deserve it. I stroked a hand over his side and pulled my medic bag from the back of the saddle. In a matter of minutes, I stitched the wound closed, making tight, neat wraps of the thread so the sutures would hold and heal while he walked.

"Half a flouncing to make him whole? Ten minutes. I can't go less than ten minutes if we're both going to enjoy it," Marcel said behind me, so close that if I so much as took a big breath, I'd have pushed my back into his front and I could only imagine what was there. He blew a soft breath against my ear and I swatted backward at him like I would a fly.

"Nope." I pulled out a jar of red sparkling paste and Marcel grunted. "That's right, I have my own magic."

"That's not really yours," he pointed out. "There is no way you made that hacka paste."

I shrugged. "Does it matter? It'll work, and Balder here and I will be leaving in a matter of minutes."

"Where did you get it?" Marcel came around to my side to peer at me while I smeared the healing paste onto Balder's stitched-up wound.

"A friend." I capped the jar and tucked it into the bag. I wasn't about to tell him that Ish made it for me. Ish didn't like other supernaturals knowing she was capable of certain things. Like healing paste.

"You aren't going to light it on fire?" Marcel leaned on Balder and the horse stepped away so Marcel stumbled. I wiped my hands on my cloak.

"Nope. It'll work, just slower without the flame." I walked up to Balder's head and took his reins.

"Wait, just like that you're leaving?" Marcel called after me. "Seriously, you're like the first *flounceable* woman I've seen in ages—"

"You'd flounce a piece of rotten twenty-day-old cheese if given the chance," I shot back.

"Ahh, you wound me. I would never flounce cheese without consent." He laughed. "Come on, just ten minutes. Pretty please?"

With my back to him, I let the smile slide over my lips. Satyrs were, if nothing else, funny as hell. As long as there was no flouncing involved, they could be good, light company. Totally untrustworthy, but fun.

Balder bumped me with his nose and gave a low snort.

"Yeah, he's a fool. But he's not a bad guy. Just a guy like all the other ones out there."

Maybe I was bitter. Shit, scratch that, I knew I was. But I was trying not to let it rule my life. Hard when the one person you thought you could trust with everything turned out to be the person you should have trusted the least.

My family hadn't helped in that department, and even my best friend . . . I shook my head. No, I wasn't going there. Not today.

From behind us came that awful goat-strangling laughter. "I heard that! And I take offense. I'm worth twice any of the other men you know! I've got the manhood to prove it. Twice as big!"

I turned as I walked, a laugh trickling through me, the lightness of the moment a balm to the anger, stealing me away from the dark place my head was going before it got too bad. "Good luck flouncing whatever woman comes through next. Or consenting cheese, as the case may be." I gave him a floppy salute and he returned the gesture.

"I'll see you again, Zam! I know it! Just you wait. We will have a great time together!" he shouted after me.

I had a feeling he was right and I'd meet him again, which was strange. I hadn't gotten that sensation in years. Not since I met Ish, I suppose, and she'd taken us from the Oasis, broken, injured, and without anyone to look after what was left of our family.

I walked beside Balder, heading northwest toward home. I tried not to think about what Ish would say when Steve got there alone. Would she care that I was dead? He'd spin his story in such a way that would make him look a hero who tried to save me, and then be overjoyed to see me survive, as though he couldn't believe that I'd made it out alive without him.

I couldn't help the anger that built with each step that took me closer to home.

And what would it do to my brother? He was there waiting to see if I survived too . . . Would he care? Something like heartbreak, an emotion I didn't want again, twisted through me and tried to set my eyes to flooding.

"No, no crying behind the wall," I whispered to myself. I refused to think that perhaps my brother would be relieved if I was dead, that he would no longer have to bear the shame of a sister who'd strayed so far from the way we were raised. I had to fight not to hunch my shoulders under the weight of those thoughts. Under the guilt of what I should have been but wasn't.

The only person who'd be happy to see me was Darcy, but that was a given. She'd been my best friend since we'd been rescued from the Oasis. My mind tried to take me back to the moment I realized she was not quite the friend I'd thought.

"You'll be glad to see Darcy and Pig, won't you?" I ran a hand over Balder and he snorted. Pig was his horse girlfriend and he adored the scruffy little bay mare Darcy rode.

I spoke to Balder to fill the space between us. "Darcy will have gotten the jewel from the Ice Witch, and then we'll only have two left to get. Ish will be okay because she'll have more of her magic back and maybe she can help Bryce then." I frowned, thinking about how long it had been since we'd started this journey. I'd made Ish swear she wouldn't tell my brother why I was so willing to be a thief. That every jewel I brought her gave us both hope she'd be able to help Bryce.

"Bryce really hates me, I think," I said softly. "He believes Father was right about everything, and he wasn't. I know he wasn't. The world is not as black and white as either of them believe." *Believed*, I should have said, in the past tense for Father. I blew out a breath.

Balder snorted and I sighed. "I know. I know. We've had this conversation a thousand times at least. But maybe this time, I'll find a way to tell him Dad was wrong. That there is no black and white, that being a thief doesn't make me a heretic or a stain on our family."

Balder flapped his lips, and I slipped him a mint I had in the front pocket of my cloak.

Around us, the world had gone quiet. Most likely, it was our presence, and not anything else more sinister, but still I kept my ears perked. Surviving was something I was very good at, and I wasn't about to let my guard down now.

I checked Balder's wound. Already it looked days old, maybe even a week. The hacka paste was good shit, as my brother would say.

"How you feeling, my friend?" I tugged on Balder's tail once and he swished it.

I turned, the sensation of being watched heavy on me, but there was no one behind us. Just in case, though . . . I held up both hands and flipped up my middle finger. "Whoever you are, I don't have time for whatever shit you want to throw at me."

Balder bobbed his head a couple times in agreement, then dropped to one knee on his front leg, inviting me to mount. I didn't argue. If he was ready, I wasn't going to question him. I leapt straight up and landed in the saddle as lightly as any cat, then picked up the reins and Balder stepped into a ground-covering trot. There was only the slightest hesitation in his stride, a mere whisper that he'd been injured.

"We might not be able to beat Steve home, but we can show up right on his ass," I murmured.

I touched the ring hanging from the chain around my neck. The bump of it under my shirt was a comfort. Without it, my life would be a mess of epic proportions. With it, I could make my own choices without a curse dragging me down. With it, I had a chance at catching up to Steve—like a burr he didn't notice stuck to him until it dug into his skin and drew blood. I grinned to myself.

HOME WAS the northernmost tip of the Caspian Sea in a town once known as Atyrau. Not that there were many people left in the town, humans or supes. Balder picked his way around the bubbling pits of waste that smelled of sulfur, cinnamon, and death. Weird combination, but I'd learned not to question why they smelled that way, just to avoid them. They burned, though not like the toxic waste that had been in the giants' home. That shit would eat you whole, an acid that cut through bone and tissue like it was nothing. No, this waste was hot, cooked from somewhere under the ground and then pushed to the surface—it would burn, but you could wash it off and survive.

Balder and I had ridden through the night, not pushing hard but keeping up the steady pace because I knew Steve. He'd push his poor horse so hard, he'd be forced to walk the last ten miles before home. At the least, if not more. At the two-mile mark, we found his horse limping his way home, head hung low.

"Batman . . ." I called to him and he lifted his dark head, his eyes fogged with pain and fatigue. I slowed Balder, slid from his back. Batman took a few stumbling steps toward me and I struggled once more to contain the anger.

Save it for the bastard. Save it for Steve. Narcissistic camel's-dung-covered asshole that he is.

The need to help Batman allowed me to put the growing anger aside and focus on the horse in front of me. I grabbed my medic pack and pulled out my oat balls I'd made for the trip. Camel fat rolled up with oats and honey, then stuffed inside a leather pouch for storage. The horses didn't take to them right away, but when they were at the end of the journey, they gulped them down like they were manna from heaven.

"Eat up, boys." I held one out to Batman and he took it with soft lips. Balder pushed on me from the other side. I gave him one ball, but saved the last two for Batman. He was not as fit for these runs as Balder; Steve didn't put the time into him he needed. I put it on my mental to-do list that I would condition Batman with me and Balder from here on out. The horse didn't deserve to suffer because of Steve's asshole-ness.

"You know that's a stupid name he gave you. That's what you get when you start hanging out with humans. Batman, who names a horse Batman? Ridiculous," I muttered as I stroked the dark horse on the neck, then slid my hands over his body checking for wounds. His legs were swollen and a bit warm, but that would be expected with the head-long gallop through rough territory. I'd have to watch him for a fallout from this bullshit.

I held up my water bottle and tipped it so Batman could drink. Once he was as fueled up as I could get him, I loosened his cinch so he could breathe deeper, and took his bridle off. He would follow us home; I wasn't concerned about that. Balder leaned over and nipped at Batman's cheek.

The dark horse flinched, which wasn't like him, and showed just how exhausted he was that he didn't try to bite the gray back. Batman was a bit on the bossy side, so Balder taking the lead was unusual. I shook my head, mounted back up, and me and the two horses walked the last two miles home.

The stables came into view first and we went straight there. What had been a stockade was now a dual-purpose sprawling living area with a stable we'd added on. I got the two boys settled into their stalls with water and food. I'd have to walk them later so they wouldn't stiffen up, but for now, they deserved to just rest and eat. I checked the other stall for Pig, Darcy's mare.

While there were a few horses, none were the scruffy little mare. Which meant Darcy wasn't back yet. My belly rolled with a sharp tang of fear. Darcy and her crew had headed out weeks before Steve and me. They were supposed to have been back by now. We'd planned it that way so we could celebrate with two jewels at once. Ish had planned it that way, really.

"Where are you, Darcy?" I whispered. Balder pushed his nose against me, shoving me out of his stall. "Yeah, yeah, I'm going." I stripped off my cloak and hung it over the stall door, which left me in nothing but dark pants, tall black riding boots, and a plain white tank top. And my weapons—I was never without those. The twin kukri blades were strapped to my upper thighs, and the flail I kept in my right hand with the two spiked balls dangling just above the ground. If I was going to carry it as an actual weapon, I'd have to look at getting a strap for it. Maybe across my back.

At the moment, though, I had only one thought outside of my concern for Darcy.

"You are about to get your ass handed to you, Steve," I muttered under my breath as I strode out of the stable toward the main hall. Darcy would love this. I only wished she was back already so she could see me finally put Steve in his place—I wasn't the only one he'd hurt. That made me grin. Perhaps it would be more than a little fun to finally give him his comeuppance. And it would take my mind off Darcy not being there. She'd be back soon. I was sure of it. That's what I told myself while my instincts screamed that something was wrong, off.

My home was huge, far bigger than it needed to be for the small number of us that served Ish, but she liked us all to have room to ourselves. Especially considering how poorly we got along.

Or at least, how poorly Steve and I got along. No, that wasn't fair. There was also Maks, the lone human in the group. Nobody liked him, but that was because he was human. He served Ish faithfully, I supposed, so that was enough for me to leave him alone.

I'd give the human one thing, he was nice to look at. If he'd been a supe, he'd have had all the women fighting over who would have been in his bed with his electric blue eyes and messy sand-colored hair, big arms, and bigger . . . well, you get the picture.

Steve picked on him, but Steve picked on anyone he thought was lesser than him. Including me. Including Bryce. Including Batman. My jaw ticked with the anger that grew and burned out other thoughts.

The main door that led into the hall was open a

crack and Steve's voice flowed out to me even though I was thirty feet away.

"Ish, I'm so, *so* sorry. I couldn't save her. I tried. I fought through the giant's legs, and I reached out to her but she wouldn't take my hand. Her hatred of me for something I didn't do . . . it killed her in the end. As I always said it would."

I pushed the door open slowly, knowing it wouldn't creak and give me away—I'd oiled the hinges myself. Steve knelt in front of Ish, his blond head bowed in submission. Ish stared down at him, her face twisted with what could only be called anger.

She was an older woman, but still beautiful, tall, slim and with thick dark hair streaked with silver strands. But in that moment, I saw only a woman who didn't know how to react to the lies—goddess of the desert help me, she *had* to know Steve was lying again. This was not the first time he'd tried to lose me on a run, or the first time he'd tried to let an accident take my life. But the thing was, Ish always gave him the benefit of the doubt, something I just didn't understand. How could she not see what a fucking tool he was? Out for his own best interests.

Which made me wary of Ish, no matter that I wanted to trust her. That she held him above me made me doubt her ability to understand fully who and what he was.

"Maks," she called out, and her human servant stepped from the shadows. Even though I didn't like Maks, it wasn't the same way I didn't like Steve. There was nothing really wrong with the servant except he was weak in a place where weakness equaled death. I should know. I was about as weak a supe as there was out there, much as it galled me. But that was why I worked so hard to fight on two legs, to improve my chances.

That was why I did all I could to be strong enough to come home every time, not in a body bag.

Ish put her hand out to him, as if to set it on Maks's broad shoulder, but he moved so her hand missed him. He didn't like being touched much more than I did. She didn't break her words, as though there was no slight toward her in his movement.

"Take a horse and ride out. Follow Steve's path backward and bring her home. Alive or dead, she does not deserve to be left behind. She has been a faithful ward of mine, and I promised her I would never leave her in the cold. *Ever.*" That last word came out as sharp as the crack of a whip and Steve flinched as a ripple of power swelled out around her. As well he should.

Ish was a strong mage, and with each jewel we brought her, her strength grew, and her ability to help others and keep us safe increased. A swell of love grew in me. Ish was looking out for me when she could have turned her back. She was going to send Maks to find me. I felt bad for doubting her in that moment, wanting nothing more than to give her the belief that she deserved.

"I swear to you, there was *no* saving her. Perhaps her horse escaped, but there is no way that Zamira made it out alive. I saw her go under the giant queen's hand. I saw the fingers close around her."

Ish leaned over him. "Did you see her body, though?"

He drew a slow breath. "I . . . could not watch her die. For all that she hates me, I still have feelings for her, Ish. I could not bear to see her beauty crushed, snuffed out like a candle in the wind."

Another time not so long ago, I would have melted with his words, but now . . . not so much.

It was about time to make my entrance into this theatrical play he had going on. Oh, I wished I could see his face when he realized I was very much alive, and about to kick him right in those cheating, shriveled balls of his.

THANK YOU FOR READING THIS PREVIEW
Download Witch's Reign to keep reading

Printed in Great Britain
by Amazon

43580697R00218